COPYRIGHT

PROLOGUE

"I DON'T disagree with you, Mother. Clarissa is a very beautiful woman. But I'm not going to date her."

Zev didn't bother trying to hide the frustration in his voice. Honestly, how many times would he have to tell his family that he wasn't interested in their setups? Exhaustion beating at him, he leaned against the back of the leather couch and rubbed his palms over his eyes. Sleep rarely came to him, and when it did, he remained partially alert, terrified of losing his humanity while he was unconscious. He was barely hanging on as it was; this intervention was the last thing he needed.

Grandma Mae's voice broke into his thoughts. Her frustration with Zev had reached such a high level that she willingly questioned him, her Alpha, a practice unheard of in her generation. Then again, maybe it wasn't just her frustration; maybe Zev's attempts to bring their pack into modern times had been more successful than he'd realized.

"I don't understand this, Zev. You're thirty years old. Your grandfather and I had already been married for close to a decade by the time we were your age. It's not natural or healthy for one of our kind to remain alone."

As if that was his cue, Grandpa Walter jumped into the conversation. Had they drawn numbers in advance to determine the order in which to beat up on him?

"I realize you feel we're intruding on your privacy, son, but any shifter with eyes can see the problems you're having, and the reason is plain. Shifters are deeply sexual beings, but the..." Walter paused and swallowed hard, as if it pained him to continue the sentence. "The women you've been using to meet your physical needs are half-souls. They aren't enough to bind your humanity, especially for this many years. You're a strong man and a strong wolf, Zev, the strongest I've seen in my lifetime. But no shifter can outrun his nature, not that I understand why you insist on trying. Whatever the reason, if you don't tie with a shifter soon, your human side will be lost."

Did his family members actually think they were telling him something he didn't already know? Their only error was underestimating his strength and determination. Though the idea of meeting his sexual needs with humans—or half-souls, as shifters called them—repulsed his family, they were certain he'd been making a practice of it. How else could he have lived with both his human and wolf sides intact for three decades? They couldn't fathom a shifter living that long without sharing at least some physical bond.

Well, they were wrong. Zev hadn't tied with anyone—human or shifter—in his life, whether they believed him or not. But for how much longer? Returning from the change was becoming more and more difficult, with his wolf clinging to its form, not wanting his human to take over. And the longer the wolf remained in control of their body, the less likely it was that the human would be able to find his way to the surface again.

"There's no point in denying it, Zev. We know what you've been doing, and we don't judge you."

Though he trusted his father's sincerity, Zev also knew he remained uncomfortable with the idea of a shifter engaging in sexual acts with humans. The only reason he accepted what he called Zev's "oddities" was because the Etzgadol pack had grown steadily since Zev had begun his Alpha training, even more so since he had taken over as pack Alpha. And Zev had had equal success with the family business, which now earned an annual gross income that was more than double what it had been before Zev had taken over.

"Move your hands away from your face and look at us, Zev. This is serious. You cannot continue to choose this lifestyle. Your body cannot survive it." Gregory Hassick's voice tightened with worry.

Zev dropped his hands to his sides and opened his eyes, knowing they were bloodshot and surrounded by dark circles. When was the last time he'd truly rested? He combed his fingers through his hair and resisted the urge to yell. His family loved him. He knew that. And this conversation, no matter how misplaced, was a reflection of that love.

"How many times do I have to explain this, Father? I'm not choosing this. I hate being alone. I haven't tied with any human women. I want to claim my mate more than anything."

Lori scooted closer to him on the couch and took his hand. The new egalitarian pack structure Zev had put in place was helped tremendously by his strong sister. She led the pack females by example, and they all admired her. She couldn't go against their elders, which was likely why Lori had agreed to take part in this little family gathering. But neither would she speak against her brother, so she remained silent and lent Zev support with her actions.

"Everyone wants a true mate, Zev," Gregory told him. "But very few shifters get them. The rest of us fall in love and feel completely satisfied with our chosen partners. Your mother and I have been happy together for well over half of our lives without the mating bond. Please, it's time to let go of childish fantasies and accept your fate. You haven't been blessed with a true mate, but you can still live a full life. Just tie with Clarissa or one of the other females in the pack. What can it hurt to try? Best-case scenario, you find this true mate you insist exists. Worst-case scenario, you have more regular companionship and a proper tie."

Zev couldn't hold back the growl in his chest. He was tired of their constant refusals to acknowledge the existence of his true mate and their never-ending setup offers. His parents had long ago stopped pretending the offers were about dinner and a movie. Were his parents honest with these women about the purely sexual role they were expected to play in his life? Probably not. Nobody outside of his family knew the truth. Hell, even those within his family denied it, despite the fact that he'd been clear with them for years.

"Clarissa isn't my true mate. And I'm not interested in her companionship." He spat out his response, his tone expressing disgust with the very idea of their brand of companionship.

"Why not, Zev? Are her breasts too small? Is her hiney too big? Just talk to us, and we can help you. If the females in our pack aren't satisfactory, we'll find a female in a neighboring pack for you so you can make a physical tie."

He winced. Now his other grandmother was engaged in the game. Had any other man ever faced an eighty-year-old woman offering him his choice of tits and ass? Dear God, please make it stop.

"I'm gay, Granny Betty. Any breasts at all are a deal-killer, and I haven't ever paid attention to Clarissa's, um, hiney."

The diminutive gray-haired woman threw her hands in the air.

"Our kind can't be gay, Zev. It just doesn't work that way. A male shifter needs to tie with a female shifter in order to bind his humanity, and the female needs to accept that tie from the male in order to release her wolf. This is basic preschool information, dear."

Zev dropped his head on top of his hands, which were crossed over his knees. Yeah, he was very familiar with their kind's version of the birds and the bees. Every shifter's soul straddled two bodies: the wolf and the human. Women were naturally connected to their human side, but their wolf side was locked away, unable to find the freedom to run. Males, on the other hand, had free rein of their wolf from childhood, but their hold on their humanity was tenuous. The only way for a male shifter to retain his human form was to tie to a female shifter and absorb a portion of her humanity. Likewise, in order for a female shifter to retain her sanity, she had to free her wolf from its cage, something that could be done only by accepting a male's tie.

So, yeah, Zev knew the basic facts, but he'd long ago rejected the idea that they were absolute. Because to believe that would be to believe he was unnatural, which couldn't be true, since he'd been blessed with the most precious gift nature could offer a shifter: a true mate.

Of course, he had told his family the reason he hadn't tied was because he was waiting for his true mate. His male true mate. The first time he'd said the words to his parents, they'd been shocked. His father yelled so loudly at him that the windows literally shook, and his mother stood in the kitchen and cried. When Zev refused to back down, despite his parents' protests, their feelings on the subject morphed into disgust, and they barred him from ever mentioning the issue again.

After several years passed without any female shifters in Zev's life, his parents started to worry. They were too embarrassed to tell people about what they called Zev's "condition," but not knowing what else to do, they eventually relented and spoke to their own parents. All four of Zev's grandparents insisted that they'd never heard of such a thing, and it couldn't be true. So after that, Zev's family grudgingly lived in a state of denial, refusing to acknowledge the possibility that he could actually be gay.

Sitting in his parents' living room and fending off setup attempts made Zev realize there was a downside to empowering his pack to speak their minds—now, he was forced to listen to them. Maybe he'd have been better off leaving things as they'd always been. Then nobody, and certainly not a female, even if she was an elder and a relative, would dare speak to the Alpha in such a condescending way.

Zev dismissed the thought as soon as it entered his head. He was glad his family cared, glad his grandmother felt confident enough to question him, and glad members of his pack felt confident enough to share their feelings. The pack was stronger for it, even if it meant Zev had to endure this emotionally debilitating family intervention. He raised his eyes and responded to his grandmother.

"I will not seek companionship with anyone other than my true mate. You know only shifters without true mates can choose a life partner. A mated wolf can be tied to his humanity only by his true mate. So having sex with Clarissa or any of the other females in the pack won't get the job done anyway. And despite what you think, I do, in fact, have a true mate. Our souls are connected at the heart; that's not something a shifter can mistake. I can feel the bond all the way down in my bones."

Oh, Zev had been confused at first, sure. The feelings he had didn't make sense in the context of what he'd been taught. But no lessons, not even those that explained the very fabric of his kind's makeup, could override the single most important truth that coursed through Zev's body: the awareness of his true mate. So before he'd reached the end of his second decade, Zev had already accepted the idea that he was gay, despite the fact that it went against everything his pack thought was natural or even possible.

Zev looked at Grandpa Hugh and Grandma Betty, imploring them to help. They were the only true mated pair in the family, and one of the few true mated pairs in the history of the pack. Surely they understood the power of the bond. It was absolute. Zev could no sooner satisfy the need to tie with his true mate by tying with another shifter than he could satisfy the need to breathe air by inhaling water.

Hugh squeezed Betty's hand and looked at Zev sympathetically.

"If you have a true mate, Zev, then you have a duty to her. She needs you in order to release her wolf or she will lose her mind. What if you're abandoning your true mate, Zev? What if you haven't found her because you're not willing to keep an open mind about females?"

Zev rolled his eyes, too frustrated to care that it was an incredibly childish and disrespectful gesture. He often wondered whether his family would believe he was gay if he told them he'd long known the identity of his true mate. Maybe then they'd stop writing off his refusal to sleep with shifter females as some stubborn philosophical exercise.

But no matter how much Zev loved and trusted his family, he wasn't willing to take that risk. Nobody would believe Zev if he identified Jonah as his mate, and the human would be perceived as a threat to the pack structure. The easiest way to eliminate that threat would be to eliminate the interloper. The basic principles of their kind were so ingrained, and so fundamentally based on the need for shifter males to tie with shifter females, that he feared harm could come to his mate if the pack knew the identity of the man destined to tie with their Alpha.

No, Zev couldn't risk his mate's safety. The only way for him to acknowledge Jonah's role in his life would be to first tie with him. Then the mating bond would be complete, and nobody would be able to dispute their relationship. Or his sexuality.

"If my mate were anywhere within ten miles of here, my senses would pick that up. Blind dates aren't how we find our true mates. But if you're so concerned that I'm abandoning my mate, I'll make you a deal. I promise to meet with whomever you want, on a platonic basis, to see if she's my mate, and in return, you promise that when I do find my mate and make the tie, you'll support the mating in every way."

The relief in his parents and grandparents was palpable. All six of the tense bodies sitting around him relaxed, and smiles took over their faces. His sister squeezed his hand and winked at him. Zev was certain she'd known his mate's identity nearly as long as he had, though neither of them had ever spoken the words out loud.

"Of course we will, dear. A mating is a blessing." His mother's pretty face shone.

"Even more so when it's for the Alpha, because it unveils the heart of our pack," Grandpa Hugh added with a wistful look on his face.

Zev knew the older shifter was likely remembering his own mating.

"You and your mate will be supported by us and the entire pack." His father's deep baritone voice left no room for debate. It was certain and sure. A vow.

Zev rose from the sofa, straightening all six feet seven inches and squared his shoulders.

"Then we have a deal. I'll tie with my mate when the time comes, and you'll stand behind us. No matter who she"—he looked pointedly at the faces of the seven people he loved most in the world, other than the man missing from the room, of course—"or he is. Good night."

And with those words, Zev turned and walked to the front door, ignoring the growls coming from behind him. They'd given him their word, and it would bring unforgivable dishonor on their ancestors to go back on that vow, so he knew his family would keep their promise. As for the rest of the pack, it'd be a challenge, a possibly insurmountable challenge, even with both past Alphas and the current Alpha standing together.

A tie between two males threatened to disrupt everything the pack had been taught about a female's connection to her human side and a male's connection to his wolf side. And, as if the idea of two males accomplishing a tie wouldn't be enough to cause widespread panic, Jonah wasn't just a male. He was a human—a half-soul—not a shifter. And everyone knew that a shifter couldn't tie with a half-soul.

But when the time came, the pack could either stand with Zev or find new territory. The Etzgadol pack land had belonged to the Hassick family for ten generations. And with his grandparents, parents, and sister by his side, Zev was guaranteed that he'd be able to continue that legacy. Even if it meant doing it while building a new pack to lead. And Zev knew if that was what it took to be with Jonah Marvel, he'd do it without a second thought. He'd do whatever was needed to claim and keep his true mate.

Zev walked out of his parents' house and over to his truck, dropped his head against the door, and took in a deep breath, letting the fresh air cool his lungs. Standing up to his family once again and garnering their support for his future mating was all well and good, but none of it meant a thing if his mate didn't return and accept his place in the pack beside Zev. If Jonah didn't come home soon, Zev wasn't sure whether there'd be a Hassick male available to lead the Etzgadol pack.

He looked up at the sky. The stars were beautiful out here. They sparkled above him, showing the spirits of those who came before. *Come back to me, Jonah. Our spirits are intertwined, and my body cannot endure without its other half for much longer.*

He felt the pain deep in his bones, the urge to shift and run. But he pushed it back, grateful that, at least for now, his human could still exert his will. His wolf was tired of waiting for his human to find their mate and the wolf wanted control of their form so he could go find Jonah and claim him. But their mate was long gone, well out of scent distance, and the chance of Zev's wolf finding him before running into hunters or vehicles was slim.

Unless he claimed his mate, the time was fast approaching when his human would no longer be able to control his wolf. When that happened, the fear driving the intervention his family had staged that night would become a reality: Zev's human would be forever lost. And without his human's wisdom to limit him, Zev's wolf would likely end his life trying to find his mate.

The black truck rumbled over the dirt and rock road, weaving through the trees and taking Zev from the family intervention at his childhood den to the place he'd been calling home for more than a decade. It was unusual for a shifter to live alone. His peers had remained in their parents' dens until they'd found a chosen partner, and then they'd built new dens together, with cubs often following shortly thereafter. But Zev had moved out of the family home when he was eighteen, hoping a little distance would help curb his frustration over his family's refusal to acknowledge the possibility that he could have a male mate.

The Etzgadol pack land encompassed thousands of acres abutting a national forest. In addition to being a place where the entire pack could run, the forest held the Hassick family ceramics business and the homes for his direct line. Every member of his family had equal rights to that land, so nobody could stop Zev from claiming a portion and setting up house. What his parents could and did do, however, was cut him off financially.

They hadn't understood his desire to live alone; "unnatural" was what they'd called it. It might have been more meaningful if they hadn't also used the word to describe his feelings when he told them he was gay. After all, his true mate was male and what could be more natural than the mating bond?

In any event, Zev's parents had hoped to keep him in their den by withholding funds, but he had taken his tent, pitched it, and lived in the woods. He'd started working for the family business by then, so he'd lived off the land and saved almost every dollar he'd made until he had enough money in the bank to build a home, the home he planned to someday share with his mate.

Zev had been too young to tie back then. Oh, he was physically able, but shifters rarely tied until they were late in their second decade. So his wolf should have been satisfied to play and hunt, like his peers. But his wolf wasn't satisfied and neither was his human. In fact, Zev hadn't felt at peace since he was eighteen. Because that was the year he'd lost Jonah.

Zev flipped on the radio, hoping some loud music would help him stay awake. His neck felt like rubber, and he rubbed one palm over his tired eyes. His body had been hurting too much for him to have found peaceful sleep in way too long. The deep-seated ache that had been his constant companion since Jonah moved away twelve years earlier was partially to blame, but most of his restlessness was caused by the wolf pacing within him, trying desperately to get out. Zev hadn't allowed himself to shift in three months.

His wolf had never gone that long without being free. In fact, Zev had always shifted more frequently and for longer periods than others. His mother bragged that it was because Zev's wolf was so powerful. And maybe that was true. Zev's wolf was bigger, stronger, and more acutely aware of his surroundings than the other wolves in the pack.

Gregory Hassick had started bringing Zev with him to interpack council meetings when the presumptive Alpha turned eighteen. It was part of the training, a way for Zev to learn what would be expected of him and to make connections with leaders of the other packs. Whenever he'd been introduced to those pack leaders, the shifters recognized the remarkable strength of Zev's wolf. Some steered clear of Zev when they first sensed him, worried that he'd challenge them for control of their packs. But it never took long for them to recognize Zev's fairness, to see that he had no desire to take what was theirs. And, as a result, he'd established some good relationships with neighboring packs over those twelve years, relationships that had already helped his pack and its members.

But the strength of his wolf was the very reason Zev could no longer allow him the freedom to roam. The fact was, Zev didn't feel confident in his ability to rein that part of himself back in once it was released. So he'd been forced to cage his strong wolf. His family was right to worry about him. Three decades was too long for a shifter to go without tying.

He'd never expected his separation from Jonah to last so long or to be so difficult. When he'd figured out that Jonah was his mate on the eve of Jonah's departure, he'd believed they'd be apart for only a few years and that those years would be interspersed with visits. No big deal.

Zev had grossly underestimated how much he'd miss his friend. He'd underestimated the ingrained need coursing through him to be with his mate. And, worst of all, he'd underestimated the length of their separation. When Jonah moved away that summer day twelve years prior, he tore a hole in Zev. And Zev was starting to wonder whether Jonah was ever going to come home to stitch that wound closed.

CHAPTER 1

"ZEV HASSICK, get back here right this instant!"

Zev wagged his tail and raised his nose in the air. He was tracking the most wonderful scent. A combination of freshly mowed grass, lemons, and mint, the scent made his belly feel all warm and tingly inside. Zev trotted through the trees, barely noticing his surroundings. His entire being was focused on that scent. He wasn't sure how far he'd gone or how long he'd been running when he noticed he could no longer feel the crunch of leaves and the snap of twigs beneath his paws. He looked around and realized that the trees were gone. He stood at the edge of a clearing that faced a playground. Children were swinging and sliding, adults stood and talked, but what about that fresh, cool scent?

Zev scanned the area with his eyes and nose until he isolated the spot. It was halfway across the clearing, next to a bench. Sitting on a red, white, and blue striped blanket was a human baby. Zev locked his gaze on that child and whined. He wanted to get closer, wanted to smell and lick. But there were so many humans around, and his parents had always told him to stay away from the half-souls, especially if he was in wolf form.

Zev raised his head and tried to howl in frustration, but his vocal cords were too new, too fresh to make that noise. He was just over a year old, and this was his first shift. It'd take some time yet before he'd completely adjust to his wolf body. Dropping to the ground on his belly and resting his chin on his front paws, Zev whimpered and kept his gaze locked on the human baby.

The humans couldn't see him where he lay, surrounded by brush and plants, but it sure seemed as if the baby knew he was there, because eyes as black as night stared right back at Zev. Then, before he realized it was happening, the baby raised himself onto unsteady feet and began toddling toward him. With the grown-ups engaged in conversation, nobody noticed the little tyke, dressed in a blue one-piece cotton jumper and no shoes, making his way over to the trees. Zev hopped back to his feet and wagged his tail furiously, making soft yipping sounds as the source of the scent came closer and closer.

When the baby stepped out of the clearing and into the brush, Zev jumped on him and knocked him down on his backside. Deep black eyes opened wide in surprise, but the human didn't cry, he just reached his small hand out and petted Zev's fur. In his wolf cub form, Zev whined with joy and pressed himself against the human baby, licking his neck and rubbing against his body. He wanted to mark himself with that lemony scent. It smelled so good and right.

Now that he was right next to the baby, Zev realized that what he'd thought was a bald head was actually covered with white-blond hair. Hair so fair and fine it hadn't been visible from across the park. Zev tilted his head to one side and carefully appraised his new friend. He'd never come across a person with hair that white or eyes that black. It was an unexpected and intriguing combination. The human wrapped both arms around Zev's neck and squeezed him tight.

"Jonah? Jonah, where are you?"

Panicked adult voices pierced the air. Zev looked toward the clearing and saw people frantically searching for his new friend. Jonah. That was the baby's name. Zev's tongue made a long swipe up Jonah's face, and the human giggled loudly.

"There he is, Kevin! Look, over by the big tree."

The humans pointed toward them, and Zev knew it was time to go back to his den. If the adults got any closer, Jonah wouldn't be blocking their view and they'd see him. But Zev didn't want to go. He didn't want to leave Jonah.

Half-souls aren't safe, Zev. Don't forget to stay away from them. The words he'd heard over and over again from his pack elders rang in his head. After one last lick and nuzzle to the human baby's neck, Zev turned and ran back through the trees.

"Why can't I go to that school, Mommy?"

Zev pointed to the pink house with the brightly colored sign in front—Sunshine and Moonlight Nursery School. He longed to step through the doors, always had, but as usual, his mother sighed and answered his question without even turning her head.

"Zev, lovey, I've already explained this to you. I realize the picture of the beautiful moon on that sign calls to your wolf, but that school is for half-souls. We need to stay with our own kind so you can learn the right things and shift and play. The half-souls don't understand the meaning of the moon, Zev; they just thought it'd make a pretty picture."

Zev whimpered and sat back in his seat. He pressed his hand to the window as if that could somehow bring him closer to the white-haired boy playing inside that pink house. It wasn't the colorful sign that called to Zev's wolf. It was Jonah. The pink building was Jonah's school. Zev knew that because he'd tracked Jonah's scent to that place.

It'd been three years since he'd seen Jonah in the half-souls' playground, and in that time, Zev had shifted and found Jonah's den and his school. He always had to stay just on the periphery, under the cover of trees, and he could never watch for long because his parents didn't like his wolf's tendency to wander. Of course, they'd like that tendency even less if they realized where Zev went when he wandered, but that didn't stop Zev. He had to track his human friend, had to know where Jonah slept and ate and played.

Sometimes, when Zev was really lucky, Jonah would catch his eye and smile. On a few occasions, the little boy had even managed to sneak away from the adults and over to Zev. Jonah would immediately wrap his golden arms around

Zev's neck and stroke his fur, and Zev would lick his friend, molding his body around the small human.

If his mother would only send him to the Sunshine and Moonlight Nursery School, then he'd get to talk to Jonah and play with him in his human form. He just knew they'd make the best of friends, even though Jonah was a half-soul.

He furrowed his brow when he thought about the distaste in the elders' voices when they used that word. Even when the humans were customers in their shops, the pack only barely tolerated them. He knew his kind was supposed to distrust the half-souls, keep their distance, but Zev didn't understand why, and he just couldn't do that with Jonah. The white-haired boy was his. Zev's wolf knew it instinctively, and Zev's human agreed. Maybe when he grew bigger, he'd be able to find a way to play with his friend.

Zev looked up from the huddle and turned his head to the other side of the field. The group of humans wearing bright red jerseys was listening intently to their coach. Well, all but one. Jonah's black eyes were aimed straight at Zev.

This was the first time Jonah had seen Zev's human. The six years since his wolf had first met the blond boy had passed without Zev ever having had the opportunity to introduce himself to his friend in this form. But now the time had finally come. Both boys played soccer in the Etzgadol City League. They were on different teams, of course. Zev's team was all shifters. He was sure the pack would have forced them to play in an all-shifter league, if there were such a thing. But the shifter population didn't have enough boys in his age group to make up a whole league, so the pack formed its own team in the Etzgadol City League.

When Zev had learned of the integrated league two years earlier, he'd immediately developed what his parents called an "almost maniacal obsession" with both soccer and baseball—not coincidentally, the two sports in the Etzgadol City League. He'd never bothered with other sports because he'd seen no point. The only reason to participate, as far as Zev was concerned, was the chance to play with his human friend.

Zev's wolf had taken the brochure for the soccer league to Jonah months ago. At first, the human boy had seemed confused by the gesture. He'd just taken the paper out of the wolf's mouth and stuffed it into his pocket before commencing with their usual greeting—a hug from Jonah and licks from Zev.

The second time Zev brought the information, Jonah had flipped through the brochure, looked into Zev's amber eyes, and asked in a hesitant voice, "You trying to tell me something, Pup?"

The final time, Jonah had just laughed as he tackled Zev's wolf to the ground. "Okay, I got the message, Pup, I talked to my dad and he said I could play soccer."

Zev was so happy he yipped and licked Jonah all over while they wrestled on the ground. He'd long since stopped being a puppy, at least in size. His human was much larger than other children his age and his wolf was the size of a full grown dog. He'd grow bigger in time, but even at his current size, he was no pup. And although that word was a schoolyard taunt among his kind, he enjoyed hearing it from his Jonah. It sounded tender and sweet.

After that day, whenever Zev came to visit Jonah, the boy snuck over to the woods at the edge of his yard and brought his soccer ball. "My dad bought me this ball. Wanna play?"

Their games never lasted longer than ten minutes. Zev had to return to his den before his parents became too angry at the length of his absence, and Jonah had to go back to his yard before his father became too curious about what he was doing. But they had fun together, with Jonah kicking and Zev blocking the ball with his head and tackling the boy with nonregulation moves that always caused giggles and rewarded him with hugs and strokes of his fur. Now Zev's human stood on a soccer field with three minutes left in the game, during which, for the first time, he had been able to look at his Jonah through human eyes.

Zev's team, the Fury, had been undefeated all season. Shifters were generally stronger than humans, even as children, so one of the two shifter teams had always been league champion. The games against human teams were really just warm-ups for the main event: a shifter versus shifter playoff. But it was different against this human team. The Storm had beaten every other human team all season long and had come close to defeating the other shifter team.

After being with Jonah on the field for nearly fifty minutes, Zev and every other player on his team understood the reason for the human team's success: Jonah was an incredible player.

The blond boy guarded his goal with a speed and agility normally reserved for shifters. His coal-colored eyes scanned the field, taking note of every player's location, and he always found a way to place his body in the perfect position to block goals. Jonah was such a skilled player, in fact, that the only two goals scored by the Fury had taken place when Jonah was on the sidelines resting and another player stood in the goal. Zev had scored both of those goals.

"We're only up one point, guys. It's time to get serious with these mutts."

Zev growled low in his throat when he heard his teammate, Brian Delgato, make the insult. He never liked hearing his pack insult the humans, but with Jonah on the receiving end of the taunt, Zev's hackles were truly up. The other shifter boys were so focused on the game they didn't realize Zev's anger was aimed at one of their own rather than at the opposing team.

Brian, Zev, and Toby took the ball up the field as the clock counted down. Toby passed to Brian, and he made a final effort to score a goal. Even with his eyes locked on Zev, Jonah was able to jump to his left and deflect the shot. The whistle blew and Brian stomped off the field. The rest of Zev's team ran over to the sidelines, happy with their victory, even if the score was tighter than they would have liked. A few boys on

Jonah's team wiped tears from their eyes, sad their season had ended. Jonah and Zev remained on the field, watching each other from their respective spots ten feet apart.

Zev's heart felt like it was beating out of his chest. He'd never questioned his reaction to Jonah. He'd been lured to the human for as long as he could remember, so it seemed as normal to Zev as running and eating. But now that he was seven years old, he was starting to realize that his draw to the boy was unusual, and not just because Jonah was a human. Even other shifters didn't seem to need each other in the way Zev's whole being told him he needed Jonah.

"My name's Jonah. What's your name?"

That voice, which Zev had heard giggle with his wolf for years, was finally speaking to his human. As if pulled by a magnetic force, Zev stepped toward the other boy. Jonah flipped his white-blond hair off his face and met Zev halfway. When they were close enough to feel each other's breath, Zev answered.

"I'm Zev."

Jonah's black eyes looked intently at Zev, so he cocked his head to the side and stood perfectly still, allowing Jonah to appraise him. His own instincts caused him to want to lean forward and smell the boy, circle around him in greeting, and maybe even lick him. But even at his young age, Zev already knew that type of behavior wasn't welcome or understood by humans, not when he was in his human form. Zev's wolf, of course, had always behaved in exactly that manner with Jonah.

"You're my friend. Right, Zev?"

No statement uttered anywhere had ever been more true.

"Yes, I am." Zev nodded earnestly.

Jonah smiled and took his hand. "Wanna meet my daddy?" Pleased all the way down to his toes with the contact, Zev wrapped his fingers around the human's and let himself get tugged toward the adults on the sidelines. In a few years, they'd be too old to touch this way. But for now, Zev noticed the humans didn't think there was anything unusual about two little boys holding hands, and he was willing to put up with reminders he knew would come from his elders about how important it was to keep a distance from half-souls.

CHAPTER 2

"PLEASE, DAD. Other pack cubs my age are starting at the Etzgadol Middle School this year too." Twelve-year-old Zev Hassick pleaded with his father, desperately hoping he could convince the man that his only son wasn't too young to leave the shifter school and become exposed to humans on a daily basis.

"Zev, we've gone over this. There are very few shifters who send their kids to the city school until high school, and the ones who do are, um, activists."

Zev was losing this argument. Again. And he didn't have any more time. School would start next week, and this was his last chance to convince his parents to let him transfer from the pack school to the Etzgadol Middle School. It was the only hope he had of spending eight hours a day with his Jonah.

"Toby's going to the city school, Dad, and he comes from a good family. You've known Mr. Harrison since you were a cub."

"Yes, I've known Tobias's father for many moons, and Jeremiah's a good man. But his mother...well, Leah's... unusual, Zev. She's not from these parts. You know Jeremiah met her when he was away studying and being hosted by the Miancarem pack."

Zev refused to back down. He kept his posture straight, his head raised, and his eyes on his father's face. He didn't like the way his father and the other pack males disregarded Mrs. Harrison. For that matter, he didn't like the way they seemed to dismiss the importance of all the women in the pack.

"Mrs. Harrison is a strong wolf, Dad. She was very well respected in her old pack, and they were devastated when she left. Toby told me that when they go visit his grandparents, the Miancarem females still come to greet his mother and beg her to return."

Gregory Hassick folded his newspaper and set it down next to him on the couch. He tilted his head to the side and appraised his son. Zev knew what his dad was thinking. How many times had he been told that he was different, different from other shifters his age, different from any shifter his father had ever known?

Even as a very young child, Zev remembered hearing his parents say that he had found his wolf more frequently and for a longer duration than they had previously thought possible. Most shifters didn't make the change until they'd been in their human skin for at least five years, but Zev had spontaneously shifted not long after his first birthday. Even when they started shifting, young boys rarely managed to maintain their wolf form for longer than a few minutes, but Zev shifted for hours at a time. Not only that, but the discomfort associated with bones moving and reshaping never plagued Zev. His parents seemed proud of Zev's unique nature when it came to strength in shifting. He'd often heard his mother brag to her friends that her boy was such a strong shifter that he needed space to run, and his father would usually follow those statements up with assertions about what a wonderful leader his son would make someday. But despite all the praise, Zev recognized his parents' concern about what they perceived as his tendency to wander.

Shifters were social animals, always keeping close together, playing, eating, and sleeping with their pack. Zev was popular with his peers and adored by his elders, so his parents didn't understand why he often wandered off alone, changing into his wolf skin and disappearing into the woods. What his parents didn't realize, what he always kept hidden, was that he didn't leave to be alone. He left to go play with Jonah.

Deciding to focus on what he knew mattered most to his father—Zev's destiny to lead his pack—he gave one final shot at his attempt to attend the human school.

"The city school is bigger than the pack school, Dad, at least twice the size. Their teachers are younger; they understand technology and have a better grasp of the outside world. Things aren't like they were when you were my age. I'll need to learn all sorts of new things in order to be a good Alpha and to run the ceramics business."

Zev immediately saw the change in his father's expression. It was as if he'd finally heard a logical reason to allow his son to attend a school filled with half-souls. Zev was the latest in a long line of Hassick Alphas. Their family had produced the strongest males in the pack for generations.

"Okay, Zev. We'll try it. I do agree that the elders teaching at the pack school are quite far removed from all the changes taking place in the world. And it will be important for the Etzgadol pack to have leaders who are ahead of the pack." Gregory laughed at his own joke.

Zev's wolf practically bounced with joy, but his human managed to portray a happy but not overly enthusiastic exterior. He couldn't let his father know how fundamentally important that decision had been. After all, nobody could ever know about Zev's attachment to a human. He got up from the couch and walked over to his father, giving the big man a loose hug.

"Thanks, Dad." Carefully calculating his next move so it'd seem unrehearsed, Zev turned toward the hallway, then looked back over his shoulder at his father. "And don't worry; I'll keep a close eye on Lori."

Gregory's eyes widened, and Zev knew his father hadn't considered Lori's attendance at the human school. Gregory wouldn't intentionally treat his children inequitably, but Lori was a female and therefore he automatically considered her vulnerable. Plus, no elder thought females had a need to learn the more modern methods they taught at the city school because those teachings wouldn't help a female run a den one day.

Zev stood still and let his father process the situation, hoping the desire to keep Lori with Zev would be enough to sway things in his direction.

Gregory grunted his acquiescence and picked his newspaper back up. Zev hurried down the hallway, closed his bedroom door, and collapsed onto his bed, a radiant smile on his face.

"Come on in, sis, I know you're waiting in there."

Lori opened the door of the Jack-and-Jill bathroom that connected their rooms.

"Well?"

"He said I could go."

She sighed and glared at her brother. "Of course he said you could go, Zev. You can be incredibly persuasive, and if he'd said no, you'd have probably managed a jailbreak. But what about me? Can I go to the city school too?" Lori bit her lip and shifted from foot to foot, her anxiety apparent. So much so that Zev felt bad about teasing his sister.

"Yes, you're coming too, Lori. Go call Toby and give him the good news."

Lori squeaked and jumped on top of her brother, giving him a big hug. Then she ran through the bathroom into her bedroom. Zev figured she'd be talking with Toby for hours. He was Zev's closest shifter friend, and it was only a matter of time before he became Lori's boyfriend.

Zev wished he could call Jonah and tell him the good news, but his human didn't have that kind of relationship with the other boy yet. They'd been playing sports in the same league for several years, and it hadn't escaped Zev's notice that he wasn't the only one who made sure to arrive excessively early to every game his team had against Jonah's. The two boys used that time to run around together, playing and laughing. Zev's heart soared when it seemed that Jonah enjoyed the time he spent with Zev's human as much as that he spent with Zev's wolf. For reasons Zev wasn't yet capable of understanding, he needed Jonah to like both parts of him.

Although Zev's human couldn't call Jonah on the phone, Zev could still share his joy about going to Jonah's school. He'd just have to do it in wolf form. Zev opened his bedroom window and shifted so quickly his clothes dropped to the floor without ripping. It was a handy trick and one he'd never seen another shifter accomplish or allowed another shifter to witness. Then Zev jumped out his bedroom window and ran through the woods, hopeful that Jonah would be playing outside or looking out his window so Zev's wolf could celebrate with his human.

CHAPTER 3

"Where's Jonah?" Toby asked Zev as he peeled off his black, lightweight sweater.

The two young men stood in the high school locker room, changing into their running shorts and T-shirts. After three years of middle school together, Zev and Jonah had become close friends, and Toby also spent a considerable amount of time with them. When he wasn't with Lori, that was.

It was their first week of high school and it'd already been difficult. Only a handful of shifter families had sent their young to the city middle school, and those families generally did so because they believed in integrating their lives with the humans'. Those particular shifter kids had been taught acceptance at home from a young age and had been easily able to blend in with the human kids. As a result, their differences weren't noticed and never caused issues.

Within ten minutes of walking into the Etzgadol High School, however, Zev knew this experience would be markedly different. The pack didn't have its own high school—there weren't enough youth in each grade to create the separate classes needed for teens—so the pack middle school, along with the other two middle schools in town, fed into the city high school. Despite being in the same building with humans, pack kids stuck together and made no effort to assimilate.

When Zev, Toby, and Lori had walked in the door on that first day, they'd seen the pack friends they'd grown up with clustered together. The humans with whom they'd spent their middle school years stood apart, looking in confusion at the kids they didn't know. Within a matter of days, all the older human kids had sent the message to the younger ones—stay away from the kids in the pack. Not that they called them "pack," of course. Some said they all belonged to a cult, others said they were part of a weird religious sect. But everyone understood the basic principles: they're different, they're not like us, don't talk to them, don't study with them, keep apart. Depending on whether a pack kid or a city kid was talking, the "they" and the "them" would interchange, but the meaning always stayed the same: shifters and humans don't mix.

Zev looked at the clock on the wall. Track practice was about to start and Jonah wasn't there, which was very out of character. The human hadn't missed a single day of school or practice throughout their middle school years. And he'd seemed fine in the sixth-period English class he shared with Zev.

"Hey! You're not supposed to be in here!"

A commotion coming from the front of the locker room disrupted Zev's thoughts. Then he heard his sister's panicked voice.

"Whatever. I'm not here to look at you, okay? I'm looking for Zev Hassick and Toby Harrison. Have you seen them?"

Toby pulled the jeans he'd lowered to his knees back up and practically tripped over himself hurrying toward Lori.

"Lori? We're right here. What's wrong?"

Zev joined his friend and carefully looked his sister over. She didn't seem injured, just scared and winded.

"It's Jonah."

Zev's stomach dropped. He clasped Lori's shoulders.

"What about Jonah? Where is he?"

Lori's shoulders slumped and her hands dropped to her knees; she was gasping for air.

"He's in the back of the school, Zev. You have to hurry. They had him surrounded and they wouldn't listen to me." She straightened herself and locked her eyes with her brother's. "Hurry!"

Zev leaped over the benches and ran out of the locker room at full speed. Thankfully, he'd already dressed in his shorts and tied his shoes before Lori had arrived, otherwise he'd have run through the school naked to get to Jonah. His heightened hearing allowed him to get an idea of the problem before he was close enough to intervene. Brian Delgato and two other shifter teens were yelling at Jonah.

"We warned you to stay away from her! She's not for you, understand? Since you're obviously too stupid to listen to reason, we have no choice but to show you what happens to people who don't do what they're told."

Zev's heart thumped wildly, and he somehow managed to increase his speed, running faster than he'd ever previously managed. Jonah was a big kid, almost as big as Zev. And he was strong. But shifters were stronger than humans, even when wearing their human skins. And with three of them surrounding Jonah, he didn't stand a chance. Hell, even very few shifters would manage to come out victorious against those odds.

The sounds of fists hitting bodies intermingled with shouting ratcheted Zev's anxiety even higher. Just as he was about to turn the corner, the noise stopped. That unexpected silence increased the fear that racked Zev's body to such high proportions that he thought he might vomit.

"Get away from..."

Zev's warning stuck in his throat as he finally managed to get around the edge of the building to survey the scene in front of him. Brian lay on the ground, cradling his arm. A shifter who was two years older than Zev was flat on his back with his eyes closed. The third shifter who'd threatened Jonah held his nose, trying to block the blood that poured out from between his fingers. And in the center of the damage stood Jonah, his fists clenched, face sweaty, blond hair disheveled, and expression fierce.

"Jonah? Are you okay?" Zev approached his friend slowly with his hand held out, palm up.

Jonah's black eyes widened as he seemed to notice for the first time what he'd done. He stepped toward Zev and then froze when more shifter boys came out of the school, saw their wounded comrades, and realized a human was responsible. They stormed toward Jonah.

"Hey! What'd you do? Get him!"

Zev completed the few steps necessary to reach Jonah. He stood in front of his friend, blocking the group of shifters, then curled his lips back over his teeth and growled low in his throat. The newly approaching boys hesitated, bumping into each other in their haste to stop in the face of the boy everyone knew would one day lead their pack.

Two of the shifters on the ground scrambled to their feet, while the third tried to rise, but swayed and landed back on his ass.

"He fought by your side. That means you help him up when he falls," Zev growled. As angry as he was at the threat to Jonah, he couldn't ignore his need to lead and teach his pack members. He wasn't their Alpha yet, but the instincts were deeply ingrained.

Brian quickly knelt down and lent support to the boy on the ground. When they were on their feet, they backed up to join the other pack kids.

"Zev, he hurt our own." Conrad, a strong shifter in his final year of high school, met Zev's eyes but kept his head slightly lowered as a sign of respect. Clearly, he wasn't sure how to deal with the Alpha's son defending a human who seemed to have attacked three pack members.

"They instigated it!" Lori's voice was frazzled and unusually high-pitched.

Zev didn't turn around, keeping his eyes on those who threatened his human friend. Within moments Lori and Toby were by his side.

"What happened, Lori?"

The surprise on the other shifters' faces was evident when Zev asked Lori to weigh in. During a standoff between males, a female shouldn't even be in the area, let alone consulted for her opinion.

Finally able to calm down now that the immediate danger had passed, Lori regained her composure. When she spoke again, it was with the strength of a young woman destined to lead the females in their pack.

"Brian and the others have the same lunch hour as me and Jonah. They weren't happy that I ate with him instead of them. So they waited for us to leave the building after school ended, and then they went after him." Her eyes blazed with anger as she turned toward Brian and looked at him accusingly. "Even after I told them to stop."

Zev growled, his body vibrating with the need to shift and punish those who had disrespected his kin and threatened the person who meant more to him than any other. The realization of just how much he cared about Jonah startled Zev, but it didn't slow him down.

"Stay here," he rumbled.

Lori and Toby complied instinctively, locking their feet in place and staring down the group of shifters, who had backed away far enough to put a comfortable distance between them.

"What do you think you're doing, Zev?" Jonah seemed to have finally snapped out of his daze. His hand landed on Zev's shoulder, holding him back.

"I'm going to take care of this so they never bother you again, that's what." Zev tried to move forward, but Jonah's grip was surprisingly strong.

"Did you happen to notice that I took care of myself just fine? I'm not some damsel in distress you need to rescue, Hassick. I can hold my own. Besides, I don't remember asking for your help."

Lori noticeably winced in reaction to Jonah's words and tone. He was questioning Zev's decisions, his leadership, his right to manage a situation involving his pack. But instead of punishing the human, or demonstrating his superior strength so Jonah would back off, Zev turned around to face his friend, his posture relaxing, head tilted to the side, and his voice soft.

"I saw what you did, Jonah, and I'm impressed. More than impressed. But I'm asking you to let me handle this. Those guys who attacked you, and the other ones over there, I've known them my whole life. They're...family friends. Will you please wait here while I talk to them?"

Toby's jaw dropped in surprise at Zev's reaction. Yeah, Zev realized his method of interacting with Jonah was unusual. After all, a stronger shifter never asked another for permission on how to act, let alone a human. Even Lori, who was well accustomed to her brother's idiosyncrasies, gasped at the quiet, placating tone Zev used when he spoke to Jonah.

Jonah's concern that his friend thought of him as weak or incapable of handling the situation dissipated in response to Zev's voice and posture. He nodded and relaxed his hands at his sides.

The bloody, swollen knuckles didn't escape Zev's notice, and he had to stifle an almost overwhelming urge to take Jonah's hands in his and lick the wounds until they healed. Pushing down the growl that wanted to escape in reaction to Jonah's injuries, Zev turned and stalked over to his pack mates. He looked only at Conrad, the oldest, strongest member of the spontaneously formed group, and spoke in a low rumble.

"They picked a fight with a human on school grounds in broad daylight. We don't need this kind of attention. It's bad for the pack."

Conrad nodded in agreement and turned to the three shifters who had been involved in the fight. Two of the boys stood with their heads arched to the side, throats exposed, and limbs loose, showing their submission in every way they knew how. Only Brian kept his head up and dared to smirk at Zev. Conrad growled at the stupidity the shifter exhibited. No matter what had led to the fight, there was no doubt Zev could take Brian down without breaking a sweat. Everyone in the pack knew of the presumptive Alpha's strength. Conrad glared at Brian.

"Explain yourself," he said in a harsh voice.

Brian crossed his arms and continued to stare at Zev defiantly, causing his coconspirators to step back, hoping to distance themselves from their disrespectful friend. "He's been eating lunch with your sister all week, Zev, even after we told him to stay away from her. Girls are weak; we have a duty to protect them. You should be thanking us for trying to keep that half-soul away from Lori."

Zev growled as loud as he could in his human skin. He curled his lips back over his teeth, pulled his shoulders back, and straightened his posture so that his height seemed even more imposing. When he towered over Brian, he spoke very quietly, barely containing his rage.

"My sister is the strongest female in the pack. She's capable of speaking her own mind and she told you not to interfere. Even if you thought she needed help, you shouldn't have instigated a fight with a human. The right action would have been to speak with me or my father. We're responsible for the females in our den, not you, Brian."

The boys who had participated in the fight all but dropped to the ground. They whimpered, expressing their regret. Brian also lowered his chin, but Zev knew the other boy did it grudgingly.

"You've never interacted with the humans, so I'm going to chalk this up to a learning experience and I won't mention it to my father or the other pack elders."

Zev finished speaking to Brian and his two friends, then looked over at Conrad, who, despite having stepped into the situation at the last minute and therefore been innocent of any involvement in the fight, had his head lowered and his eyes pointing downward.

"And, Conrad, I don't know what went on at this school before I came, but this animosity toward humans stops now. I can't force you to be friends with them, but I will demand civility. If I hear of any pack members fighting with humans, I will step in. And the next time, it won't end on school grounds. Any shifter who exposes our pack to unflattering attention by fighting with our human schoolmates will be facing my wolf under the full moon."

Zev looked at every boy and made sure his threat had sunk in. The frightened expressions, exposed throats, and slight twitches let him know he had made the intended impression.

"Spread the word around," he finished before returning to his place at Jonah's side.

CHAPTER 4

"YOU'RE OUR class salutatorian, Zev. College should be a given. I don't understand why you're not going." Jonah repeated the same words he'd said dozens of times during their senior year.

Zev elbowed Jonah and laughed.

"If I didn't know better, Blondie, I'd say that little comment was just an excuse for you to once again point out your higher grade point average. Even though it's only higher by two hundredths of a point."

"Oh, I don't need any excuses to point out my outrageous and advanced awesomeness. My grades are better than yours, I scored more home runs this year, and you couldn't block a ball from the goal if your life depended on it. Bottom line, dude, I'm superior."

Zev laughed and reached into the bag of chips on his lap. He took out a handful, throwing them at Jonah one by one as he spoke. "I pitched more perfect games than any kid in the history of our school. Ditto for my score average in soccer, Mr. Hides-in-the-Goal. Plus, I have a bigger dick."

"Oh, such violence! Not sure if I can handle it. Save me! Save me!" Jonah yelled and laughed as he protected his face from the onslaught of chips with his hands and swayed on his feet.

Zev dropped the chip bag and tackled Jonah onto the bed, landing on top of him. The two friends were pressed together, their bodies connected from ankle to thigh to chest. Somehow, lying that way made Zev's lungs work harder than when he'd been jumping around Jonah's bedroom. Zev's amber eyes locked onto Jonah's intense black gaze. What was it about this person that impacted him so deeply?

"You weren't kidding about that last one, were you?" Jonah asked breathlessly, and Zev realized that the close physical contact had caused his cock to harden against his friend's hip.

He should get up. The feelings coursing through his body were wrong. But being close to Jonah didn't feel wrong. In fact, for as long as Zev could remember, he'd felt most right in his life whenever his human or his wolf was with Jonah. And that moment, lying together on Jonah's bed, was no exception.

"What is this, Jonah?" Zev asked, his voice sounding rough and uncertain to his own ears. He was sure his confusion—hell, his fear—was evident by his expression. Jonah knew him too well to miss that. And even if he didn't, lying as close together as they were, Jonah was surely able to feel Zev's racing heart.

Jonah reached up and brushed Zev's brown locks off his forehead, the expression on his face tender.

"We're done with high school now, Zev. I'm leaving for college in two days. I'm tired of pretending." Jonah took a deep breath before continuing. "This is attraction," he finished softly.

Fright turned to terror as Zev's eyes widened, and he shook his head furiously.

"No, that can't be. I can't feel that way about you. It's not possible."

Despite his panic, Zev was still hard, and he'd made no move to separate their bodies. But Jonah didn't mention that. Instead, he continued stroking Zev's hair and spoke softly, as if he were calming a wild animal.

"Why can't you be attracted to me, Zev? Or is it that you think you shouldn't feel the way you do about guys in general?"

Zev's head swam. How did he feel about guys in general? He let the thought take root and reflected on it. He didn't feel anything in particular about guys; he never thought about them. Well, except for Jonah. He always thought about Jonah.

"I don't have a thing for guys in general. I swear." His tone sounded desperate, but he couldn't help it. It was how he felt.

Jonah kept his caress constant, motivating Zev to press his face toward the welcome contact. He sniffed the palm of Jonah's hand, and the familiar scent both excited and calmed him. Why did he always react that way to Jonah's scent?

"So you're saying you like girls, Zev? As far as I know, you've never had a girlfriend or even a date."

Jonah's words stunned Zev, not that they should have been a revelation. After all, Zev was fully aware of his own dating history. Or lack thereof. It was just that he'd never given it any thought. How did he feel about girls? Zev thought about it and came to the same conclusion as he had about guys—he didn't think about them. He shook his head again, his entire body trembling as he came dangerously close to a dawning realization.

"I don't like girls either. I mean, I like them, you know. Just not like that."

Jonah smiled sweetly.

"Zev, you're an eighteen-year-old guy. You can't possibly expect me to believe that you're asexual or something. You must have those feelings. You don't have to pretend with me. I'm your friend. Your best friend. You're safe with me, Zev. No matter what you tell me about yourself, I won't judge you. Hell, I might even surprise you with some things about the way I'm made."

Although Zev knew Jonah was talking about his own desires, the statement had highlighted the crux of the problem. Zev was a shifter. He couldn't be attracted to another male. His kind wasn't made that way.

"I have to go." Zev scrambled to his feet, his eyes darting around the room as if he were a caged animal, then he flung himself at the door, yanked it open, and ran out.

Zev ran through the woods, his normal grace replaced by wild, frantic movements. Twigs and leaves crumbled under his feet and branches slapped across his face and forearms, leaving cuts and welts in their wake. Shifters healed rapidly, but that didn't mean injuries didn't hurt. Nevertheless, in his immensely agitated state, Zev couldn't feel any external pain. Every ounce of mental power he had was focused on his conversation with Jonah, on the way his heart raced when he was with his best friend, on the delicious scent of the young man, on the word Jonah had used to describe all of those feelings: attraction.

Zev reached his house and pushed his way inside. He stumbled toward his bedroom, dragging air into his lungs.

"Zev? Honey, is that you?"

The sound of his mother's warm voice drifting over from the kitchen forced Zev to get himself under control. He slowed his pace but kept walking toward his room.

"Yeah, it's me, Mama. I need to go for a run. I'm going to leave my clothes in my room, and then I'll get going."

Zev had reached his doorway by the time she responded. Based on the volume of her voice, he knew she was right behind him.

"What about dinner, Zev? You must be hungry."

He walked into his room and stripped off his shirt, keeping his back turned to her. When he was alone, he allowed his wolf to take over so quickly that undressing wasn't necessary because the clothes fell easily to the wayside. But with his mother present, Zev forced himself to slowly undress. He wasn't ready to explain his ability to shift more quickly than others. His parents already knew he was

different, stronger than the other shifters. They didn't need
to know all the details.

"I'll hunt something for dinner, Mama. I need to clear my
head, my wolf needs to roam."

She hesitated, aware of her son's unusual penchant for
running on his own, then relented.

"I understand, dear. You go have a nice run and hunt.
Stay out as long as your wolf demands."

Zev's clothes were in a pile by the window by the time his
mother had finished her sentence, and then he was outside,
letting his animal control his impulses and desires. He was
certain that shifting into his wolf would solve the dilemma
that had been plaguing his human. After all, his beast was
more primal than his man; he worked on instinct rather than
logic. But much like his human, Zev's wolf insisted that he
was attracted to Jonah.

It was as if Jonah's act of speaking the words out loud had
knocked down the walls. Zev's conscious knowledge of this
now obvious attraction was no longer blocked. He couldn't
continue to hide or pretend he didn't know. How was this
possible? How could he be attracted to a male human—
two factors that would prevent him from tying and should
therefore repel him, or at the very least his wolf?

He caught a rabbit for dinner, climbed the highest peak
in the forest, and howled at the moon in frustration. As if the
attraction to his best friend wasn't confusing enough on its
own, it wasn't the only thing the conversation with Jonah had
brought to the forefront of Zev's mind. The other realization

now consuming him was that he'd never been attracted to anybody other than Jonah in his entire life.

It didn't make sense. Shifters were, if anything, more sexual than humans. His peers had long been sexually active within the pack. In fact, the only time Zev had ever heard of a shifter having such a limited attraction was when... Zev's wolf sucked in a deep breath as shock radiated through his body. The only time he'd ever heard of a shifter being attracted to only one other was when that shifter had a true mate. And in that circumstance, the shifter would never want anyone other than his true mate because that shifter's spirit was already bound with that of his mate, and he could never tie with another.

Jonah was Zev's true mate.

He waited for his wolf to brush off the thought, but instead all he felt was a deep sense of peace fall over his body, as if he'd been tense his entire life just waiting for that truth to make itself known. Zev didn't understand how it was possible; it was completely inconsistent with everything he'd been taught. Yet, no matter how illogical the realization, in his wolf form, Zev couldn't deny it. His wolf was all primal feeling, and the only thing he felt was the absolute truth, the undeniable fact that the human whose scent had called to him seventeen years earlier and had inspired his first shift, his best friend, the only person to whom his body had ever responded on any level, was his mate. Jonah Marvel was Zev's true mate.

CHAPTER 5

BEFORE HIS mind could process what his body was doing, the brown wolf, larger than many twice his age, was weaving through trees at a breakneck speed. He had to be with his mate, at that very moment and for every other moment in time. When he finally had Jonah's house in sight, Zev froze. He'd never gone farther than the edge of the clearing in his wolf form, knowing it wasn't safe to risk exposure to humans. But it was the middle of the night, so Jonah wasn't outside and wouldn't see him unless he got closer to the house. Zev needed his mate. With that overpowering force driving him, Zev's wolf stalked closer to the house just as Jonah's bedroom window opened.

"Zev? Is that you?" a sleepy whisper sounded out from the window.

Like a puppy receiving the most delicious bone possible, Zev's wolf bounded over to Jonah, jumping up and resting his large paws on the windowsill. The young man laughed, reached his hand out, and stroked Zev's thick coat.

"Oh, it's you, Pup. I thought I heard my friend out here."

Zev tilted his head to the side and looked at Jonah, really looked at him. The young man couldn't have heard anything.

The window had been shut, and Zev had barely made a sound. Even a shifter wouldn't have been able to hear him approach.

As Zev pondered the situation, he remembered other times over the past seventeen years when his wolf had visited Jonah. Sure, there were instances when Jonah had been outside playing. But those days were by far the minority. Usually, Zev's wolf would sit for a few minutes and Jonah would come out, always delighted to see him.

The shifter wondered whether the human even realized why he had been drawn outside. No, he couldn't know. Zev hadn't recognized it until that very moment, and he was a shifter, familiar with their history, well-versed in their powers and, as it turned out, personally acquainted with the internal call between mates. He was certain Jonah had felt more than heard him—that Jonah could sense the call too. It was likely that the mate's call had led Jonah out to his yard over the years when Zev's wolf had come to visit.

Zev pushed his muzzle against Jonah's hand and whimpered, his amber eyes locking on the black orbs shining from the beloved face above him. *Let me in, Jonah. I need to be with you.*

Jonah's brow furrowed in confusion. He backed away a step and patted the sill.

"Do you want to come in, Pup?"

Had his mate heard his thoughts? True mates sometimes shared a mental link. But Zev had been taught that this rare gift presented itself, if at all, only after the mates had been tying for many moons. Like most aspects of the mating bond, the connections were cumulative, strengthening and growing over time. With each tie, mates grew closer together, so close that some true mates had been said to hear each other's unspoken thoughts. Not possible. Jonah couldn't have heard me. It was a coincidence.

Whatever the impetus for the invitation, Zev intended to take it. He backed up from the window and pushed off the ground, leaping into the air, above the sill, and landing smack dab against Jonah, who stumbled backward and crumpled to the floor. And just like that, Zev found himself in the same position he'd been earlier that day, his body covering his best friend's, his eyes looking down at Jonah's, and, yes, his dick hard as a rock from the close proximity to this man, from the touch of his hands stroking Zev's fur, from his stimulating scent. Zev wanted Jonah like he'd never wanted anything else in his life. The need was so strong it made his bones ache.

The human buried within the wolf's skin exerted every ounce of control he had and forced his wolf to move back, lest he frighten his best friend. Zev raised himself off Jonah on shaky legs and backed away into the corner. He rolled himself into a ball and whimpered quietly. He hurt. Every nerve ending in his body wanted to touch Jonah. He needed to claim his mate, but he couldn't because Jonah was male and human. Zev had never known pain as intense as that which coursed through him as a result of the denied need to be with his mate, to tie together and join with him in all ways possible.

"What's wrong, Pup?" Jonah approached Zev with his hand out, palm up. He squatted down and looked at him with concern. "Are you sick?"

Jonah's position brought his crotch dangerously close to Zev's face. The young man's enticing scent was strongest in that part of his body, and Zev couldn't stop himself from raising his head and resting it in Jonah's lap, sniffing at him and burrowing as close as he could through the protective barrier of his mate's pajama pants. He rolled onto his stomach, hiding an arousal that he knew would frighten and repulse the human, but kept his head in place on Jonah's thigh with his nose close to Jonah's sex.

With his mate near, he could feel Jonah's heat, smell Jonah's scent. They were together. It was enough. It had to be enough. For now. The last thought—an internal promise from Zev's human to his wolf that the separation from Jonah's body was only temporary—was what Zev's body needed to soothe the cramping that had taken over his intestines.

Jonah lowered himself onto his backside and scooted against the wall. He kept his hand on the thick fur and petted the wolf that he'd seen on an almost daily basis for as long as he could remember.

For the first time since that afternoon's debacle with Zev, Jonah felt calm. He'd had trouble falling asleep, still anxious about Zev's reaction to their encounter and Jonah's assertion that Zev was attracted to him. Even when he'd finally drifted into slumber, Jonah had tossed around restlessly, terrified that he'd driven away his best friend for good. But in that moment, sitting on the floor with his arms around the brown wolf, he felt better. There was something about the animal that tempered Jonah's worry and relaxed him from the inside out.

Jonah sighed. His eyelids felt heavy and his body was worn out from the stressful day. But more than that, he felt complete and at peace. So much so, that with the wolf's warm body pressed against his, Jonah succumbed to sleep, too tired to consider why his cock had lengthened and hardened as soon as he'd embraced the creature.

Jonah snuggled up against the soft, warm pillow and sighed happily. An answering rumble caused him to reassess the pillow theory. As sleep started clearing from his mind, Jonah became aware of the strong heartbeat close to his ear and the sound of someone else breathing. Zev. He sensed Zev.

But the last time he'd seen his best friend, Zev had seemingly had a panic attack and fled, so that didn't make sense.

Jonah opened one eye and was greeted with an amber gaze. Except these amber eyes weren't attached to the body of the young man who'd played front and center in Jonah's every fantasy. They were attached to the brown wolf Jonah had known even longer. His arm was already wrapped around the large canine, so Jonah just moved his hand back and forth over the soft coat, petting his animal friend.

"Morning, Pup. Anyone ever tell you that you make a great teddy bear?"

Jonah laughed when the wolf growled. He actually looked affronted. Who knew that expression was possible for a dog?

"Oh, Pup, did I offend you? Sorry, boy." Jonah squeezed the large animal into a tight hug. It felt so comforting, he didn't want to let go.

"Jonah?"

His father's voice outside his bedroom door forced Jonah to release his hold on the wild creature. The wolf rose to his feet and licked Jonah's neck. Then he walked over to the window and jumped out.

"Coming, Dad."

Jonah watched the wolf run across the yard. Just as the wolf reached the thick trees, Jonah heard a loud gasp. He turned to see his father standing right behind him, staring out the window, his eyes wide and his expression petrified.

"Dad? Are you okay?"

Kevin Marvel didn't respond to his son. His sudden loss of color and panting breath worried Jonah. He grasped his father's shoulders and shook him lightly, hoping to get his attention.

"Dad! What's wrong?"

Kevin swallowed hard a few times and shook his head. "Nothing. Must have been my imagination. Thought I saw a wolf."

Jonah's father was allergic to dogs. It was why he'd never been allowed to have one as a pet. But he hadn't realized there was fear in addition to the allergy. He wondered if his father had been bitten as a child. He was about to ask his dad about the oddly intense reaction he'd just had, but Kevin spoke first.

"I have breakfast ready. Come join me, Jonah. I have some good news I want to share with you."

Well, that tone made for the least persuasive pitch of something good Jonah had ever heard. Was his father tense about the good news or was he still in the throes of his odd reaction to the wolf? Only one way to find out.

"'Kay. I'll be out in a sec."

His father nodded and walked away. Jonah pulled a T-shirt from his drawer and slipped it over his head. Then he made a quick stop in the bathroom before stepping out of his bedroom, down the hallway, through the family room, and into the kitchen, where his father sat at the table waiting for him.

"What's up?" he asked as he reached for his glass of juice and lifted it to his mouth.

"The hospital near the college had an open position. I applied and they offered me the job. That means I'll be able to sell the house and move with you."

Jonah didn't know how to respond. He had a great relationship with his father, but the man had always been a bit overprotective. For the most part, Jonah didn't mind. The long-standing crush on his best friend meant Jonah hadn't ever wanted to sneak off with girls, and until yesterday, Jonah had never been brave enough to express his feelings for Zev. Good relationship or not, though, having your father follow you to college was just weird.

"Look, I can tell you're concerned about this, but don't worry. I won't hold you back, son." Kevin Marvel reached his hand across the table and rested it on his son's cheek. "You're my only family, Jonah. I know you think you're all grown, but you'll always be my baby, and I want to keep you safe."

How was he supposed to respond to that? Jonah had never known his mother. She'd died when he was a baby. His father had never dated again, devoting his life completely to his son. Sometimes Jonah felt it was too much pressure, but he loved his father and felt grateful for their close relationship.

"Okay, Dad. I'm glad we'll be moving together. It'll be great."

When he saw the tension leave his father's body and a smile grace his father's face, Jonah knew he'd said the right thing. He dug into his meal and tried to focus on how wonderful it would be to move to a new place, how much fun he'd have in college, how much he'd learn. Basically, Jonah tried to think about everything except the fact that, with his father's move, there'd be no reason for him to return to Etzgadol. No reason for him to ever see Zev Hassick again, even if his friend was willing to spend time with him after the previous afternoon's fiasco. An ache deep in his chest told Jonah that if he didn't make up with his friend, he'd never be able to recover from the loss.

CHAPTER 6

AFTER HELPING his father clean up the breakfast dishes, Jonah walked into the bathroom adjoining his bedroom, stripped off his pajama pants and T-shirt, and stepped into the shower. He leaned his head back and enjoyed the feeling of the water flowing over his hair and shoulders, caressing his body. As usual, any thoughts of stimulation to his body immediately made Jonah think of Zev. At eighteen years old, Jonah was already over six feet tall, taller than most other guys his age. But his best friend had several inches on him.

Jonah snickered. Based on the feeling of Zev's hard cock pressed against his hip the previous afternoon, Jonah guessed height wasn't the only place where Zev was bigger than other guys. A strange feeling deep within Jonah's body distracted him from his internal stand-up comedy routine. He suddenly felt...empty. That was the only word that fit. His body felt empty. And without any conscious action, his insides were moving, contracting and releasing of their own accord. The feeling should have been uncomfortable, but instead it was arousing.

Blood pulsed into Jonah's dick in time with the contractions in his ass. His member lengthened and hardened, and he felt light-headed from the intensity of his sudden arousal. Jonah closed his eyes and rested his forehead and arms against the cool tile. His heart raced, and he needed something, but he didn't know what it was.

"Holy damn!"

Jonah's head snapped up to see Zev's face peeking into the shower. Zev had the shower curtain clenched in his fist and his eyes roved over Jonah's naked body, taking him in from head to toe. Jonah's cock, which had already been hard from the start of a fantasy about his friend, twitched in response to the real life Zev standing next to him.

"W-what are you doing here?" Jonah stuttered.

"Your dad let me in just as he was leaving for work. Told me you were back in your room. I heard the shower and just..."

Zev looked at the drops of liquid leaking from the crown of Jonah's cock and moaned. He licked his lips and stepped into the shower, fully clothed. Reaching a shaking hand over to his friend, Zev touched Jonah's shoulder, the nape of his neck, his chest, ribs, and hip—and then wrapped his hand around his hot, pulsing dick.

Oh, God, it felt so right. Zev closed his eyes. The pleasure of touching Jonah intimately was so very right. Up and down the shaft he went, enjoying the pleasure of his fingers wrapped around the smooth skin covering hard steel.

Clutching Zev's waist, Jonah said, "Feels so good. Makes my legs weak." He thrust his hips back and forth into Zev's fist. "I'm gonna… Gonna…" Jonah trembled and panted, and he squeezed Zev so tightly, he was sure there'd be bruises later.

Zev continued to move his hand up and down, his grip slightly tighter, pace slightly faster.

"So good. So good. Zev!" White cream shot from Jonah's cock and ran over Zev's hand. His body went limp, he dropped his head against Zev's neck, and he kept his hands on Zev's waist.

Zev wrapped his arms around his mate and held him tight. By the time Jonah finally lifted his head and looked into Zev's eyes, the shower had soaked them both.

"You're wet," Jonah whispered.

"So are you," Zev responded as he rubbed circles on Jonah's back.

"But you're dressed and I'm naked."

"Yeah, I sorta noticed that. It was the whole you-naked thing that made me climb in here so fast."

Zev sighed. It was going to be hard to think around this man. His wolf wanted to claim his mate and any disruptions were unwelcome. But there would have to be a long conversation between them before that could happen. Not only about their relationship, but about Zev being something other than completely human. One step at a time. Relationship first; revelations that shifters weren't fictional characters from horror movies later. Zev held Jonah closer.

"This okay, Jonah?"

Jonah nodded.

"Yeah, it's okay. I've wanted this for a long time." He raised his hands and stopped inches from Zev's head. "Damn it, you're my best friend. I shouldn't worry about saying stuff to you."

"Don't hold back with me, Blondie." Zev frowned, not liking the idea of his mate keeping any part of himself hidden, despite his doing that very thing.

Jonah gulped nervously. "Can I touch you too, Zev?"

"Yeah, you can touch me." Zev reached behind Jonah and turned off the water. "But we should get out of the bathroom. These wet clothes are starting to feel uncomfortable."

With a dip of his chin, Jonah stepped out of the shower and lifted his towel from the hook. He dried off quickly, then wrapped it around his waist and walked toward the door.

"I'll go get you a towel. Be right back."

Zev pulled his wet shirt off over his head and pushed his soaking jeans down to his feet, where they caught on his sneakers. He growled in frustration and was about to bend down to wrestle the shoes off his feet when Jonah returned. Jonah laughed at his predicament, handed him the towel, then dropped to his knees and unlaced Zev's shoes as Zev dried himself.

Once Zev was free of his shoes and socks, he stepped out of his pants and briefs and onto the mat outside the shower. Jonah was still crouched down on the ground. He raised his gaze and slid it slowly up Zev's body, resting his eyes on Zev's towel-covered groin.

"I'm going to throw your things in the dryer." Jonah gathered Zev's dripping clothes into his arms and stood back up. "You can borrow something of mine to wear if you want, Zev, but..." Jonah shifted from foot to foot nervously and dropped his gaze to the ground. "But I'd rather you didn't get dressed," he finished in a whisper, his tone and expression uncharacteristically shy.

Zev took Jonah's chin in his hand and lifted it so the other man was forced to meet his eyes. Okay, so he'd been blind to his own feelings for this man for years. But now that he knew, he wasn't going to hide, wasn't willing to waste more time. Zev had been born and raised to lead, and he'd never struggled with that role. It was who he was. Power had rolled off him since he was a cub, letting every shifter know he was destined to run their pack. He'd always been decisive, strong-willed, and determined, and those traits weren't going to change.

The denial and hesitancy he'd initially expressed when Jonah was forced to point out Zev's own feelings were gone. He didn't know how it was possible to have a human mate or how to tie with a male, and he'd need to figure it out, but he wasn't going to deny it, wasn't going to hide from it. No, Zev would embrace his true mate. Jonah was a gift. A handsome, funny, strong, brilliant gift.

"I won't get dressed. And, Jonah, don't hide from me. I'm your best friend. You're safe with me. No matter what you tell me about yourself, I won't judge you." Zev repeated the words Jonah had used with him the previous day.

Jonah smiled and nodded, then walked out of the bathroom, through the bedroom, and out to the hallway. Zev finished drying his body, hung his towel, and then headed into Jonah's bedroom. He noted the stacks of boxes in the corner, Jonah's belongings ready for his move, and felt a stab in his chest. With a hand pressing down against his heart, Zev settled into Jonah's bed and thought about how to handle the situation facing him.

True mates didn't separate. Not ever, not for any length of time. True mates were said to be incomplete without each other, a single spirit torn in half, residing in two separate vessels. When true mates finally found each other, they tied together, allowing the spirit to reconnect, becoming whole once again. Tribal lore said true mates were rarely apart for even a few hours; most found jobs together during the day to ensure an almost constant connection. And because of the reverence paid to the rare mating bond, packs did everything in their power to ensure true mates were able to remain together at all times.

So what was Zev supposed to do? He had a true mate, but his mate was human. Jonah didn't know about spirits. He didn't understand the concept of true mates or tying. Jonah was human. How could Zev tie with a human? Hell, how could Zev tie with a male? None of it made sense, and Zev didn't have the time to figure it all out because Jonah was going to move away for college. With that thought, the pain in his chest sharpened once again and Zev had trouble breathing.

"Hey." Jonah stood at the door, a towel still draped around his waist, his hands in tight fists by his sides.

"Hey yourself." The pressure in Zev's body ebbed at the sight of his friend. He grinned, lifted one end of the blanket, and gestured for the human to join him in bed.

Jonah's hands relaxed and a glowing smile came over his adorable face. He took the two steps necessary to reach the bed, dropped the towel, and then crawled under the covers, stopping when he was a couple of inches apart from Zev. They lay on their sides, looking at one another's faces. Soon their hands reached out and stroked skin, moved over bodies, and explored.

After so many years of wondering what this would feel like, Jonah's curiosity was finally being sated. It felt amazing. Every part of Jonah was engaged—his body, his mind, his heart. He wanted his friend to crawl under his skin, wedge himself inside his body. It seemed to Jonah that was the only way to get Zev close enough.

When Zev's hand caressed his cheek and Zev's fingers roamed over the side of his ear, Jonah raised his eyes and locked onto an amber gaze. With a light nudge, Zev pulled him closer and met him halfway. Firm red lips landed on his and Jonah was in heaven. He melted against his friend, parted his lips, and moaned when Zev's tongue entered his mouth. Their nude bodies bridged the few-inch gap between them and pressed together. Tongues danced, hands brushed through hair, and dicks rubbed against hot skin.

Jonah felt the pace of Zev's thrusts against him increase, heard Zev's breath coming faster, felt Zev's heart beating harder, and he knew his friend was nearing the precipice. Suddenly Zev rolled on top of Jonah, pinning him down against the mattress and pushing his hips back and forth against Jonah's as long fingers tangled in Jonah's hair and a talented tongue continued its assault on Jonah's mouth. He met Zev every step of the way, clutching the other man's hips and bucking up to meet every thrust.

He moaned into Zev's mouth, and just as his climax approached, Jonah instinctively turned his head to the side, baring his neck to Zev. Jonah heard a growl, felt it vibrating against his skin, inside his skin. Zev moved his teeth over Jonah's neck, but he didn't bite down. Just the slight pressure against that part of his body was enough to set Jonah off. He cried out Zev's name and felt his cock pulsing between their bodies, joined seconds later by Zev's release.

They lay together, sticky from their combined seed, gasping for air and waiting for their racing hearts to slow. Zev rained kisses down on Jonah's neck, his shoulder, his face. Jonah wrapped his arms around his friend's imposing frame, stroked Zev's skin, and shivered with delight at their new connection.

"Wow. That was so much better than beating off." Jonah practically giggled.

Zev laughed. And then nodded and kissed Jonah's cheek.

"Yeah, it's way better."

"What took you so long, Hassick?"

CHAPTER 7

WHAT HAD taken Zev so long? How could he have missed the signs all those years? They were all there, laid out before him as clear as day. It was just that Zev didn't think it was possible for shifters to mate with humans, didn't think it was possible for shifters to be gay. Add to that the fact that true mates were incredibly rare, and the only things he knew about them he'd heard from stories handed down from the elders or from watching his grandparents together, and... Hell, not one of those reasons was a good excuse for why he'd been blind to the mating bond.

"I was an idiot. Guess maybe you really are the smarter one, Blondie."

Jonah stretched his neck up and kissed Zev chastely with closed lips. One kiss wasn't enough, so Zev reached down and took another. Jonah relaxed back on the bed and grinned as Zev continued to pepper his mouth with little kisses.

"You laughing at me?" Zev asked. "Maybe you're not as smart as I thought."

Jonah's smile graduated to a chuckle. "So what if I am laughing, Hassick? What're you gonna do about it? Kiss me to death?"

Zev glared at Jonah, trying to keep his expression stern, then he leaped off Jonah, pinned his golden arms down by his sides, and held them in place with his knees.

"What are you doing?" Jonah asked, his bright smile and happy laugh proving that Zev hadn't succeeded in masking his amusement.

"Isn't it obvious?"

"No, if it was obvious, I wouldn't have—"

Zev attacked his friend's sides and stomach with a flurry of tickles.

"Zev!" Jonah shrieked with surprise, a blush covering his face for that not-so-masculine sound. He tried to wriggle himself out of his predicament, but Zev had weakened him with the onslaught of tickles so he couldn't get loose.

"Damn it, Hassick!" Jonah protested as he gasped for air and squirmed under the assault. He laughed so hard that no sound left his mouth and tears streaked his cheeks. "Stop!" It was more a mime than a verbal word because he couldn't get enough air into his mouth to actually speak. But it was enough to accomplish his goal.

The tickles turned into soft caresses. Zev bent down and kissed the tears off his face, eventually finding his mouth, darting his tongue out and entering when Jonah opened those full lips in welcome. Zev released his hold on Jonah's arms and melted against his mate. His body relaxed and splayed on top of Jonah's, his hands combed through that soft blond hair, and his mouth merged with Jonah's, enjoying the delicious flavor.

Without moving apart, Zev moaned and whispered into Jonah's mouth, "Damn, Blondie, you're a great kisser."

Jonah moved his arms up to Zev's back, wrapping him in his embrace and stroking his skin. "You're not so bad yourself, Hassick. You been practicing this with someone without me knowing?"

Zev snickered. "You jealous?"

Instead of returning the smile, Jonah looked into Zev's eyes and, without any guile, said, "Yeah. I'm jealous of anyone who got to touch you." Then he held his breath and stared at Zev, clearly waiting for a negative reaction to his confession.

But now that Zev understood who Jonah was to him, he was done freaking out. Completely calm, he gazed into Jonah's eyes and tried to convey the power of his emotions. "Unless you can manage being jealous of yourself, you don't have to worry. Like I told you yesterday, I haven't ever thought about anyone else—girls or guys—let alone touched anyone else. It's just you, Blondie. It's always been you." Zev let his words sink in, then he reversed the tables on the discussion. "What about you? Been hiding out behind the bleachers sneaking kisses with cheerleaders?"

Jonah snorted more than laughed. "Uh, Zev, I was teasing about the whole not-so-smart thing earlier, but now I'm thinking I may have been on to something. That hardness you feel against your stomach isn't a banana. That's me happy to see you, or feel you, in this case. And you're a guy. With that background in place, we can add two and two together here and even someone with your limited math skills can come up with the correct answer. I'm gay. I've got no deep dark cheerleader secrets in my past."

Zev was amazed at how easily Jonah said the words. He admired how his friend so completely accepted this part of himself. No shame, no hesitation. Just a matter-of-fact statement. In that moment, Zev decided he'd take the same approach. He knew it'd shock his parents. Hell, it'd rock his whole community. But he was attracted to a man. He had a male mate. That meant he was gay. Zev Hassick was a gay shifter. The pack would just have to find a way to deal with that truth even though they'd always believed it to be impossible.

"And in case you're wondering," Jonah continued, his hand still rubbing Zev's back but now moving lower, skating over his ass, "I don't have any deep dark football player secrets, either. I've had a crush on one guy for as long as I can remember and I kinda put all my eggs in that basket."

Zev took another kiss, slow, soft, and sweet this time.

"I better be the egg-basket guy in that story, Blondie, or the tickles are coming back in full force."

Taking Zev off guard, Jonah responded by pushing up against him and rolling Zev onto his back, reversing their positions. Then Jonah retaliated against the earlier tickle attack by launching one of his own. Zev laughed and wiggled underneath him but made no attempt to buck him off. Apparently deciding Zev had had enough, Jonah settled back against him, pushed a lock of hair off his forehead, and replied to his last comment, completely deadpan.

"Yeah, I was referring to your basket."

Zev groaned loudly and rolled his eyes. "It's a good thing you're so incredibly good-looking, because your sense of humor is for shit. Was that supposed to be a joke? Weak double entendres do not count as humor."

"You...you think I'm good-looking?" Jonah hated the whiny, insecure tone of his question, but he was surprised to hear Zev describe him that way.

Zev was honestly the best looking guy Jonah had ever seen. And not only in person; that included men in movies and magazines. His features were strong and masculine, brown hair with a hint of chestnut highlights, remarkable amber eyes set the perfect distance apart, nose the right proportion to the rest of his face, a strong chin—he even had dimples. And that was just his face. Zev's body was downright incredible. So tall and broad that huge wasn't an overstatement, and covered in rippling muscles. Jonah was always the strongest, fastest, biggest guy around until Zev walked into the room, and then he felt almost small in comparison. It should have been annoying, but instead, it aroused Jonah. Everything about Zev turned him on.

"I think you're beautiful, Jonah. I've always thought you're beautiful."

Zev seemed sincere, the look in his eyes adoring, so Jonah realized he believed Zev even though it wasn't true.

Jonah knew he had a good body, tall, strong, well-defined. But there was something about his face that didn't look quite right. Every individual feature was fine, but combined they didn't seem to fit. His eyes were a bit too large for the shape of his face, his nose somewhat small. And he'd never seen a natural blond with black eyes.

Well, if Zev's physical reaction to him was any indication, his best friend had no issues with his personal appearance, and that was all that mattered. Jonah moved his hips forward, pressing his belly against Zev's renewed erection.

"Are you already hard again, Hassick?"

"You complaining about my remarkable regenerative powers, Blondie?"

Jonah settled his body on top of Zev's, rested his head on that broad, hard chest, and sighed.

"I like your regenerative powers."

They lay quietly together, Zev stroking Jonah's head, Jonah playing with the hair on Zev's chest.

"Hey, Zev?"

"Yeah?"

"What inspired the about-face?" Jonah asked quietly.

"What do you mean?"

Jonah didn't want to tempt fate by reminding Zev of his reaction to their encounter the previous day, lest he run away again. But this was Zev—his oldest friend, his best friend. They'd stuck together even when all the kids Jonah had grown up with told him to stay away from Zev because he and his family friends belonged to some cult. And Jonah knew Zev had faced similar pressure from those very family friends who didn't understand or like their relationship.

But neither of them had kept away from the other; if anything, they'd grown closer. And their now-former classmates had eventually backed off and even learned to tolerate each other. So standing together, trusting each other, had always served Jonah and Zev well. No reason to think that had changed.

"Yesterday you ran out of here like your ass was on fire when I suggested that you might be attracted to me. And now you're lying naked in my bed. I'd say that's quite a turnaround."

Zev stilled for a few seconds but then continued to caress Jonah's hair.

"I'm sorry about yesterday, Jonah. I was confused. I just..." Jonah could sense Zev's frustration, so he stayed perfectly still and let his friend answer at his own pace. "I never thought I could feel this way about you. I've been taught that it isn't possible. So when you said those things yesterday, they just didn't make sense in the context of my life."

Jonah had met Zev's parents, but only in passing. They'd cheered for their son at almost every soccer and baseball game through high school, but a brief, "Hi, Mr. and Mrs. Hassick," wasn't enough to give Jonah insight into their beliefs. If anything, it was the lack of time spent together that spoke volumes.

Zev had never invited Jonah to his house and he'd never been allowed to spend the night at Jonah's. While the reasons remained unspoken, Jonah knew it was because he wasn't one of Zev's family friends. Jonah respected Zev too much to call them a cult, but he certainly recognized that it was strange, the attachment all those kids had to each other, their unwillingness to let anyone else in. But as odd as they'd always seemed, the Hassicks hadn't struck him as cruel or hateful. And they'd certainly raised children who were open and accepting. Zev and Lori were two of the nicest people Jonah knew.

"What do you mean, it isn't possible? Your family doesn't believe people can be gay?"

Zev was quiet for so long that Jonah wondered whether he'd heard him.

"No, they realize people can be gay, they just..." Zev squirmed uncomfortably underneath him, and Jonah decided to let his friend off the hook. He'd gotten the basic point: Zev's family wasn't going to make things easy for Zev, and there was no reason for Jonah to add to the stress by talking about them any further.

"I get it. I'm sorry, Zev. Do you, uh..." Jonah cleared his throat and found the strength to continue his sentence. "Do you wish you weren't like this? Do you wish you didn't, um, feel this way about me?"

Zev wrapped his arms more tightly around Jonah's body and held him close.

"Oh, hell no. Having you for a true ma—feeling this way about you is a gift, Jonah. I'm just sorry it took me this long to figure it out."

Jonah relaxed into Zev's embrace. He'd been worried that he'd opened Pandora's box and was then going to leave Zev alone to clean up the devastation when he moved away for school the following day. But the other man didn't seem to be struggling with his newly acknowledged feelings. There was no anger, no shame in Zev's voice or actions. He was the same strong, confident person Jonah had always admired and adored. The thought of leaving Zev had been painful, but after what they'd just shared, it had escalated to crippling.

"Zev, are you sure about skipping college? I know your family wants you to take over their business, but is it what you want? And even if it is, don't you want to go to college first?" Jonah's voice lowered as he finished his plea. "Come with me."

Zev stretched and kissed the top of Jonah's head, which was still resting on his broad chest. He rubbed the back of Jonah's neck.

"I can't move away from Etzgadol, Blondie. I have responsibilities here, things I can only learn from my father and grandfather. Besides, your school is in the middle of the city. I don't think I could handle being closed in by those tall buildings with no trees or meadows. You know how much I love the woods."

Yeah, Jonah knew. He couldn't even imagine his friend surrounded by smog and traffic.

"I'm gonna miss you, Hassick."

"Missing doesn't cover it, Blondie. But you'll be home for vacations, right? School breaks and long weekends and..."

"No vacations. My dad's moving away with me. He's selling the house."

Jonah felt tension suddenly consume his friend's large, strong body. "What do you mean he's moving? This is your home. He can't just sell your home."

Zev's voice sounded panicked, and Jonah sensed how Zev's heart had started to race.

"He just told me this morning. Said he wants to stay together so he got a new job. He's gonna sell the house. So, yeah, no vacations in Etzgadol."

Zev's amber eyes closed, the pace of his breath sped, and his hold on Jonah tightened. Nothing made sense. He'd spent his entire life thinking certain things were absolute and suddenly up was down, light was dark, and true mates were forced to separate. Of course, that wasn't the only thing that didn't make sense about the situation with Jonah. The reality was the situation didn't make sense from beginning to end.

First, true mates didn't meet in childhood. It was said to be a protection thing. Because the desire to tie with a true mate was so all-consuming, if mates met during youth, they'd tie too young. Having preteens or teens carrying cubs could be dangerous, and the elders had always explained this was why true mates never came from the same pack. Instead, those lucky and rare shifters who were honored with a true mate would feel the existence of the other half of their soul but would be blessed with a meeting only when their physical bodies were ready to make the tie, usually late in their second decade or early in their third. But Zev had known Jonah for as long as he could remember. His earliest memories were of his wolf rolling with Jonah in the grass of Jonah's backyard.

But it wasn't only the young age when they'd met that distinguished Zev's relationship with Jonah from what he'd been taught took place between true mates. The biggest issues, of course, were that Jonah wasn't a shifter and was a male. Even if a human female were willing to tie with a male shifter, Zev wasn't sure whether the tie would be sufficient to bind the shifter's humanity. But tying with a male was physically impossible.

The combination of all these discrepancies should have been enough to make Zev reject the possibility that Jonah was his true mate. But now that he knew the truth, both his human and his wolf would never allow Zev to deny it again.

He rolled them over so his larger frame blanketed Jonah's, then pressed his nose into Jonah's soft, white-blond hair and inhaled the fresh, clean scent. He burrowed his face against Jonah's neck and licked the spot next to his ear tentatively. The flavor of the other man exploded in his mouth and his tongue sought out more. He nuzzled and nibbled, licked and sucked, until he saw that he'd drawn up a mark on his friend's neck.

Zev raised his head and looked at Jonah lying beneath him, body trembling, heart racing, head arched to the side so his neck was exposed for his ministrations, and wearing Zev's mark. This was his mate. There was not a single doubt in his mind or in his heart. Sure, there were questions to answer, things to learn, but Zev would figure them out. Maybe that was why Jonah was leaving, to give Zev the time he'd need to understand how to tie to a human male.

Yeah, that makes sense, Zev thought. *I've been given an introduction to my mate early because I'll need time to learn how to tie. He'll return to me at the right mating age.*

With this explanation in place, Zev's body calmed. He'd think and research and solve the quandary of how to tie with his mate. And until they could live together and complete the bond, he'd find a way to see Jonah.

"Well, I'll come visit you, Blondie. Not sure how frequently I can do it, but I'll make it work. And it's only four years. Then you can come back permanently and we'll be old enough to... we'll be old enough to, um..."

Zev didn't know how to verbalize his thought. He wasn't ready to explain tying and true mates to Jonah. He needed more time to get his own mind wrapped around their unique situation.

"Are you saying you want to do some sort of long-distance thing, Zev? Like, uh, see each other or whatever?"

"See each other or whatever?" Zev repeated the sentence back to his friend slowly. He had no idea what Jonah was asking, and the confusion was obvious in his voice.

A blush crept up Jonah's cheeks, which Zev found remarkably adorable, and then Jonah stammered, "I guess what I meant was, is this like a one-time thing between us, Hassick, or are you saying you want more?"

Jonah's question made no sense until Zev reminded himself that his friend was human. The other man didn't have the same mating instinct, didn't understand that they were literally made to be together. Zev couldn't be with another even if he wanted to, not that he could ever imagine such a ridiculous desire.

"There is no one-time thing for us, Blondie. We're it. The real deal."

Jonah grinned, caressing the sides of Zev's face, and he mumbled into Zev's mouth.

"The real deal, huh?"

Zev bit that plump bottom lip and returned his friend's smile.

"Uh-huh," he answered before tilting his head and pressing his tongue into Jonah's sweet mouth.

Jonah sucked on Zev's tongue, enjoying the warmth of the smooth skin skating under his fingertips, and tilted his pelvis up against the hard body above him. Zev rubbed Jonah's shoulders, smoothed over his chest and down to his waist, and clung to him as the kiss grew deeper and more passionate.

"Damn, you feel good, Zev."

"So do you, Blondie," Zev replied as he rolled to his side and took Jonah with him. Then he lined up their hard dicks and wrapped his large hand around them, stroking up and down slowly. Jonah looked between their bodies and enjoyed the sight of his friend's hand moving over their joined cocks. He cupped Zev's cheek in his hand and pulled him in for another kiss, then ran his fingers lower on their bodies and curled them around their cocks until his fingertips met Zev's.

They moved together seamlessly, drawing pleasure from each other's bodies as well as their own. Jonah could feel Zev's warm breath on his face, hear his quiet moans, and taste his unique flavor as they continued kissing, continued stroking, and allowed the pleasure of their coupling to overtake them.

"I've wanted you for so long, Zev."

The confession snuck out of Jonah's mouth without thought or warning. The emotions of the moment were too great to allow him to keep holding back the feelings he'd long harbored for his friend.

"You have me, Jonah. I'm yours. All yours."

Jonah arched his back, flung his head back, and closed his eyes as his body found release and pulsed over the joined hands wrapped around his firm member.

"Oh, look at you, Jonah," Zev whispered. "So beautiful." Zev's mouth found its place on Jonah's neck and bit gently as he joined him in ecstasy.

As their trembling bodies clung together and mouths met again, Jonah wondered how he'd survive the coming years apart.

CHAPTER 8

"THIS IS the great room. Right over here is the office. To the left is the bedroom. We're standing in the kitchenette, and the bathroom's through that door. There you go, tour complete. Welcome to my humble abode."

Jonah smiled hesitantly at Zev as he gave a tour that consisted of him standing in the center of his two-hundred-square-foot dorm room and moving his hand in various directions. He hoped his nervousness over this visit wasn't too obvious. After all those years growing up together, being best friends, and then finally coming to terms with the depth of their feelings, Jonah had moved away to school and left his heart behind. He'd been aware of his crush on Zev for years, but it wasn't until he no longer saw his friend every day that he realized the enormity of his desire for the other man.

It'd been six months since he'd last seen Zev. They'd kept in close touch, of course, but it hadn't been enough. Jonah had dreamed of Zev every night since he'd moved away. He'd compared every man he met on campus to the man he'd left behind and nobody came close to measuring up.

Jonah had been looking forward to his friend's visit since the day they'd said goodbye. But now that he had Zev standing inches away from him, he was nervous. Would they still have their effortless connection or would things be strained? Would Zev want to continue their all-too-brief explorations or was he just there to visit his old friend in the platonic sense of the word?

"Okay, couch with stained cushions, check. Two desks, check. Set of bunk beds, check. And a microwave and mini-fridge, check. You're living the high life here, Blondie." Zev chuckled as he closed the dorm room door behind him and dropped his duffel bag to the ground.

"Hey, screw you, Hassick. I'll have you know this is premier student housing. There's even a waiting list for this place."

Zev walked over to his friend and wrapped his arms around Jonah's waist.

"I wasn't teasing, Jonah. Believe me, this is way better than where I'm crashing these days. At least you have running water."

The familiar back and forth banter, and the feeling of Zev's body so close to his, comforted Jonah. This was still his Zev; time and distance had kept them apart physically, but nothing had changed between them. Relief quickly turned to desire when Jonah felt Zev's hardness press against his hip. And suddenly, Jonah could no longer remember what they'd been discussing.

Wait. Did Zev say something about not having running water? Jonah reached up and stroked Zev's cheek, enjoying the rough whiskers rubbing against his hand.

"What're you talking about, Zev? Aren't you living with your folks?"

"Nah. Moved out months ago. Been camping out in a tent, saving up for my own place."

Damn, but Zev smelled good. Standing as close as they were, Jonah could feel the heat that radiated off that hard, muscular body, could feel Zev's breath brush against his face, could see amber eyes that seemed to glow look at him with an expression that matched the longing Jonah felt in his own gut every time he so much as thought about his friend.

"You never said anything on the phone. Why'd you move out?"

Jonah could hear the roughness in his own voice. He tried to swallow down his need. They'd been apart for months. They should talk, catch up on things. He should tell Zev about school, hear about how Zev was doing working for his family business, ask about Lori and Toby.

"Do you really want to talk about my living arrangements right now, Blondie?"

Zev bent down, licked at Jonah's neck, and groaned. The sound vibrated against Jonah's skin, causing ripples of pleasure and desire to make their way down his chest to his groin. He was already painfully hard and they'd barely touched each other.

"Ehm." Jonah cleared his throat. "No, we don't have to talk about that. What do you want to talk about, Hassick?"

"Don't wanna talk at all, Blondie," Zev said, his voice husky.

Jonah didn't get a chance to respond because Zev tightened his strong arms around Jonah, caressed his flank, and then pressed his firm lips over Jonah's. The pressure of Zev's mouth was warm and welcome. Zev's tongue swiped across Jonah's lips and pressed into his mouth, and both men moaned with pleasure. Zev's body felt so good, tasted so good, that Jonah's brain completely shut down and his body took over, relishing the sensations of touch and taste and smell. The real Zev was so much better than what Jonah had remembered in his many, many fantasies.

Before Jonah knew he was moving, Zev had steered them toward the bed and the larger man was pulling at Jonah's zipper with a desperation that comforted him; he wasn't alone in this all-consuming need. The lack of oxygen was making Jonah light-headed, but still he whimpered with regret when Zev pulled that delicious mouth away. Then Zev's full lips made their way across Jonah's jaw, behind his ear, and down his neck with licks and nibbles, and Jonah moaned out his gratitude.

"Want you, Blondie." Zev's voice caused a familiar aching need to travel over Jonah's entire body.

"Yes." Jonah wasn't sure if Zev had actually asked him anything, but he wanted his friend to know that he was on board for everything.

Zev yanked off Jonah's shirt, pushed his jeans and boxer briefs down to his ankles, and then lowered him onto the bed. Jonah looked up at Zev, pleasure and desire coursing through him. He kicked his feet, trying to dislodge the clothing trapped at his ankles, but he wasn't having any success.

Zev chuckled, dropped to his haunches, and unlaced Jonah's All Stars. Strong, thick fingers pulled Jonah's shoes off his feet while Zev's talented mouth covered whatever skin was available with kisses and licks. When Jonah was finally nude, Zev gripped the bottom of his own shirt and peeled it off over his head. He had begun to rise to his feet, but paused when he was at eye level with Jonah's erection. Darting his tongue out, he licked his lips and glanced up.

"Jonah?"

It took a few seconds for Jonah's brain to register the change in Zev's tone and several more seconds to gather the brain cells necessary to speak.

"Yeah?"

"I want... I want..."

Jonah sat up, gazed appreciatively at Zev's hard chest, and trailed his fingers through the soft, dark hair covering bulging muscles.

"What do you want, Zev?"

Intense amber eyes peered at Jonah's face, then down to his lap, and back to his face again.

"I want to put my mouth there. To, uh, taste you there." Zev looked pointedly at Jonah's hard dick with every *there*.

An embarrassingly needy noise snuck out of Jonah's mouth. The thought of Zev's lips wrapped around his cock was so damn hot it was a wonder Jonah didn't explode from the words alone.

"P-p-please."

Jonah's stuttered acquiescence seemed to be the only motivation Zev needed to move forward. He wrapped sure, steady fingers around the base of Jonah's cock and dipped his face forward until his wet lips met the hot skin. Zev moved his hand up and down Jonah's length and peppered gentle kisses along Jonah's shaft. Jonah melted onto the bed. He lay on his back, propped up on pillows, and watched his friend with a heated gaze.

The gentle kisses turned to sucks, and then Zev darted his tongue out to taste and lick. Though his first attempts were tentative, Jonah's flavor triggered something primal deep within him and he quickly needed more. With long swipes of his tongue, he moved up and down every inch of skin, then kisses and sucks followed the prominent vein that pulsed with Jonah's increased excitement, and eventually, Zev opened his lips over Jonah's cock and sucked the crown into the wet heat of his mouth.

"Nnnh, Zev!" Jonah cried out. Clutching the sheets at his side, he threw his head back and clenched his eyes shut as his chest heaved.

Zev popped his mouth off the velvety heat that had felt so perfect on his tongue.

"Did...did I hurt you, Blondie? Want me to stop?"

Jonah tightened his stomach muscles and raised his upper body off the bed. His eyes were wild and desperate as he looked at Zev.

"Please, Zev. Don't stop. Please don't stop."

"Oh, damn. You're so hot, Blondie!"

With those words, Zev opened his mouth and fell forward, taking Jonah deep inside. He twisted his hand while it moved over the base of Jonah's dick and pumped up to meet his mouth as he bobbed up and down, taking in as much of that hardness as he could.

"I'm gonna... Zev, oh God. You need to move your mouth before I... Zev!"

Jonah twined his fingers in Zev's hair and tried to pull him off, but there was no way Zev was going to release his prize. He was so turned on by Jonah's noises, by the feel of Jonah's erection, by the taste of his skin. And he wanted more. He wanted to taste Jonah's release.

Without hardly realizing what he was doing, Zev moved his right hand down to his jeans. He pried open the button, lowered the zipper, and tugged his painfully hard dick out of his briefs. Then Zev fisted his hand over his own engorged length as he sucked and pulled Jonah's pleasure from him.

"Zev, Zev, nnnh, Zev!"

Jonah cried out Zev's name with a triumphant shout and thrust his hips up just as his seed shot into Zev's waiting mouth. The taste of his mate was an erotic elixir that pushed every one of Zev's sensual buttons. He swallowed down Jonah's offering and moaned as his own hot, wet release covered his hand. Zev was still suckling on Jonah's softening dick when tender hands caressed his hair and gently urged him up.

"Too sensitive, Zev. C'mere."

Zev moved off his mate's glorious dick and gave it a final swipe.

"You have an unusually long and coordinated tongue."

Ignoring the observation, Zev crawled over his mate and petted his warm skin.

His nose twitching, Jonah turned his head to the side. His eyes widened as he stared at Zev's cum-covered palm. He curled his fingers around the back of Zev's hand and brought it forward, leaning up and licking the fluid into his mouth.

"Holy damn, Blondie!"

Zev gasped at the sexy show taking place in front of him. He dipped his head until his mouth met Jonah's and pushed his tongue inside. Their tastes mingled together and sent his body into overdrive.

Jonah felt an odd clenching and releasing deep within himself. He'd only had that sensation one other time: the day before he'd left Etzgadol, when he'd been fantasizing about Zev in the shower. But this time, the feelings were stronger, more insistent. He needed...something. No, not something. He needed Zev. Needed Zev inside his body.

Although Jonah's sexual experiences were limited to those he'd shared with Zev, he'd spent more computer time surfing for porn than he had doing class work over the past six months. He'd watch hard bodies writhe together in various poses and always imagined himself and Zev in their places. And while most of the scenes and positions led to fantasies of Jonah in either actor's role, there was a notable exception. Whenever he saw two actors engaged in penetration, Jonah imagined himself on the receiving end. Every single time.

At first, Jonah wondered whether that was strange. Whether it held some deeper meaning into him as a person. But then he found various websites catering to gay men, read articles and advice columns, and decided that it didn't mean anything. It just was. He only hoped that Zev would prefer to take the opposite role. If not, they'd take turns. Jonah wasn't about to walk away from Zev over something like who was on top.

CHAPTER 9

"WHEN'S YOUR roommate coming back? Should we get dressed?"

Zev's voice suddenly sounded strained. Jonah ran his hand against his friend's stubbly cheek. It felt warm and rough and perfect.

"He's staying at his girlfriend's place all weekend. We have the room to ourselves."

Although there was something arousing about having his naked body covered by Zev's denim-covered form, Jonah wanted to feel skin against skin. So he moved his hands to the waistband of Zev's jeans, tucked his thumbs under the heavy fabric and the soft briefs beneath, and pushed the barriers down over his friend's hips and midway to his thighs.

"Kick off your shoes, Hassick."

Zev complied and wiggled until his jeans were at his ankles, at which point he toed off his shoes, pushed off his jeans, and then settled his naked warmth on top of Jonah. Instinctively, Jonah's legs spread, making room for Zev between them. He rubbed his calves against the sides of Zev's legs, bent his knees and draped his ankles over the back of Zev's thighs, and then moved them up and down the back of Zev's legs in a gentle caress. And the entire time, Jonah looked up into Zev's eyes, enjoying the warmth and affection that so clearly poured out.

But there was something else in those eyes too. Something Jonah had rarely seen in his friend. There was a glimpse of uncertainty and anxiety. The last time Jonah had seen those emotions in Zev was when he'd confronted his friend with their attraction, and Zev had responded by running out of Jonah's childhood bedroom. Jonah suddenly worried that they were back in that place, that Zev was overwhelmed by what they'd shared and that he'd changed his mind.

"Zev?"

He couldn't do anything more than say the name. Jonah wanted to beg Zev to stay, but his throat constricted and his entire body tensed. He strengthened the grip of his legs around Zev in an attempt to prevent the other man from escaping.

"You showing off those strong gams, Blondie?" Zev asked with a chuckle as he caressed one thigh with his firm fingers, massaging the muscle and relaxing Jonah's hold on his body.

"Sorry, you just got me worried there for a minute," Jonah replied quietly. He bit his lower lip and looked up at Zev through his eyelashes. "Thought you might make a run for it or something."

"Nah. I'm not gonna run from you, Blondie. I was just a little freaked out. I don't have my bearings with this whole, um, this whole being-with-another-guy thing."

Jonah wondered, and not for the first time, exactly what went on at Zev's church, or whatever it was they called it in their religion. Come to think of it, Jonah had never heard Zev, Lori, or Toby call it a religion. He'd never heard them give it a title at all. People at school called it a cult, but Jonah knew that wasn't true. It just seemed like Zev and the kids he referred to as family friends all knew each other. They all went to some private elementary school that nobody else knew a thing about, and they all seemed to distrust anybody who wasn't part of their little community. Well, not all of them. Zev had always been open to Jonah and the other kids at their school. And Lori and Toby weren't bad, either. They were nice to everyone, though they definitely didn't have Zev's charm and open, friendly demeanor.

"Are you worried about your family finding out? About what they'll think of you? Or if your dad will fire you or something? I'm not a huge expert, Hassick, but my guess is that I've had an easier time of, um, coming out to my dad. Talk to me. Maybe I can help. Or are you worried about, uh, going to hell or whatever?"

Wow. That was eloquent. Well, at least he was trying. This wasn't an easy conversation for Jonah to have, either. Jonah felt Zev shaking above him and a hint of liquid dripped onto his cheek. His heart fell, and he snapped his gaze up to look into Zev's eyes, expecting to see sadness. Instead, Zev was laughing at him so hard that he was crying.

"Hey!" Jonah smacked his friend's shoulder. "Cut that out! I'm trying to be all sensitive and shit here, and you're totally spoiling my mojo."

"Sorry," Zev gasped out, pausing to catch his breath. He wiped at his eyes with the back of his hand. "That was deep, man, seriously. Going to hell or whatever... Ow!" Zev shouted when Jonah smacked the side of his head, hard.

"Shut up, asshole. How am I supposed to know what had you all worked up? They were legitimate questions. Now stop laughing at me."

A few more chuckles, and then Zev slid off Jonah and settled on his side, his head propped up on one hand, the other hand petting Jonah's chest.

"Okay, okay. You're right. Sorry. No, I wasn't worried about my family or being fired or any of that crap. I just don't know what to do with you, Jonah. I never know if my, uh, urges are weird, you know?"

"Your urges?" Jonah pushed himself up so his cheek was also resting on his propped-up hand, mirroring Zev's pose. Then he pushed his knee between both of Zev's.

"Yeah, you know, like what I just did to you," Zev responded, looking pointedly at Jonah's crotch while he licked his lips. "Is that okay or is it weird?"

Zev knew his question wasn't coming out right, but he didn't know how else to ask. He didn't know how humans had sex. Frankly, he didn't know all that much about how shifters had sex, just what his father had told him when he was twelve.

His closest friends were Jonah and Toby, and sex wasn't something they'd ever discussed. With Toby it was because the other shifter had always had a thing for Zev's sister and she'd been his only girlfriend. No way did Zev want to hear about Lori's sex life, and Toby probably wasn't particularly eager to share that information with him, either. And with Jonah, well, in hindsight Zev guessed they'd both avoided the topic for the same reason—how do you talk about sex with the guy you want when you don't know if he wants you back?

Jonah gave Zev an odd look.

"I don't understand what you're asking me, Zev."

The conversation should have been uncomfortable, but it really wasn't. Jonah was Zev's friend first and foremost. He felt safe and comfortable with Jonah, like they could talk about anything and Jonah wouldn't judge him. Well, almost anything. Zev wasn't quite ready to spill the beans about the whole "I'm a wolf" thing quite yet.

"I'm asking whether huma—uh, whether people use their mouths on each other like that."

"Well, uh, yeah. I think so. Blow jobs are pretty common, Zev."

Zev's tension eased. He flopped onto his back, folded his arms beneath his head, and looked up at the ceiling. "Okay. Cool. 'Cause I liked doing it."

Jonah rolled on top of him and straightened his arms, raising himself above Zev in a push-up position and looking down into Zev's impossibly handsome face. "Think you might like feeling it too? 'Cause I wanna get my turn." The hardness that suddenly poked into his hip answered Jonah's question. "I'll take that as a yes, Hassick."

"Oh, it's definitely a yes, Blondie. Show me what you got," Zev responded with a smirk and raised his eyebrows up and down comically.

Jonah chuckled. "Quit making me laugh, Zev. You're spoiling the romance. And I went through great efforts to seduce you here. I put away the dirty socks, threw out the pizza boxes, and I even changed the sheets on this bed."

"Oh, wow. How could I possibly resist when you bring out the big guns of seduction like that? Nothing turns me on like basic housekeeping."

A grumble was Jonah's only response, and then he started kissing and licking his way down Zev's neck, taking breaks to suck on sensitive spots. When he got to Zev's nipple, Jonah traced it with his tongue before taking it into his mouth and sucking until it hardened. Zev shuddered and moaned beneath him.

"Not such a big talker now, are you, Hassick?" Jonah asked as he switched his attentions to the other nipple and ran his fingers over Zev's hard cock and down to his heavy balls. "Turns out I know the Kryptonite to curb your super-sarcasm power."

"Uh-huh. Less talking more licking, Blondie," gasped Zev.

"Pushy asshole," Jonah replied, but there was no animosity behind the words, just affectionate amusement.

By the time Jonah had made his way down to Zev's cock, both men were done talking, done thinking, and operating on pure instinct. A few strokes of Zev's erection had Jonah moaning, and the first swipe of his tongue across the glistening glans took Jonah's breath away. Before he knew it, his lips were stretched around a hard cock. He felt a tender caress over his forehead and warm fingers pushing his hair back. He looked up to see Zev watching him.

Jonah didn't move his mouth, just darted his tongue out and licked the salty skin. Zev's fingers made their way through his hair to the back of his neck, where they massaged and nudged Jonah downward. He whimpered in agreement and sucked more of that hard cock into his mouth. He loved feeling Zev's need, loved it when the other man gave into it and asked for what he wanted, loved that what Zev wanted was him.

He cupped Zev's balls, squeezing and rolling them as he enjoyed their weight and texture. Without stopping that caress, Jonah popped his mouth off Zev's dick, licked his lips, then gathered saliva in his mouth and plunged back down, letting the wetness seep out and over Zev, easing Jonah's descent. His free hand went to the base of Zev's dick and met his mouth on its downward approach.

Both of Zev's hands touched Jonah, petting his cheeks and combing through his hair. "Feels so good, Jonah. Never thought anything could feel so good."

Zev's breathless voice praising him added another layer to the sensual maelstrom Jonah was experiencing. He rocked his hips against Zev's leg, wanting to feel the friction against his own need.

"Mmm, hmm. Mmm, hmm." Jonah moaned as he increased the speed of his up and down motions and tightened his mouth even further around Zev's cock.

He pushed his hips harder against Zev's leg, pumped faster, and it wasn't long before Jonah was wailing around Zev's dick as he released his seed onto Zev's skin and the mattress. Zev's answering howl came just as his large body shuddered, his thick fingers tightened in Jonah's hair, and his hard cock exploded in Jonah's mouth.

After he finished swallowing his friend's offering, Jonah rested his cheek against Zev's thigh and tried to catch his breath.

"So." Zev's husky voice broke the silence once their gasps died down. "What do you think? Did you enjoy your turn?"

Jonah rubbed his hand up and down Zev's leg, kissed the man's softening dick, and then crawled back up his muscular body.

"I think that's definitely a keeper. Let's add it to the rotation."

Zev laughed, wrapped his arms around Jonah, and held him tightly.

"Whatever you say, Blondie. After all, you are the brains of this operation. Or at least that's what you keep telling me."

"Ha ha." Jonah's sarcastic tone was muffled because he couldn't seem to move his mouth from Zev's skin. He kissed a stubbly cheek and sighed contentedly as he wiggled around, getting comfortable against the warm body beneath him.

"Missed you, Blondie."

"Me too. It's not too late to change your mind about school, you know. I'm sure you can still get in here."

Zev stroked Jonah's hair and kissed his forehead.

"I can't leave Etzgadol, Jonah."

Jonah didn't want to push, but he truly didn't understand. It wasn't just his own desire to be near his friend that caused him to bring up college once again. He also thought it'd be good for Zev. Jonah's father had always raised him to know he'd go on to college and then graduate school. It was a given. He couldn't understand why Zev's parents wouldn't want the same thing for their son.

"Explain it to me, Zev. Because from where I'm sitting, you're living in a tent in the woods working for your dad's business. Isn't that same life going to be there for you after graduation? Why not study first? Maybe you'll be able to add more to the company that way. Toby's going to school. Can't his parents talk to yours? They're friends, aren't they?"

There was no answer from his friend for several long minutes, but Jonah knew Zev wasn't angry at his question, because that large hand continued its caress and several more kisses landed on Jonah's head.

"It's different for Toby. He wants to learn a trade that requires school. What I'm going to do isn't something I can learn in college. And even if I could, it couldn't be here." Zev paused, trying to think of how he could explain that even shifters who went to college did so in towns that had packs. They'd get accepted into the pack as a hosted student, live among them while they learned, then return to their home pack with a new trade. There were no packs in the middle of the city because there wasn't room to run and hunt. Besides, urban areas were occupied by vampires. And shifters didn't mix with bloodsuckers.

"I know. You need to be in the forest. You already told me that." Though he clearly wasn't pleased about the situation, instead of arguing, Jonah changed the topic. "All right, what do you want to do while you're here? Anything you want to see?"

Zev moved his hands down Jonah's neck and over his back to land on his ass. He massaged the firm globes as he answered.

"I'm up for anything. I just have to stop at a couple of stores to see if they're interested in carrying Etzgadol Ceramics."

"Sounds good. We can do that tomorrow and then have lunch in Old Town."

"'Kay. What else do you wanna do, Blondie?"

Jonah laid his head on Zev's chest and snuggled against him.

"I just wanna be with you. So catch me up on things. Tell me how Lori and Toby are doing. Tell me about work. Oh, and tell me why you're living in a tent."

CHAPTER 10

"So when did you say Zev's getting here?"

Jonah saved the term paper he was writing, stuffed his books into his backpack, and turned around to look at his roommate, Dennis. The man was sitting on the beat-up couch in their shared room, playing Xbox with another guy from their frat.

"He should be here anytime. His flight came in this morning, but he had some work meetings today. It's after five, though, so I bet he's almost done. You sure you don't mind clearing out for the weekend?"

Dennis popped open a beer and took a few gulps before wiping his mouth with the back of his hand and answering Jonah's question. "Nah, man. It's fine. I'm gonna bunk with Cohen 'cause Alex is never there. He'd save his parents a bunch of coin if he and Sheila would just give up the charade and admit that they're living together."

The man sitting next to Dennis threw the controller on the ground and stalked over to the mini-fridge to get himself another beer. "I hate that fucking game!"

Dennis rolled his eyes at that outburst. "You didn't suck as much as usual today, Mathews. And you're better on the screen than when we play ball for real. You want a turn, Jonah?"

"Sure." Jonah picked up the controller, joined his roommate on the couch, and started a new game, but his mind wasn't really in it. His body was strung so tight waiting to see Zev that it was hard to concentrate on anything else.

"I'm looking for Jonah Marvel's room." Zev's deep voice floated through the fraternity house hallway and immediately brought Jonah to his feet.

"In here, Hassick," he called out as he walked toward his doorway.

A huge smile spread over Zev's face when he caught sight of Jonah. When they were within touching distance, Zev reached his long arms around Jonah's waist and pulled him in for a tight hug.

"Missed you," Jonah mumbled into Zev's neck. It had become their usual greeting.

"Missed you too," Zev whispered back before straightening and taking in his surroundings. "Wow, this place is an even bigger shithole than that dorm room you used to live in."

Jonah laughed.

"Yeah, well, the dorm was owned by the university, and they had a maintenance staff. This house is looked after by a bunch of freshman pledges. But I promise my room is clean." Jonah lowered his voice and looked at Zev knowingly. "I remember how important basic housekeeping is to you."

That comment got a laugh out of Zev. He dropped his duffel bag on the ground next to Jonah's desk and walked over to the two men sitting on the couch, reaching his hand out in introduction.

"Hi. I'm Zev Hassick. I'm guessing one of you is Dennis."

Jonah's roommate grinned at Zev, got up off the couch, and took his hand.

"Yeah, that's me. Nice to finally meet you in person, man. Looking forward to getting to know you better while you're here this weekend."

After shaking Dennis's hand, Zev turned to Bob, who seemed intent on whatever game he was playing.

"That well-mannered dipshit is Bob Mathews," Jonah said with a chuckle. "You hungry or did you have time to grab lunch today?"

"I could eat." Zev walked back to him, pushed a lock off his forehead, and tucked it behind his ear. "Your hair's longer."

"Haven't had time for a haircut." Jonah could hear the breathlessness of his own voice. Having Zev close to him, touching him, even innocently, was enough to make his body feel primed and ready for more contact.

"Looks good, Blondie." Zev's voice had a husky rumble that Jonah knew meant the arousal he was feeling was reciprocated by his friend.

The litany of cuss words from the couch told Jonah that Bob had once again lost the game. He didn't bother turning around; all of his attention was focused on Zev. Those amber eyes were gazing at him, an adoring expression on that handsome face. Jonah moved even closer to Zev, not stopping until he could feel the other man's breath blowing across his face.

"A bunch of us are going to Tens tonight, Jonah. You should bring your friend," Bob said as he walked to the mini-fridge and picked up another beer.

"You aren't any smarter now than you were three beers ago, Mathews. Put down the can. Let's go." Dennis put his hand on Bob's shoulder and tried to steer him toward the door.

"What?" Bob asked as he shook off Dennis's hand. "Why're we leaving? What'd I say?"

"Dude. I don't think Jonah and his boyfriend want to come to a girl strip club with you. Now, let's get out of here and give them some space."

Silence filled the room as Bob's eyes widened, taking in the sight of Jonah and Zev standing close together.

"Jonah's gay? That's sick, man!"

"Wow, Mathews, you just managed to go from zero to bigot in sixty seconds flat. Impressive. Clear the room, man. Come on." Dennis pushed Bob toward the door as he looked apologetically at Jonah and Zev.

Bob pulled himself out of Dennis's grasp and kept talking, his voice raised and his face red.

"You've known about this, Dennis? And you still live with him? Are you a fag too?"

Jonah and Zev froze and looked over at the scene playing out in the small room. Dennis leaned over Bob with his fists clenched at his sides.

"I'm straight, but my sister's a lesbian, so watch your fucking language."

Apparently unable to just walk away, Bob kept sputtering. "It's not the same with chicks, Dennis. Gay guys like to, uh, fuck each other up the ass, man! Do the other guys know about Jonah? He shouldn't be living here. What if he tries something on us while we're sleeping?"

"You know what, Mathews? None of us signed up for passage on your boat of bigotry, so get the fuck out of our room. Swift sailing. Bu-bye. Don't let the door hit your ass on the way out." With those words, Dennis finally managed to drag Bob out of the room and into the hallway. He followed and looked back inside as he took the door handle in his hand to close it behind them. "Sorry about that, guys. Zev, don't let that little incident make you think you're not welcome. You can be sure Bob doesn't speak for the rest of us. In fact, I think he just got himself named the World's Most Close-Minded and Oblivious Asshole of the Year with that little tirade. See you guys later."

Jonah stared at the closed door, afraid to look back at Zev. Shit. Shit. Shit. This was the last thing he wanted Zev to witness. It'd be yet another reason for Zev to worry about being gay, to keep hiding from his family and friends back in Etzgadol.

"Uh, Jonah?" Zev's voice was frighteningly quiet, his words drawn out slow as molasses.

Jonah took a few deep breaths then turned to look at Zev. "Yeah?"

"What was he talking about?"

Jonah couldn't get a good read on Zev's emotions. He didn't seem ashamed or angry. More like he was curious. The reaction didn't make sense.

"Listen, Zev, he's a jerk. There are gonna be jerks in the world. We can't let them dictate how we live our lives. And I know you're worried about what your family will say when you come out, but come on, your folks are smarter than that dumbass."

Zev shook his head and waved his hand back and forth in the air. "Yeah, yeah. But what did he mean about gay guys fucking each other's asses. That's not true, right? I mean, of course it's not. He was just being an idiot, right?"

Jonah's jaw dropped in shock. Was Zev serious? Sure, Etzgadol was a small, secluded town, but how could any twenty-year-old gay man not know about gay sex? But Zev's furrowed brow and the concern etched on his face told Jonah that his friend wasn't kidding around.

Jonah reminded himself that Zev's family was nothing like his. His father had moved to Etzgadol when Jonah was a baby, but he'd lived all over the country before then, and Jonah had learned about a lot of things over the dinner table. Zev's family members, on the other hand, were all from Etzgadol. They'd been raised in that small town.

Plus, Jonah had gone on lots of trips with his father as a kid, whereas the first time Zev had gone anywhere out of state, it was to visit Jonah at school. And school was another difference. Jonah had almost two years of college under his belt, where he'd made new friends and joined a couple of gay students' groups, while Zev was still back home with the same guys they'd known in high school.

"Come on, let's sit down. You look kinda pale." Jonah took Zev's hand in his and led him to the couch. After his friend was seated, Jonah joined him. He spread his knees and leaned down, resting his forearms against them. "All right, so yeah, Bob's an idiot, but he was right about that part. That is how some men have sex."

Jonah paused, gathering his courage. He'd planned to bring this up during Zev's visit anyway, though certainly not like this. He figured they'd be naked, aroused, and in bed when he asked Zev to take him. But since they were already talking about it...

"I'd like to try it, Zev. With you. I'd like you to, um, make love to me like that." Okay, so he was blushing. At least he'd said the words. Even if they had sounded incredibly asinine coming out of his mouth.

Zev shook his head furiously and pulled Jonah up against him. He kissed his friend gently and petted his hair.

"I couldn't hurt you like that, Jonah. I never want to hurt you."

Jonah was reeling. What would Zev have done if Jonah hadn't essentially dragged his ass out of the closet? Would he have ever realized he was gay? Jonah was truly starting to wonder whether his friend lived in a bubble. Maybe "cult" wasn't as outrageous a description of Zev's church, or whatever it was, as Jonah previously thought.

"It doesn't have to hurt, Zev. In fact, I'm pretty sure it feels good. Guys enjoy it. At least, I think I'd enjoy it."

The disbelieving expression on Zev's face made Jonah laugh. He was actually explaining the ins and outs of sex to a six and a half foot, two hundred twenty pound man as if he were a pubescent teenager. The whole thing was kind of endearing. He looked at Zev tenderly and kissed his way across that strong jaw. Letting his tongue lead the way, Jonah traced a path down Zev's neck and over to his ear, where he took a few moments to suck on the lobe.

"You ever watch porn online, Hassick?"

Zev pushed his hands under Jonah's shirt and massaged his back.

"Nuh-uh."

The idea hadn't even crossed Zev's mind. Zev's every sexual fantasy involved Jonah, so he hadn't ever wanted to watch other men. Plus, he didn't have a computer in the tiny trailer he was now calling home. It was an improvement over the tent, especially since he'd dug a well and put in a septic tank, but it was still pretty rudimentary. Zev spent very little on the trailer so he could keep saving to build a house Jonah would want to call home.

After nuzzling Jonah's neck, Zev moved one hand from Jonah's chest to the back of his friend's head and drew the blond into a kiss. He gnawed on Jonah's lip, sucking it into his mouth, and licking it. Jonah gave as good as he got, and it wasn't long before he was straddling Zev's lap, pushing his hard dick against Zev's stomach and sucking Zev's tongue into his hot mouth.

When the men finally separated in search of air, Jonah rested his forehead against Zev's shoulder and continued their conversation.

"I wanna show you, Zev." He reluctantly moved off Zev's lap and pulled him off the couch. "Come on."

Zev followed Jonah to the desk and stood behind him, massaging his shoulders as Jonah clicked a few buttons on the keyboard. It didn't take long for the screen to be filled by a view of two naked men in a bed. One was on his hands and knees and the other was behind him, pressing first fingers and then a hard dick into his waiting ass. The blissful expression on both men's faces and the happy moans that streamed from their mouths seemed to prove Jonah's point.

"See. It feels good." Jonah's husky voice was accompanied by a motion from his rear end against Zev's crotch. Zev was leaning over his shoulder, staring at the screen. "Damn, Zev, from the feel of things back there, I think you might be interested. Wanna try it?"

Jonah's hands went to the sides of his track pants, and he hooked his thumbs in his pants and briefs together, pushing both of them down to his knees.

Zev couldn't stay away from the enticing sight, so he reverently moved his hands over the firm globes of Jonah's ass as he sucked and nibbled his neck.

"Can't do that, Blondie. Not yet. Need to think first. But, oh, man, do I want you."

Zev moved his hand to the button of his pants and managed to get them down. His briefs were next, and then his cock was free to rub against Jonah's ass.

"Lotion." Jonah gasped. "I have lotion in the right drawer." Jonah scrambled to the side, yanked open the drawer, and pulled out a bottle of lotion. "I use this to, uh, beat off when I watch these videos." He flipped the cap and pulled Zev's hand in front of him, squeezing some of the liquid onto it. "Coat your dick with it. Do whatever you want to me, Zev. I want it. Want you."

And with those words, Jonah stopped talking. He bent over the desk, rested his face on the surface, raised his ass in the air, and reached back, spreading his cheeks.

"Holy shit, Jonah. Damn."

Zev moved his finger up and down Jonah's cleft and soon replaced the finger with his cock. Once the hard member was settled between Jonah's cheeks, they moved together, back and forth. Merely paying attention to that part of Jonah's body spun him into overdrive. He met Zev's thrusts and moaned his pleasure. When Zev's hand reached around him and started stroking his cock, Jonah shouted and came all over his desk.

"Jonah! Oh, Jonah." Zev bucked against his firm body, groaned and shuddered, coating Jonah's lower back with his seed and biting into the muscle where Jonah's neck met his shoulder.

Although he'd previously licked and nibbled on that area, Zev had never truly bitten him. Even at that moment, he hadn't let his wolf canines out or broken the skin, but this bite was definitely harder than any other he'd bestowed on his mate. Before he could worry about whether he was hurting Jonah with the firm grip his teeth had on the other man's neck, Jonah cried out his name, and Zev felt the dick he was still holding come back to life and climax once again.

With his muscles too spent to hold himself up, Jonah's knees buckled and he collapsed. Zev put one arm around his mate's shoulders and the other under his knees. Then he lifted Jonah in his arms and made his way to the bed. His motions were slow and awkward since his pants were still pushed down around his ankles, but once he reached the bed, he yanked off his clothes, undressed Jonah, then wrapped the other man in a tight embrace.

"What the hell was that, Zev?" Jonah asked as he burrowed against Zev, trembling. "I've never come that hard in my life. Or twice that quickly. Damn, I never thought I was into pain, but when you bit me, my entire body felt like it was on fire. A good fire."

"It's not the pain." Zev stopped himself before he said anything else and blew his secret. He wanted to tell Jonah everything. Wanted to explain shifting, mates, and the claiming bite. That was what had aroused Jonah, a bite so very close to the one Zev would one day use to permanently mark his mate and let the world know Jonah was taken. Based on Jonah's reaction, Zev knew his mate's body was ready for that step, but it couldn't happen until they finally tied together.

Oh God, did Zev want to explain tying. He'd been wondering how tying would work with a male mate and now he knew. And if his mate's words earlier that evening were any indication, Jonah was very much up for it. Well, Jonah was up for sex. The human didn't know about tying.

But there was no way for Zev to tie with Jonah and then let him go. It was already hard enough to live apart from his mate. The distance between them went against every one of Zev's instincts. He had to regularly remind himself that he had to let Jonah follow his dreams and couldn't drag his mate back to Etzgadol and force the man to stay by his side.

Once they were tied together, Zev knew his wolf wouldn't allow Jonah to leave. Hell, Zev wasn't at all convinced his human form could remain civilized enough to allow the distance between them after he tied with his mate. So there was no other choice. Tying would have to wait until Jonah graduated from college and moved back home.

CHAPTER 11

"YOU GOING to eat the last slice, Zev, or can I have it?" Toby asked through a mouthful of pizza.

"Nah, you go ahead. I don't know how you can eat like that after a run."

Zev grabbed a bottle of water from the fridge and collapsed on the couch. Toby was in town visiting for a few days. Between all the time the man had been spending with Lori, and with his own family, Zev hadn't gotten to see his friend much. But that evening Toby had shown up with an extra-large pizza and a six-pack of beer.

They'd eaten some of the food, then shifted and gone out for a long run. It had felt good to let his wolf free and feel the wind running through his fur. So good, in fact, that Zev was almost smiling. A foreign expression on his face these days.

"Look, Zev, I know you'd rather sit on my lap while I'm taking a dump than talk about your feelings, but what's going on with you?"

Zev coughed at the visual image that little comment painted in his mind. "I don't know what you're talking about," he replied none too convincingly. Then he flopped his head on the back of the couch and draped his arm across his eyes.

"Sure you don't. The puking noises Lori tells me she hears when you go into the bathroom are just a friendly reminder of how well you're doing." There was a pause, and then Zev heard Toby moving his CDs around. "Damn it, don't you have any decent music in this house? Be right back, I'm getting my iPod out of my truck."

"I keep a loaded shotgun under this couch, Toby, and I'm bringing it out if I hear Michael Bolton. And this isn't a house. It's a small tin can."

Toby grumbled. "Why the hate, dude? That man's voice is beautiful. I'm telling you, if he showed up at my door singing a ballad, I'd give him anything he wanted without blinking an eye. My social security number, where I keep the hidden house key, the secret ending to *The Crying Game*, anything."

"If I pretend to be deaf, will it get me out of a continued discussion about whiny singers? And does my sister know about this sick obsession of yours? 'Cause I imagine the best thing about your taste in music is all the money you save on buying condoms."

"Fine. But I don't want to hear your head-banging crap, so no music." Toby walked over to the couch and flopped down next to Zev, then threw his feet onto the file boxes serving as a coffee table and smacked Zev in the stomach.

"Ow. Fuck, Toby, that hurt."

"Yeah, right. Come on, Zev, I haven't got all night. I need to go home, shower, pretend to go to bed, then meet your sister outside your parents' house so I can corrupt her. And

I'm not gonna get very far with her if she isn't convinced that I got you to open up, so spill."

Zev winced. "There are so many things wrong with that sentence that I can't even prioritize. Can you please pass me the brain bleach?"

"Okay, fine. Lori and I are going to play chess and braid each other's hair all night. Is that what you want to hear? Or maybe you want her to get mad at me and start dating Brian Delgato? 'Cause that jerk's still after her. Come on, Zev, you've lost at least thirty pounds since the last time I saw you. There're dark circles under your eyes. Basically, you look like shit. Talk to me."

"I'm fine, Toby. I've just been working out."

Toby cocked an eyebrow at Zev in clear disbelief. "Working out, huh? Is that what you call drinking before the sun goes down most days and then crawling into bed? I should tell you that you're only going to continue to lose muscle mass with that approach. Come on, Zev."

When Zev still didn't say anything, Toby visibly stiffened, seemingly steeling his courage, and then continued speaking. "Is something going on with Jonah?"

"We haven't talked about Jonah since he moved away," Zev answered after a short pause.

"I know."

"That was three and a half years ago," Zev continued.

"I know."

He probably should have been surprised that Toby had known he'd kept in touch with Jonah, but Zev wasn't. Lori was pretty perceptive, and she probably knew exactly where Zev went when he traveled for business. And what Lori knew, Toby knew. Whether they were aware of the nature of Zev's feelings for the human wasn't clear, but Zev was too tired to try to make excuses.

"He's gonna go to medical school." Zev still hadn't moved his arm from his face, so he couldn't see Toby's reaction.

"Medical school?" Toby's voice was tempered but confused.

"That's, like, four years of school and then four years of residency. Which means eight more years away from Etzgadol." *Eight more years away from me.*

The last part was really the crux of the problem, but Zev didn't dare say it out loud. It'd give away too much. Still, it didn't make sense. A few years away so they could grow up and be old enough to tie when they came back together, Zev was almost able to understand. But that time had passed, Zev had figured out how to tie with a male, and he was ready for his mate to join him.

Why would nature give him a mate who insisted on staying away? Zev had to be missing something, but he had no clue what it was. Instead of learning a lesson or gaining wisdom, he felt frustrated and angry. So many thoughts were swirling in his mind that he hadn't registered Toby's long silence until the other man spoke again.

"You know my mom works with Doc Carson."

The change in topic was weird, but welcome, so Zev engaged Toby in the conversation.

"Yeah, I know."

"So I was asking her the other day if she thinks he'd take me on at the clinic when I get my nursing degree, and you know what she told me?"

The conversation was about as interesting as watching paint peel, but at least it got Zev thinking about something other than Jonah. Almost.

"What?"

"She said I may want to look at the hospital in town because she wasn't sure how much longer Doc'll be practicing. He's getting up there in years and apparently he's had enough. He wants to retire."

Zev was sufficiently distracted from his own personal problems by that statement to finally pay attention to the conversation. He sat up straight and jerked his eyes toward Toby. Damn it. Doc Carson was the only healer in the pack. If he retired, they'd be left without any medical aid other than Toby's mother, who was a nurse. Well, and Toby, too, when he graduated. But that wasn't enough for a pack their size.

Their pack had grown slowly but steadily over the past few years. Families were asking for admission on an increasingly more frequent basis, and Zev knew that at least part of the growth was a result of the improvements and infrastructure they'd put in place in the shared spaces. Most of those had been funded with the extra money the ceramics business had been bringing in from the new accounts Zev had nurtured.

It turned out that interacting well with humans was profitable. And while Zev had started traveling for business as an excuse to see Jonah, the trips truly had helped the business grow. He'd come home from every trip with several new accounts, and word of mouth from those often led to others. Whatever the reason for the pack's growth, it showed no signs of stopping, and even if they had two nurses, a pack their size still needed a healer.

"We're going to need to find a new doctor to take over when Doc Carson steps down. And it's not easy to find a healer. All the trades are supposed to have succession plans in place, but that one is so rare that we haven't lined anything up. Does my father know about this?"

Toby shook his head. "I'm pretty sure he doesn't know yet. My mom's not even supposed to know, she's just heard Doc mumbling to himself in the clinic when he thought nobody was listening." Toby looked intently at Zev. "Listen, Zev, I'm not sure how much time we're talking about here, but it's probably not immediate. There's no way Doc would do something like that without giving the Alpha plenty of notice, and your dad would probably tell you, right?"

"Yeah, he would. He's including me in all the pack-governance things. It's part of my Alpha training. I'm taking over in a few years so I'm involved in every decision now."

"Right. So if your dad hasn't told you, that means Doc hasn't told him. And if Doc hasn't told him, then he's probably planning to stick around for at least five or six more years."

A switch clicked in Zev's head and everything suddenly became clear.

"Jonah said he'd be in school for eight more years," Zev said, looking at Toby's face to gauge his reaction to the implication of that statement. Would he balk at the idea of a human working for the pack? In order to be the pack healer, Jonah would have to understand what they were. And the pack never shared that secret with humans.

"Eight years, huh? I bet Doc would stick around that long if he was asked."

Toby wasn't even fazed. Zev relaxed for the first time since Jonah had told him the news about medical school. Maybe this was all part of the plan. Jonah would come to the pack not only as Zev's mate, but also as a healer—a skill they'd need. That'd help the shifters accept the human into their pack. It made sense, which meant the separation made sense. It sucked, but it made sense.

"Yeah, I bet he would. I'll make a point of subtly saying something to Doc next time I see him. Thanks, Toby."

"Anytime, man." Toby patted Zev's knee, then raised himself off the couch and stepped toward the door. "Try to get some sleep, dude. You seriously look like shit."

Zev followed his friend to the door and waved as he walked toward his truck.

"Have fun tonight. Keep Lori happy. The last thing I want is Brian Delgato for a brother-in-law."

Toby had settled into his seat and was about to close his door when he added one final comment. "I got it covered. No worries on that front. And next time you talk to Jonah, tell him Lori and I miss him. You're not the only one waiting for that boy to come home."

CHAPTER 12

"DAMN BUT you're beautiful, Blondie. How do you manage to get better-looking every time I see you?"

Jonah was naked, standing in the doorway to his small off-campus apartment. His blond hair was disheveled, his cheeks were rosy, and his eyes were blinking in a just-woke-up way. Zev stepped inside, dropped his bag next to the door, and pulled that tight body against his chest, holding Jonah close and rocking them from side to side.

"What're you doing here, Zev?" The chill in Jonah's voice and the tension in his body felt like a punch to Zev's stomach.

"I'm here for your graduation, Blondie."

The four years apart hadn't been easy. Hell, they'd been downright miserable, but the two of them had survived. Zev had managed to find reasons to make trips to see Jonah several times a year, and they both had unlimited minutes on their cell phone plans. It wasn't enough—not nearly enough—but there hadn't been another choice. Not if Jonah was going to get the education that was clearly so important to him.

"Is that right? Guess I'm surprised you're here given the way you've been acting every time we've talked over the past few months."

Zev sighed and rubbed his hands up and down Jonah's bare arms. They felt thinner, and Zev wondered if his friend had been studying so much that he'd forgotten to eat.

"I'm sorry, Jonah. I was being an ass. I'm really proud of you for getting into medical school. I should have said that when you first told me the good news. I guess I was being selfish. I was hoping you'd be coming home now, not starting another long period away. But I understand."

The previous few months had been pure hell. Ever since Jonah had told Zev that he wanted to continue his education, their calls had been strained. And this was the first visit Zev had made since Jonah had given him what he had considered exciting news. Given the way Zev had been acting, Jonah had honestly thought his friend would skip his graduation, but that hadn't been his biggest worry. He'd actually been wondering whether Zev was angry enough to break things off between them.

That fear had felt like a cut to Jonah's heart, paralyzing him. So much so that Jonah had been thinking about walking away from medical school and moving back to Etzgadol. Just the fact that he'd had those worries, that he'd considered giving up a career he really wanted while Zev refused to even consider the possibility of making a life with him away from their home town, made Jonah feel resentful.

"You understand, huh? Well, I don't. What do you expect from me, Zev? You say you want me to move back to Etzgadol, but what's your master plan when I do? You gonna hide me somewhere? Are we gonna go back to being buddies? I don't want to live my life in the closet, Zev."

Jonah tried not to sound angry, but it was hard to keep at least a tinge of bitterness out of his voice. Given Zev's ever increasing role in his family business, it seemed virtually impossible to tear the man away from Etzgadol. So a future with Zev meant a future living under the scrutiny of his strange and overbearing family. Jonah was mostly upset with Zev's parents for making their son feel like he had to hide, but he'd be lying if he said some of that resentment hadn't bled over toward Zev. Being kept a secret made Jonah feel like Zev was ashamed of him, of what they shared.

"Please don't be mad, Blondie. It's hard to explain, but my parents just wouldn't understand."

Jonah snorted.

"Let me guess, you told your dad this was some kind of a business trip, right? Does he even know we keep in touch? Did you tell your parents you were coming to town for my graduation?"

Jonah rested his forehead against Zev's chest and slipped his hand under Zev's shirt, stroking the dark hair that covered rippling muscles. He wasn't sure why he was picking this fight when all he'd been wanting for months was to see Zev again. The situation with Zev's family had been the same for years; nothing had changed. Okay, that wasn't true. He knew exactly why he was picking the fight. He was frustrated. And not just with his friend's family situation or the tension between them since he'd told Zev about medical school.

"I promise you, Jonah, I will never hide you from them once you come home. I just can't tell them about you until then. I need them to see us together, and then I know they'll understand. Please trust me on this. It's the only way it'll work."

The sincerity in Zev's voice and the feel of the man he'd missed beyond reason in his arms took all the fight out of Jonah. He still wasn't happy about being hidden from Zev's family, but he trusted his best friend, his boyfriend, his lover, his everything. He believed Zev would tell the Hassicks about their relationship when Jonah moved back to Etzgadol.

They'd walked farther into the apartment as they'd talked, and they now stood in the small kitchen space. Without conscious realization, Jonah had turned his body so that he was leaning on the counter with his back pressed against Zev's chest and his naked ass pressed against Zev's cloth-covered groin. The feeling of Zev's large erection against that part of his body caused the usual reaction: Jonah's insides tingled and clenched, his skin broke out in goose bumps, and his cock stood at attention. He wanted Zev so badly that he sometimes thought he'd lose his mind from it.

"I missed you so much, Blondie." Zev's husky voice ghosted over his ear.

"Missed you too."

Jonah wiggled and pressed farther back as he replied, hoping to encourage Zev to do what he'd so far refused. Reaching behind him, he found the button on Zev's pants and popped it open. Then he pushed the zipper down and moaned when Zev's hard dick broke free and thumped against his lower back.

"Oh, yes, going commando. I like that." Jonah moaned, continuing the wiggle. He bent over, resting his forehead against the counter and lifting his ass up and out in a silent invitation. Zev groaned and pressed against him, peppering his shoulders with kisses.

"Blondie, you're killing me here. You can't imagine how much I want you."

"Then take me, Zev. I want you. You want me. Nothing's holding us back."

Zev sighed and hugged him tightly.

"Medical school is holding us back, Jonah. We have to wait until we're done with this long-distance thing."

Having Zev constantly refuse to take that next step was increasingly difficult for Jonah to understand. They'd been together for four years. Why did they have to live in the same city before they could have sex? Wasn't their relationship solid enough, even for someone as old-fashioned as Zev? Jonah's need to have his lover fill him had become so intense that he thought he might break into tears or punch a hole in the damn wall if Zev kept denying him.

"Shhh, Jonah. I'll make you feel good even without that. I promise."

Jonah hadn't realized he was shaking until Zev whispered those words into his ear. He wanted to argue, demand, cajole, hell, do anything to change Zev's mind, but then he became distracted by the loss of Zev's body heat against his back. One protesting moan was all he could get out before he felt Zev lick down his spine to the top of his ass. After landing a few light kisses on his lower back, Zev parted Jonah's cheeks and continued the path his tongue had been taking, moving down Jonah's cleft and then back up again.

"Zev," Jonah whimpered as his body went completely limp, resting on the counter. Damn, that felt good. Zev caressed him with his tongue, making broad swipes over that hidden area. And then, when Jonah thought he'd die from the pleasure, Zev took it a step further and began sucking on his pucker.

"Oh, dear God," Jonah cried out while pushing his ass farther back, hoping to encourage Zev to continue. And continue he did, with licks and sucks, and eventually a thick, talented tongue pressed its way into Jonah's body. Just the feeling of being penetrated was all it took for Jonah to cry out Zev's name and climax, coating the front of the cabinet with his release. He thrust back and forth against Zev's face, riding out the pleasure until his body could take no more.

And then he crumpled onto the floor, where Zev caught him and cradled him in strong arms.

"So good, Zev. So good," Jonah sighed, just before his eyes shut and he fell into a deep sleep.

Zev held Jonah against his chest and stood up, carrying his mate to the bedroom. He'd known that Jonah wanted them to tie—or, as Jonah described it, have sex—but until he'd seen the desperation on that beloved face, he hadn't realized that the mating instinct was at least partially responsible for that desire.

With Jonah being human, Zev hadn't known whether the man would have the same connections and needs that accompanied shifters with a true mate. Well, if the past thirty minutes were anything to go by, those needs and connections were just as strong in Zev's human mate as they could ever be in a shifter. In fact, Zev sometimes wondered if the mating bond between him and Jonah was stronger than what he'd heard could be possible. What else could account for Jonah's ability to sense his presence and sometimes even hear his thoughts? They'd long ago moved past any chance that those occasions were coincidences.

Take that morning, for example. Jonah hadn't been expecting Zev. The man had clearly been asleep in bed. Yet the blond had the front door open before Zev had put his key in the lock. There was no way Jonah could have heard him, and he was sure his mate wasn't in the habit of yanking the front door open for no reason without wearing any clothes. Thankfully Jonah had been too groggy from sleep to question his own actions, but Zev had certainly noticed.

For true mates to have that depth of connection even after decades together would be unusual and a sign of a deep bond. But to have it before they'd tied, before they'd been able to live together, and while both of them were in human form? Well, that was unheard of.

There was no doubt in Zev's mind that he'd been truly blessed. Even if he did have to suffer through eight more years before he could tie with his mate, his bond with Jonah was a blessing. But would he be able to survive that long?

After laying Jonah down on the bed, Zev stripped off his own clothes and crawled under the covers. His mate immediately rolled toward him and snuggled into his embrace, moving one leg in between both of Zev's and draping one arm across Zev's waist. The way Jonah liked to sleep tangled together with Zev was another characteristic that Zev adored. It reminded him of being a cub and sleeping in a pile with other shifters his age.

His kind were very tactile. They bonded through touch and smell. Zev hadn't expected a human to have the same need for physical contact. But Jonah did. He seemed to revel in Zev's touch, always standing close to him, kissing him, holding his hand.

So, yeah, Jonah was a human, but he was still the perfect mate, Zev thought with a smile as he fell asleep.

CHAPTER 13

"Who in the hell are you?"

Jonah flushed the toilet, yanked up his briefs, and ran into his bedroom as soon as he heard the loud shout. That sounded like a woman's voice. It took him a few minutes to take in the scene before him.

A very pregnant woman stood just inside the bedroom door, shaking keys menacingly at Peter. Or was it Paul? Hell, what difference did it make? The woman was yelling at the Mary he'd picked up at the bar that night. When Jonah had gone into the bathroom, his date (wow, was that ever a strained use of the word) had been naked in the bed. Now the man was feverishly yanking his pants back up and stuffing his feet into his shoes.

"I'm leaving. I'm leaving. I didn't know he was married. I swear."

Married? What was Peter...Paul...fuck it, Jonah would have to do a better job getting names next time he picked up a guy. That is, if there would be a next time.

The first time he'd tried to bring someone home, he'd ended up throwing up all over whatever that guy's name was. He managed not to upchuck on the next guy, but in an even more embarrassing physical malfunction, he couldn't get it up, so he ended up calling the whole thing off on the grounds of ED. Now, he had guy number three in his bedroom, and a strange lady had shown up and started shouting before they'd been able to get anything started. Clearly, this wasn't meant to be. As if he didn't know that already. The whole idea of being with someone other than Zev made Jonah feel ill.

"I don't want to hear your excuses, you slut. Get out!"

Despite the fact that the woman was smaller than him, well, other than in the belly, Jonah cowered a bit when he heard the tone of her voice. She sounded pissed as hell and not like someone you'd want to mess with. The guy in Jonah's apartment certainly agreed, because he got his ass out the door before he'd even put on his shirt. Jonah was about to ask the woman who she was and what she was doing in his apartment when she turned and flipped her hair back. He got a look at her face for the first time and almost fell down.

"Lori?"

He didn't think he'd had all that much to drink. Just one beer and two diet sodas. That wasn't enough to cause hallucinations. Plus, he was usually asleep when the disturbing childhood-related visions entered his head.

"Not now, Jonah. We don't have any time. I know you're only human, but that's no excuse for this kind of behavior!"

The way Lori said that sentence, it seemed to take on a meaning different from the traditional "you're only human, you're bound to make mistakes" shtick. But Jonah didn't have time to focus on that.

"What...what are you doing here?"

Lori dropped her purse and keys to the floor and stalked around the room, looking at everything. The way she kept sniffling, Jonah wondered whether she had developed allergies with her pregnancy.

"I'm here to celebrate your med school graduation with you, Jonah Marvel. My brother thought you'd like to have Toby and me here, so we left the twins with my folks and spent half a day traveling." She walked over to the bed as she kept talking. "I get motion sickness even when I'm not pregnant, and carrying the next generation in my body just makes it worse, so Zev dropped me off here while he and Toby look for a parking spot. He gave me your keys so I'd be able to let myself in if you weren't home, but I had to pee so I didn't bother knocking." She turned to Jonah and put her hands on her hips in a straight-from-television mother move. "With that useful background in place, do you have any other pressing questions for me or do you want to start fixing this mess?"

Jonah was struck dumb. He just stared at Lori and tried to process what she'd said. He was stuck somewhere around the part where Zev was outside his apartment.

"But...but Zev isn't coming to town until Friday."

"Seriously, Jonah? That's your focus? Fine! Toby needs to be back for work on Saturday so the two of us can't stay for the weekend. This trip is too long for just one night so we all decided to surprise you by coming a couple of days early."

Lori elbowed past him and walked into the bathroom.

"Sorry to interrupt your fun," she said, not sounding the least bit sorry. "Now, take your sheets off the bed and put them in a thick garbage bag. No, make that two thick garbage bags. I really need to pee."

Those were Lori's last words before the bathroom door slammed shut. Jonah still hadn't moved from his spot when he heard the toilet flush and the sink run, and then watched a still furious Lori walk out of the bathroom.

"Jonah! Were you listening to me? If my brother comes in here and smells another man, he'll lose it! And if you hurt him that way, pregnant or not, I'll kick your ass from here to next Sunday." She threw her hands up in the air in frustration. "You know what? Forget about the sheets, I'll take care of them. Go get in the shower and scrub until you take off the entire top layer of skin." She walked over to the window and pried it open, then turned back to Jonah. "Now!"

That scream was the final push Jonah needed to unglue his feet from the floor and run into the shower. He put the water on a higher temperature than he'd usually use and poured a liberal amount of bath gel on his sponge. He hadn't seen Lori in eight years. Not since they'd graduated from high school. And this was not how he'd imagined their reunion. When he was sure he couldn't get any cleaner, Jonah turned off the water and pulled the shower curtain open.

"Ahh!" he shouted when he saw Lori standing in front of him, stuffing the clothes he'd worn that night into a garbage bag. He automatically covered his groin with his hands. Lori rolled her eyes.

"Save it, Jonah. Your dignity's already shot. Go get dressed. If we're lucky, we can get out of here and meet Zev and Toby downstairs. Then by the time you come back here tonight, there'll be a chance this place will have aired out."

He didn't understand what Lori was talking about. It wasn't as if his apartment smelled of sex. The clothes had just come off before Lori had walked in, so truly, nothing had happened. Besides, Zev hadn't told his family about their relationship, so she couldn't be worried about her brother being jealous.

Maybe she was just disgusted with the idea of Jonah being gay and thought Zev would be too? Yeah, that made sense given the way Zev had first reacted to their feelings toward each other. He did say his family didn't think he could be gay. Jonah snorted at that one. Like family had any control over how a person was made.

Still, Jonah had no desire to argue with a furious, pregnant Lori. That was just stupid and possibly suicidal. He dried off frantically and hurried into the bedroom, where he pulled on clothes as quickly as possible. He noticed the open window and considered making a snarky remark about how environmentally destructive it was for them to air-condition the entire neighborhood, but then thought better of it. Good thing at least some synapses were still firing.

"Where's your laundry room?"

Jonah took a break from bouncing on one foot and yanking on his sock to answer Lori's question.

"I don't have a laundry room. This is a two-room apartment. This bedroom and the living room slash kitchen area."

"Huh. Well, that won't work," she said as she marched over to the window and threw the trash bag out into the alley.

"Hey! Were those my clothes?"

"Yeah, and your sheets."

Jonah ran to the window and looked outside, not that he could see anything in the dark from seven stories up.

"Why'd you do that, Lori? I'm a student. I'm not rolling in dough here. I can't afford to just throw out my clothes and bedding!"

Lori turned on him with an anger so ferocious that Jonah backed away several steps and held his hands in front of him in a defensive posture.

"That person you had in here was naked in your bed, Jonah. And even I could smell him all over your clothes. You think my brother won't notice that?" She scoffed and looked at him in disgust. "Finish getting dressed. We need to get out of this apartment before..."

She never got to finish her sentence because they both heard the front door open.

"Shit!" she whispered. "I guess your lover boy didn't lock up on his way out."

"He's not my lover. Honest, Lori, nothing..."

"Not now, Jonah!" she hissed in an angry whisper. Then she smoothed down her skirt, tucked her hair behind her ears, and walked into the living room. She seemed to be going for casual indifference, but Jonah could still hear the tension in her voice when she spoke.

"Hey, I caught Jonah in the shower, he's just finishing getting dressed, and we thought we could go out and grab a late bite."

With Lori out of the room, Jonah took a moment to sit down and collect himself. What the hell just happened?

He'd been completely out of control lately. More than usual. He snorted out loud with that thought.

He no longer knew what was usual. He'd been slowly losing his mind, and he didn't have the ability to rein it in. How else could he explain the feelings he'd been having? It was like he wanted to tear his skin open, like his own body was a prison from which he couldn't escape.

At first he thought the feelings were a stress-induced reaction. That medical school was getting to him. He wouldn't be the first person to suffer that fate. One of the women who'd started school with him ended up dropping out after six months when the police found her wandering the streets late at night, completely unaware of her own name. After a few nights in the psych hospital, she got herself together but she refused to go back to school. He heard she was happily running a flower shop in Austin now.

But Jonah truly loved what he was doing. His last couple of years had been spent more on clinical work than classroom work. Patients reacted well to him. He seemed to have a knack for making them feel at ease. And he enjoyed helping them. So school wasn't the problem; the problem was rooted inside him.

Jonah knew his father's family pretty well and didn't think there was a history of mental illness there, but he knew nothing about his mother or her family. Over the years, he'd wanted to ask his father many times, but the pain in Kevin Marvel's eyes when the man so much as looked at the picture he still kept on his nightstand told Jonah more than any words ever could. Bringing up his mother would cause immense pain to his father.

So Jonah hadn't asked, but now he wondered whether there was some medical condition on his mother's side that would explain what was happening to him. He rubbed his hands over his tired eyes. The early to midtwenties were the right age for several different mental disorders to manifest. And, if he were honest, the signs had already been around for the past couple of years. But Jonah had done some research on his symptoms, and they didn't quite fit anything he'd learned about in his psych block.

Unable to get to the crux of the problem, he had made a decision to just move on with his life. He forced himself to focus on school, friends, when he could next see Zev, and just ignore the pain in his body and the skitters in his mind, hoping they'd get bored and go away. But then the dreams had started, and Jonah could no longer ignore what was going on in his body. He had to stop the dreams.

That was what had led to the bar pickups. He'd hoped that sating the deep-seated desire he had to be filled by a man could stop the disturbing images that plagued him in sleep. Of course his desire was for only one man, but Zev continued to refuse him, and eventually, Jonah's frustration beat out his good sense and common decency. Good thing his body hadn't allowed him to actually have sex with those strangers. Even if Zev would have found it in his heart to forgive him, Jonah was pretty sure he'd never have been able to forgive himself.

Shaking his head free of the distracting thoughts, Jonah tried to focus on the here and now. He hadn't cheated. Zev was here. And the man had brought Toby and Lori.

Oh, damn it, Lori. That had been an unpleasant reunion. Seriously, like an adult version of the "showing up to school in your underwear" dream. Speaking of Lori, she was being awfully quiet. For that matter, so were Zev and Toby.

Jonah had lost track of time while he was lost in his own head, but now that he was paying attention, he couldn't help but notice the silence. His apartment wasn't that big. How could he hear nothing if three people were waiting for him in the living room? Jonah's heart began slamming against his ribcage as he had a horrifying thought that he'd imagined the whole thing. Would he have to add visual and auditory hallucinations to his list of symptoms?

He willed his body to get up and walk into the living room. His friends would be out there. They would. Lori's visit wasn't some elaborate vision his mind had conjured. But he couldn't force himself to get up, couldn't take the risk that he'd slid farther down the rabbit hole.

CHAPTER 14

"Come on, Blondie. I need you to get up for just a couple of minutes while I make the bed." Zev's familiar voice coated Jonah's mind like a soothing balm.

He could almost feel the tension seeping away as a strong arm cradled his neck, another made its way underneath his knees, and he was scooped into familiar arms. He rested his cheek against the broad chest and felt grateful for this dream.

At well over six feet in height with a muscular frame weighing in at over a hundred and eighty pounds, Jonah was not the kind of man that could be easily carried. But Zev was scary powerful. So much so that when Jonah had bought a new-to-him sofa, Zev had moved the heavy piece of furniture up seven flights of stairs into his apartment without even getting winded. By the time the sofa was set on the floor, Jonah was so turned on by that display of strength that he'd shoved Zev onto it and practically ripped his lover's pants down before dropping to his knees and taking Zev's delicious cock into his mouth.

The rough fabric of that same tweed couch scratched Jonah's skin as he was lowered away from the hot body holding him, distracting him from the happy memory. He clung to the large biceps, not wanting to let go yet. Not wanting to wake up alone again.

"Shhh. I won't take long, Blondie. Just rest here and I'll be right back."

A whimper was Jonah's only response. It did no good to fight the separation. It always happened eventually. Morning would come and take Zev away again, leaving Jonah feeling desolate. Violent shivers ran through his body. He curled into a ball, hoping to find warmth, but knowing he wouldn't. How could he drive away a chill that came from inside?

"Okay, here we go. Open up so I can take you to bed. It's okay, Jonah. I'm here and I'll take care of you."

He willed his muscles to relax and felt the strong grip take hold of him again. Zev felt so real. Smelled so real. Jonah refused to open his eyes, not wanting the feeling of being wrapped in that comfortable warmth to end. Once crisp sheets were under his body, sure fingers removed his shoes, socks, and jeans.

"Head up."

He complied, lifting his neck as his shirt was pulled up and over his head. Then a hard body pressed against him, and sure, solid arms encircled his waist and pulled him tight. He immediately relaxed into the embrace.

"Night, Pup," Jonah murmured as he let sleep take him, wondering all the while whether the disturbing visions would infiltrate his mind once again.

Zev gasped and forced his body to remain still despite what he'd heard. Pup. Jonah had called him Pup. Did the other man know? Had he somehow recognized the connection between his boyfriend and the wolf he'd befriended during his youth?

No, he couldn't know. At least not on a conscious level. But their mating bond was so strong, stronger than anything Zev had heard the elders describe, that he could imagine Jonah realizing who Zev was in both forms. In fact, Zev thought Jonah likely would have put it together himself by now if they'd been back in Etzgadol, where Jonah could see Zev's wolf.

The man hadn't seen Zev in his wolf skin since the night they'd slept curled together, after Zev had run away from Jonah's house and before he'd come back in his human form and taken ownership of his true feelings for his mate. After all they'd shared over the past eight years, both physically and emotionally, Zev knew their mating bond was exponentially stronger than it had been when they were kids.

After all, Zev hadn't even been aware of the bond back then. But all the denial and outright stupidity in the world couldn't prevent Zev from feeling it now. The link he shared with his mate was an almost tangible thing. It was undeniable. And he knew Jonah felt it too. The human just didn't have the context or words to articulate what he felt.

Should he tell Jonah the truth? It was a question Zev asked himself almost every day. He'd go over his options, wondering if there was any way for Jonah to learn about this unusual facet of his boyfriend, and about their roles in each other's lives, without the other man either running for the hills or having a complete mental break.

No, Jonah wouldn't run away from him. He couldn't. Even without being pack, Jonah seemed to have an ingrained need to be with Zev. His desire to tie had progressively increased over the years, to the point where almost every sexual contact they'd shared during their last couple of visits had involved Jonah doing everything in his power to get Zev's dick up his ass.

Refusing was difficult, but Zev's commitment to see Jonah achieve his dream of becoming a physician gave Zev the strength to push down his own needs and Jonah's. They'd have to wait. Only a few more years now, and Jonah would be done with his education. Then Zev's mate would come home to Etzgadol and they would join together. Zev got hard just thinking about it. Now he had to figure out what Jonah had been doing before Zev had arrived at his mate's apartment that night.

"Zev?" Jonah mumbled, his voice sounding sleepy. He blinked open his black eyes, confusion clear on his face. "Are you really here? What time is it?"

"Yeah, I'm here. It's the middle of the night. You can get more sleep."

Jonah rubbed his eyes and sat up. He cupped Zev's cheek, ran a finger across the stubbly jaw and down the corded muscles of Zev's neck, then took Zev's hand in his and brought it up to his mouth for a kiss.

"What the hell?" Jonah's gaze darted from Zev's bloody knuckles to his eyes. He reached for the nightstand and flipped on the light. "What'd you do, Hassick? I think you might need stitches."

Zev pulled his hand back.

"I'm fine. It'll be better in the morning. I'm a fast healer."

"Yeah, I know, but this is bad. Come into the bathroom with me so I can see it in better light."

"I'm fine, Jonah. Promise."

Jonah stopped focusing on Zev's hand and looked at his face. "You don't sound fine." He stared at Zev and furrowed his brow, as if he was trying to put something together. "You sound...angry."

Unable to deny that, Zev sighed and pulled his hand away. "What happened tonight, Jonah?"

After a beat, Jonah's eyes widened and he reared back, clearly having remembered what had happened that evening.

Instead of playing dumb or playing games, his posture slumped, and he mumbled, "There was a guy in my apartment when Lori got here."

Zev heard those words and a sharp pain stabbed his heart. He'd already known there'd been a man in Jonah's place. He'd smelled the human as soon as he'd walked in. So why did it hurt so much to hear Jonah say it?

"Oh. Is he a classmate? Were you studying?" Even to his own ears, Zev's voice sounded desperate.

He took a few calming breaths. Everything was fine. His mate was with him. Nothing to get worked up over.

"No, Zev, he isn't a classmate." Jonah sighed heavily. "I...I think I might be messed up, Zev. Like, seriously messed up."

Whatever else had happened that night, Zev cared more about the source of his mate's pain. And it was clear that there was pain. Jonah looked thinner than the last time Zev had seen him, and the dark circles under his eyes weren't from one night of uninterrupted sleep.

"What kind of messed up, Blondie? Talk to me."

Jonah scooted until his back was pressed against the wall. He closed his eyes, tilted his head back, and reached one hand in Zev's direction. His hand was immediately gripped by a bigger one, thick fingers were twined with his, and he felt better.

"I don't know how to explain it. I just... I don't feel right. I don't have a fever, don't have symptoms that fit any particular illness, but I'm just not right." Although he didn't want to continue, Jonah forced himself to carry on. He owed Zev the whole truth and, frankly, he needed his friend's support. "And then there are these dreams, Zev, these terrible dreams."

Warmth against his right side caused Jonah to open his eyes and turn his head. Zev was sitting up right next to him. Jonah sighed and got even closer to that hot body. He rested his head on Zev's shoulder.

"It's like I'm constantly itching. Awake, asleep, it doesn't matter. This is the most comfortable I've been in my own skin for the first time in weeks, maybe longer." He closed his eyes again and took a calming breath.

"Tell me about the dreams," Zev said, his voice tense.

"They're all childhood dreams, but not anything I actually remember. Not even things I could remember. Some of them are about my mom."

"She died when you were a baby, right? Before you moved to Etzgadol?"

Jonah nodded. "Right; car accident. I don't remember her, obviously. I know I'm named after her—her name was Joan, so, yeah, Jonah. And I've seen a couple of pictures, but that's it. My dad doesn't talk about her, so it's not like anything I'm dreaming is a real story. But it still..." Jonah swallowed hard. "It still scares me. There's always so much blood in the dreams. Sometimes she's screaming, begging for help. Sometimes she's still, her body twisted at weird angles, her eyes vacant. Sometimes we're alone. Other times, there are a bunch of men I don't recognize with us."

"What do you think it means?" Zev whispered.

"Hell if I know. That I miss her? Miss having a mother? I have no idea. They're nightmares; they're not supposed to make sense. A few times she's even been a wolf in the dreams, but I still know she's my mom. Like I said, none of it makes sense, but it makes me feel sick."

The hand holding Jonah's squeezed tightly, and he heard Zev gasp.

"She's a wolf? You dream that your mother turns into a wolf?"

"Not all the dreams are about my mom, Zev. Some of them are about you." Zev didn't say anything, so Jonah continued, keeping his eyes closed. He couldn't bear to finish his explanation if he saw pain on Zev's face. "Sometimes you're a wolf too, one I used to play with when I was a kid. That makes sense because my brain is probably just replacing one childhood friend with another, but Zev..." Jonah sighed and met Zev's gaze. "Most of the ones with you are, well, they're pretty erotic. Truth is, they make me crazy. And lately, I just can't stop thinking about them. I know you won't...you know. But I need to. I really need to."

"So you went out and found someone else to have sex with you."

The cold, almost detached way Zev summarized the situation hurt more than any shouts or strikes ever could.

"I didn't. I couldn't go through with it, but...yeah, I tried. I know it was wrong. I know. I know. I don't have a good excuse, Zev. I'm sorry." Jonah wiped tears off his cheek with a shaky hand. "Nothing happened. Not that it justifies my behavior, but I thought you might want to know."

Silence. Not one word in response. Jonah forced himself to open his eyes and look at the person he felt closest to in the entire world, even if they did spend most of their time several states apart.

"Say something, Zev. Tell me you forgive me."

It took another long couple of minutes, but Zev eventually pulled Jonah onto his lap and hugged him.

"I forgive you, Blondie. And I know that I can't stop you from..." Zev clenched his eyes shut and gulped. "I can't stop you from being with other guys, but I wish you wouldn't."

Jonah shook his head furiously. "Won't. I promise that I won't."

"Listen to me, Jonah, listen. I get that it's hard being apart, okay? I get that you're...frustrated. I know you might not believe me, but I feel the same way."

"Then why are we doing this, Zev? I'm sorry to push again, but I don't understand." Jonah hoped he didn't sound whiny, but he doubted that he'd been able to pull that off.

"Because you need to finish school and become a doctor. And I can't leave Etzgadol. Jonah, there are hundreds of families depending on me."

Jonah understood that Zev couldn't leave his job. Over the years, it'd become clear that Zev wasn't just some employee. His father had been grooming him to take over, and by the sound of things, Zev was practically running the family business already. It was only a matter of time before Mr. Hassick would retire and Zev would hold the reins completely. But that didn't answer Jonah's question.

"You know that's not what I mean, Zev. I get that we can't live in the same place yet, and that sucks. But we can still..."

"No, we can't." For the first time that night, Zev sounded truly frustrated. "I don't know how to explain it to you. I've tried and I never seem to have the right words." He dragged his fingers through his hair. "If we, um, have sex, Jonah, we won't be able to tolerate the separation from each other. Believe me. The frustration you're feeling now, you can handle it. It sucks, it hurts, I get that. But we aren't given more than we can handle. That's not how it works. Yeah, it's harder for us than most ma—people. We found each other and got torn apart. But we can do this."

Zev kissed Jonah's temple and stroked his hair. When he continued talking, his voice was softer.

"You'll finish school, become a great healer, and come home. Then we can be together in the way we both want. If we do this now, we won't be able to keep living apart. That means you'll have to leave school or I'll have to leave Etzgadol. Neither of those are acceptable options. People are counting on us. We have to hang in there just a little bit longer."

They'd had this conversation so many times that Jonah had practically committed it to memory. Zev was smart, fun, and sexy as hell, but he was also an absolute throwback. That weird religion of his was so deeply ingrained that he'd created his own version of the no-sex-before-marriage rule. Despite Jonah's best efforts, he hadn't been able to change Zev's views on the matter. But after what he'd been doing— picking up men, intending to have sex with them—Jonah had no room to question Zev's decision. He had to respect Zev's wishes, even if he didn't understand them.

"Okay, we'll wait," Jonah agreed. Strangely, a sense of peace washed over him with those words. "Now give me a proper hello kiss, Hassick."

Zev tilted Jonah's chin and moved his lips against Jonah's in a gentle caress.

"Missed you."

"Missed you too."

CHAPTER 15

ZEV WOKE before Jonah the following morning. His arm was wrapped around Jonah's chest, Jonah's arm was draped over his waist, and their legs were tangled together. He licked and kissed Jonah's neck, tenderly caressed his back, and rubbed his calf up and down Jonah's muscular leg.

With his eyes still closed, Jonah whispered, "If I believed in a deity of any kind, I'd be thanking her right now."

"Why's that?" Zev brushed his lips over Jonah's.

"For bringing you into my life." Jonah's eyes fluttered open, the dark gaze landing on Zev. "There isn't another person alive who turns me on like you do, or makes me laugh so freely, or challenges me in the same way intellectually. There's nobody with your integrity and compassion." Jonah traced Zev's eyebrow with one fingertip. "Bottom line— nobody comes close to matching up to you, Zev." Sadness flooded Jonah's face right before he buried it in the base of Zev's neck.

So how could I possibly have thought it was a good idea to risk this by picking up strangers in bars and bringing them home?

Tightening his grip around Jonah, Zev said, "It's okay. Being apart from each other is really hard, and you're going through a lot right now." He kissed the top of Jonah's head. "I'm not going to say I'm happy about what you did, but I do understand. I don't hold it against you, Blondie." His throat thickened, making his voice sound rougher as he finished. "What we have goes way too deep for a few moments of desperation to get in the way."

Jonah nodded in acknowledgement. "You know me so well. You practically read my mind just now."

Zev froze, thinking about whether Jonah had been talking out loud.

"You're so damn sexy, Hassick." Strong hands roamed over his chest, distracting him. "Have I ever told you how much I enjoy this silky hair?" Jonah ran his fingers through the hair on Zev's chest and rubbed his cheek against Zev's heavily whiskered jaw. "Or how sexy you are in the morning before you shave? All rough and tumble."

Unable to resist his mate, Zev grasped Jonah's head and slammed their mouths together. Sharp need robbed him of finesse so the kiss was ferocious. He breached Jonah's mouth with his tongue, ground his erection against Jonah's, and then flipped them over so he pinned Jonah to the bed.

"I want you." Zev's voice sounded gruff to his own ears but Jonah didn't seem to mind.

His nostrils flared and body trembled as he rasped, "Anything, Zev. Take anything you want." Jonah spread his legs, leaving himself completely open and available.

Zev moaned and kissed Jonah again, hard and desperate. Then he crawled up Jonah's body until he straddled Jonah's chest. He caressed Jonah's jaw and traced his lips. "Tilt your head back and open up for me."

Jonah complied, licking his lips and opening his mouth widely.

Zev didn't waste time. He guided his dick into Jonah's waiting mouth, then supported himself by placing both hands on the wall behind the bed. He slowly pushed his way past Jonah's welcoming lips, enjoying the warmth and wetness, the tongue darting around him.

Looking down, Zev saw himself sliding deep into Jonah's wet, eager mouth. He saw the blissful, adoring expression as Jonah looked up at him. Then he began a slow rhythm, pumping past those stretched lips, reminding himself and Jonah of his strength, of the fact that he could take care of Jonah. Of the fact that the man was his. His. Nothing and no one could change that.

"Do you feel me, Jonah? Feel my cock deep in your mouth?"

Jonah couldn't respond verbally, his mouth was too full, but Zev could see his agreement in his eyes. He could practically hear his mate's "yes" in his mind.

"I'm going deeper, Jonah. Going in all the way. Gonna remind you where you belong."

And with those words, Zev knew he really could hear Jonah in his head, answering him with moans and exuberant agreement. He let go of any restraint and let his body claim what was his—his mate. He rocked his hips forward and back, filling Jonah's throat, then pulling back and dragging his cockhead against the other man's tongue, only to push back in again.

In and out he went, not slowing down, just pushing into his mate, feeling the pleasure wash over him and take him higher and higher, until he was at the edge of the precipice.

"Gonna come now. Wanna taste me, Jonah?"

Oh, God, yes. Please!

The words weren't spoken, obviously, since Jonah had his mouth full. But they were still communicating, their mental link stronger than ever. That knowledge—that he was so in tune with his mate, despite the fact they hadn't yet tied, despite the distance, despite...the rest of it—excited Zev even further.

"Now, Jonah. Now!" Zev shouted as he pulled his cock out so just the crown was in Jonah's mouth. He wrapped his hand around the base to keep himself steady and threw his head back as he let go and released his pleasure into Jonah's mouth.

He remained leaning against the wall with one hand, the other stroking Jonah's cheek as he continued to suckle on his softening cock, a reverent expression on his face. Eventually, he slid down Jonah's body, noticing with satisfaction that the other man's stomach was wet with his own release. When his big frame blanketed Jonah, he cupped his mate's cheeks and looked deep into his eyes.

"Mine."

Jonah whimpered and nodded before closing his eyes and falling asleep.

After resting together for a short time, they forced themselves out of bed and took turns in the shower. When Jonah got out, Zev was standing naked in the bathroom, leaning over the sink and shaving. He looked so damn big, so damn strong, so damn hot.

"So what's the plan for today?"

Jonah pressed his naked body against Zev's, enjoying the skin-on-skin contact.

"Mmm. You feel good," Zev said as he dropped the razor, turned around and took Jonah's cock into his hand and squeezed it, causing blood to immediately flow in that direction. "Lori and Toby want to hang out with you. I need to meet a few clients in the morning, but I should be done in time to meet you guys for a late lunch. That work?"

The entire time he spoke, Zev caressed Jonah's dick with one hand and his ass with the other. Every conversation should feel that good.

"Mmm hmm. That works."

They got dressed at a snail's pace because neither man could keep his hands off the other. Whether it was goofing around with tickles or pinches, petting with tenderness, or kissing with arousal, Jonah was sufficiently distracted to forget all about the fact that Lori was probably still mad at him. It wasn't until he was knocking on the hotel room door that the memory of the previous night's interaction with Lori hit him like a bucket of cold water and wiped the smile from his face.

The door swung open. Toby stepped out and pulled the door shut behind him.

"Hey, man. It's been too long," Jonah said and reached over for a hug.

Toby shrugged him off.

"I'm starved. Is there a breakfast place around here? Someplace that makes good steak and eggs?"

Jonah noticed the chill from Toby and figured that Lori had told her husband about what had happened the night before. Toby quickly walked toward the elevator.

"Aren't we waiting for Lori?" Jonah asked.

Toby didn't turn around as he answered. "Nah, she isn't coming. We'll meet up with her later today."

Great. Lori was too pissed to see him and Toby was like Antarctica. Jonah still wasn't completely sure why they were so angry, given the fact that Zev hadn't told anyone back home about their relationship. Well, there was one option; his old friends weren't comfortable with him being gay. Tough shit.

Jonah figured the best way to deal with the situation was to face it head on. But as soon as they got into Jonah's car, Toby started fiddling with the radio. Jonah decided to bide his time and wait for Toby to finish what he was doing so they could talk. He almost lost his composure when the other man landed on a Barry Manilow song and kept it there. Toby had to be the only Fanilow under the age of fifty.

"So I'm guessing Lori told you about that guy in my apartment last night."

Toby's posture immediately stiffened. Several long moments passed before he answered.

"Yeah, she did."

"Anything you want to ask me about it, Toby? Might as well get it out there. No reason to walk on eggshells around each other."

"Ooookay," Toby responded, drawing out the word. He took a deep breath and turned to face Jonah. "Did you stumble across a clearance sale on jackass cream or something? Maybe they were running a special on lobotomies?"

Well, that was an unexpected response.

"Huh? What do you mean?"

"What I mean, Jonah..." Toby said in a louder voice, "is that I know we're all just a couple of bad decisions away from being one of those weirdos who buys fake nuts and hangs them on the back of his pickup truck, but you really managed to win the stupid cake last night."

Okay, this conversation wasn't going exactly how Jonah had planned, but he still felt the need to defend himself.

"Stupid? Why? Because I'm gay? That's not a bad decision, Toby. It's not a decision at all."

Jonah pulled into a parking lot of a decent diner, turned off the car, and twisted to face Toby. The conversation was tense and awkward, but at least Toby's atrocious music no longer made Jonah's ears bleed. Jonah would have preferred hearing his car engine drop out and drag across the asphalt than another cheesy ballad.

"No shit, Sherlock. But cheating on Zev is a decision. A really bad decision."

Jonah's mouth dropped open, and he snapped his eyes toward Toby in shock. Holy crap. Toby knew about his relationship with Zev. That meant Lori knew. As much as he hated being hidden from Zev's family and life back in Etzgadol, Jonah didn't want the man to be forced out against his will.

"You know?"

"Know what?"

"About, um, me and Zev?"

Toby rolled his eyes.

"Of course I know. Just because I was blessed in the looks department doesn't mean I was shorted anything upstairs. I'm not an idiot, Jonah."

"Yeah, and you're not lacking in the ego department, either. Listen, Toby, you can't tell anyone. Zev isn't ready for his family to know he's gay."

"Honestly, Jonah, it feels like we're living in two different worlds. Zev came out to his family years ago. Not long after you moved away, actually."

Jonah was left momentarily speechless by that bit of news.

"But he told me that he couldn't tell his family about us."

Toby's face softened. He cleared his throat.

"Oh, yeah. Well, that's true. If he'd have told them about you, they'd have seriously lost their shit. But Lori and I figured out the deal with the two of you. We won't tell anyone, though. No worries about that."

Jonah nodded. It made a strange kind of sense. Telling your parents you're gay and telling them you're actually dating a guy are two different things. Even though Zev hadn't told his parents they were together, Jonah was still relieved to hear that his friend had come out of the closet and his home life hadn't come to an end as a result.

Toby took a deep breath, distracting Jonah from his thoughts.

"Listen, Jonah, I know we haven't talked in a few years, but we've known each other a long time and you're family. You've always been a good guy. Someone I trusted. But the way you were acting last night, I have to assume that you misplaced your moral compass when you moved away or something, because the Jonah I knew never would've betrayed Zev."

Jonah winced at the words. Toby was right. He'd made a mistake. He felt like he owed Toby an explanation, but he didn't know how to give it.

"I know, Toby. Look, it's hard to explain what happened. You wouldn't understand."

Toby crossed his arms over his chest. "I understand a lot more than you realize, Jonah. Try me."

Toby seemed calmer than he'd been previously, now sitting quietly and waiting for Jonah to talk.

"I don't take Zev for granted, Toby. I spent way too many years wanting him to forget just how lucky I am that he wants me too. Zev's wonderful, but he's also really old-fashioned, you know?"

Toby snorted. "Zev? Are you kidding? He's probably the most progressive guy I know."

"Not in all things," Jonah muttered under his breath.

"What things are you talking about?"

"You heard that?"

"I have great hearing."

Jonah shrugged. "Yeah, so does Zev." He took a breath and tried to figure out what to say without making Toby uncomfortable. He turned to look at Toby. "Did you and Lori have sex before you got married?"

"Married?" Toby snorted. "Lori and I had sex before we got out of high school."

Jonah leaned back in his seat and closed his eyes.

"Well, there you go. Zev won't. Have sex with me, I mean. Not until I'm done with my residency and move back to Etzgadol. And I know it shouldn't matter, but it does." He said the last part quietly.

"He won't have sex with you?" Toby's tone was disbelieving.

"Well, he'll have sex with me, but he won't, you know, have sex with me."

Jonah hoped Toby understood what he meant, because explaining the ins and outs of gay sex to Zev was one thing, but he wasn't prepared to do it with Toby. Etzgadol seriously needed to come into the twenty-first century. How all these people could be so sheltered was inconceivable. Weird religion or not.

"Oh, I see. Well, that makes sense."

He seriously doubted Toby understood what he meant.

"No, it doesn't make sense. Men can have sex with each other, Toby."

"Oh, save it, Mr. High and Mighty. You're not the first gay man I've met. I get the basics."

Well, that was good news. Maybe Toby had broadened his horizons when he left Etzgadol to go to nursing school. Although, from what Jonah knew about the town in which Toby had studied, it was just as small and rural as their hometown. It seemed like Toby shared Zev's aversion to metropolitan areas.

"You have gay friends in Etzgadol?"

Toby shook his head.

"Gay uncle. I've spent a good bit of time with him and his, er, husband."

Huh. Jonah didn't remember Zev ever mentioning Toby's uncle. Maybe Zev didn't know about the man. He forced himself to focus on their conversation.

"Okay, then, how does Zev not having sex with me make sense? You just said you've been sleeping with Lori since high school. You went to nursing school out of state, so clearly that didn't stop you."

"That's different, Jonah. My relationship with Lori isn't like your relationship with Zev."

Jonah wasn't surprised, he was just tired. Of course Toby would see the relationships as different. Two men couldn't possibly feel about each other the way a man feels about a woman. Apparently having a gay uncle couldn't change that type of thinking.

"Right. Because we're gay. Our relationship can't be as meaningful as yours," he responded sarcastically.

"No," Toby replied, looking straight into Jonah's eyes with a somber expression. "What you have with Zev is much deeper."

Jonah's mouth dropped open, and he stared at Toby. As long as Jonah had known the other man, he'd had a thing for Lori, and, as far as Jonah knew, they were very happy together.

"Last night when we came to your place, Zev flipped out. Did you know that?" Toby said.

Jonah shook his head. He'd been sitting in his bedroom and hadn't heard a thing.

"Well, he did. He lost it and ran outside. I followed him and caught up to him in the alley. He'd punched a hole in the side of your apartment building, and he was kneeling on the ground, vomiting and crying."

Jonah's heart broke. So that was how Zev had acquired those injured knuckles. He didn't want to hear any more.

"I didn't know what the hell was wrong," Toby continued. "I couldn't get him to come inside and I didn't want to leave him out there alone. Once his stomach was empty, he just kept dry heaving and shaking. Eventually Lori came out and told me what'd been going on before we got there." Toby glared at Jonah. "I wanted to go upstairs and kick your ass myself when I heard there'd been another man in your bedroom. You wanna know what stopped me?"

Jonah couldn't bring himself to respond. He was still thinking about Zev crying on the street. The man was always so strong, so steady and confident. He'd never seen Zev cry, and the knowledge that he'd caused that level of pain made Jonah feel sick.

"I knew that if I so much as looked at you crosswise, Zev would've crippled me. No matter what you'd done to him." Toby's voice got louder and more agitated as he kept speaking. "Zev deserves better than this. Do you have any idea how hard things are for him? He puts up with endless shit because he's waiting for you to finish your education, and this is how you treat him?"

Jonah shook his head.

"No, I...I..."

"You think he's being old-fashioned. I guess it can seem that way. But believe me when I tell you that he wants the same thing you want, uh, as far as sex goes. He's just strong enough to be patient. Zev is the most powerful shi...person I know, physically and mentally. If you want to be with him, Jonah, it's time you stepped up to the plate and showed the same strength."

"I get it, Toby. I was a weak, selfish asshole. It won't happen again."

Toby dragged his fingers through his hair, and Jonah could see him relax slightly.

"Glad to hear it. Because if you don't get your shit together, man, I'm going to gift wrap it, slap a big, ugly bow on top, and send it to you for your birthday."

Jonah nodded. There was nothing else to say. They got out of the car and started walking toward the diner. Out of the corner of his eye, Jonah noticed a man standing in the shadows of the building, staring at them. He was tall and fit, with cafe au lait skin and jet-black hair.

"You know that guy?" Jonah tilted his head in the direction where the man was standing.

Toby looked over. He froze for several long moments before the dark-haired man gave a brisk nod, then walked farther into the shadows and out of sight. Toby turned back to Jonah and draped an arm over his shoulder.

"Hey, who do you think wins in a challenge, Superman or the Incredible Hulk?" Toby asked.

Jonah chuckled. He'd missed Toby. It was nice to be with his old friend again. He was so happy they were back on solid ground that he barely noticed the fact that his question hadn't been answered.

CHAPTER 16

THE NEXT couple of years were so busy that Jonah barely had time to think, let alone fret about his nightmares. Not that they were gone. No, the visions of his mother still plagued his sleep just as often as the erotic dreams featuring Zev. And the dreams continued to share the strange wolf connection. In fact, the dreams about his mother now had a new twist where the men he saw with her were sometimes wolves. That is, they looked like wolves, but Jonah always knew they were the same men he'd seen in previous dreams. None of it made sense.

"What are you up to tonight, Jonah?"

Jonah looked over at the staff room door and saw his friend Katie walking in. The petite blonde flopped down on the couch next to Jonah and moved a coffee cup sitting on the table so she could rest her feet on it. After looking around for a new place to put the cup, Katie sniffed the liquid, shrugged, and drank it.

"You're disgusting." Jonah shook his head and laughed in spite of himself.

"Hey, it's not as if this sludge they call coffee tastes good when it's fresh, so what's the difference? At this point, it's medicinal. I need the caffeine so I can stay awake tonight. I just pulled a sixty."

"Aren't you off now? Go home and get some sleep," Jonah said.

"Nah, I need to get laid. It's been an embarrassingly long time." Katie took another sip as she furrowed her brow, looking like she was in deep thought. "Shit, I think it's been almost a month. I haven't had a dry spell like this since... I've never had a dry spell like this."

As pretty and smart as Katie was, Jonah had no doubt that was true.

"Poor baby. A month. Welcome to my world," Jonah replied. He rolled his neck around and felt it crack.

"No thank you. Your world scares me. It's all sunshine and roses with Mr. High School Sweetheart."

"What kind of a lesbian are you? Aren't you supposed to be renting U-Hauls on your second date and not gallivanting around from one woman to another?"

Katie smiled and shrugged. "I have a short attention span."

Jonah shook his head and chuckled. "All right," he said as he rubbed his hands over his face and forced his tired body off the couch. "Are you taking off now? I'll walk out with you."

The hospital wasn't in a bad neighborhood, and it wasn't as if Katie could protect Jonah if they were attacked—the woman barely cleared five and a half feet and was thin enough that a strong wind would probably blow her away—but Jonah still felt better with company. Over the past several months, he'd constantly felt like he was being watched when he was outside at night. He'd never actually seen anyone, but the feeling was still disconcerting.

"Yeah, let's go. I have just enough time to go home and change into something slutty before hitting the bars."

"And what, pray tell, would that be? A flannel shirt and some cargo pants?"

Katie smacked Jonah's chest without turning her head. "You're an ass."

"Kidding," he said with a laugh. "I'm kidding! I know you're the femme. Speaking of which, I get that you're into girls who keep their hair short, but what's the deal with the scissors in bed? Can't they wait until later to get a trim?"

"I'm officially ignoring you," she said and shook her head as they kept walking to their cars. "Oh, I forgot to tell you. I blew it with Dr. Hottie again."

"I seriously doubt that, Katie. The woman wants you. Trust me."

"Right, because you're the authority on women," Katie said and rolled her eyes. "Besides, even if she wanted me before, she's changed her mind after the latest fiasco. The other day Lucy and I were practicing wraps and she walked in. I smiled and gave her my best 'come and get me' look. Then I tried to flick my hair back, totally forgetting that my arm was covered in a splint and gauze, and almost gave myself a black eye. She thinks I'm an idiot."

Jonah laughed and put an arm around Katie's slender shoulders.

"That's doubtful, given your resume. But whatever else she thinks, she also knows you're hot. And I'm pretty sure that's the feeling that's gonna win out in the end."

"Spoken like a true guy," Katie said. "You have no idea how women work. Besides, you wouldn't want me to go out with someone who just wants me for my looks, would you?" she asked with feigned horror.

"When has that ever stopped you?" Jonah said drolly.

Katie grinned and put her arm around Jonah's waist. "Stopped me? Hell, it's a plus. I was just confirming what you meant."

"Uh-huh," Jonah said. "What was that you said about me not having a clue about how you work?"

"Whatever." Katie waved her free hand in Jonah's direction. "What about you? Gonna take off anytime soon to see Mr. Wonderful again?"

Jonah smiled dreamily and nodded. "His name's Zev. And, yeah, I have three days off in a row."

Katie tightened her grip and gave him a squeeze. "Glad to hear it. This couldn't have come a moment too soon."

"You having sympathy pains from my empty-bed syndrome?" he asked.

"Nah. I'm too busy worrying about my empty bed to think about yours. But you've seriously looked like shit lately. You need to relax, and you always seem better after your trips to meet your guy."

"Aww, Katie. I didn't know you cared," Jonah said with one hand on his heart and his eyes blinking rapidly in a mock fluttering motion.

"I don't. But if you run yourself down any further, you'll end up getting admitted for exhaustion and I'll have to work more shifts. So, you see, it's in my best interest for you to keep your act together."

"Now, there's the self-absorbed woman I know and love. Glad to see all the sleepless nights haven't made you go soft."

She scoffed and smacked Jonah's ass before walking to her car.

"Have fun with your man, Jonah. And don't do anything I wouldn't do."

"I will. And from what you've told me, there isn't anything you wouldn't do."

She turned back and waggled her eyebrows, Groucho Marx-style. "Exactly! That's why it's fun."

Jonah laughed and waved goodbye, then walked over to his own car. Just as he was opening his door, the hairs on the back of his neck stood on end and he was overcome once again with a disconcerting feeling of being watched. He quickly scanned of the parking lot, but he didn't see anyone. Then he heard the sound of a heavy door opening and turned around just in time to see a small, brown-haired man disappearing into the stairwell.

"Shit," Jonah said, shaking his head. "I probably have at least a foot on that guy. Apparently my paranoia knows no bounds. Maybe tomorrow I'll get the heebie-jeebies from an old lady with a walker." He hesitated and then added with disgust, "And now I'm talking to myself out loud in public. Wonderful."

"This room's great," Zev said as he followed Jonah into the hotel room.

"Yeah, it is. Oh, God. Remember that first motel we slept in a couple of years back?" Jonah crinkled his nose and shivered at the gross memory. "I'd call it a rathole, but I think even rats knew better than to go in there. Wish I could say the same for the cockroaches. I almost had a heart attack when that one crawled across my arm in the middle of the night."

"That cockroach was probably cleaner than the sheets on that bed. I don't even want to hazard a guess about the origin of some of the stains," Zev replied.

Jonah laughed as he unzipped his bag and moved the clothes into the dresser. They had three days to spend together almost uninterrupted. Zev would need to meet with a couple of retailers, maybe take a few calls, but they both knew these business trips were just an excuse for them to get together.

After Jonah had been called into the hospital during Zev's first couple of visits once Jonah had started his residency, even though he wasn't on-call, they'd instituted a new game plan. Jonah would tell Zev his schedule as soon as it was posted, and Zev would make business appointments in neighboring cities and states during times when Jonah had two days off in a row. Then Jonah would meet Zev at his hotel. Jonah rested while Zev worked, and the rest of the time was theirs to spend together. It was a great way to ensure uninterrupted time, but it didn't happen nearly as frequently as either of them wanted.

"Well, we have you to thank for the improved digs, Blondie."

"How do you figure, Hassick? I'm just a poor resident. You're the one covering the bill, Mr. Fancy Businessman."

A muscular chest pressed against Jonah's back and strong arms enveloped him.

"I can afford to foot the bill because the business is doing so well. We've tripled sales since I started traveling. And we both know you're the reason for my trips, Blondie."

Zev stood behind Jonah and rubbed his bare chest against Jonah's clothed frame. He moved his hands up and down Jonah's chest, then reached with nimble fingers for the buttons and slowly opened the shirt. Once the fabric draped open, Zev made his way back to Jonah's chest and caressed his skin.

Moaning, Jonah draped his arms over Zev's and pushed back against him.

"Mmm." Zev kept petting him while he kissed his way from Jonah's ear to his neck and then rained openmouthed kisses on his skin, making Jonah shiver and whimper. Then Zev moved his right hand over to Jonah's hair, caressing it until Jonah turned his head and took Zev's finger into his mouth, licking and sucking it.

Zev groaned and bucked, his erection dragging against Jonah. He circled Jonah's chest with his left hand, trailed around his nipple. Then he pushed down into Jonah's pants, taking Jonah's hard cock in a gentle grip and stroking it.

Tilting his head back, Jonah rested against Zev's shoulder. He closed his eyes and reveled in the feeling of Zev's skin touching his, Zev's hand pumping him, Zev's finger pushing in and out of his mouth. He groaned when the finger pulled out and began playing with his nipples.

"'S good, Zev."

"Yeah, it is," Zev mumbled into his neck, his hand continuing the up and down motion. "How's work going? Any interesting patients?"

"Umm." Jonah tried to concentrate on something other than Zev's body. It wasn't easy. "Oh, there was one patient who came into the ER wanting the aliens removed from his body." His breath caught when Zev's palm skirted over the top of his glans, sliding fluid down the shaft. "Said if the surgery went well, he'd bring in his brother, 'cause he had 'em too."

Zev's hands suddenly disappeared from his body, leaving Jonah feeling lost. He turned back to look at his friend.

"Why'd you stop?"

"I'm comin' back. Don't worry."

Zev pushed Jonah's pants down, and a few seconds later, a suddenly slick hand returned to his cock, continuing to jack him. Jonah sighed and rested his head against Zev's shoulder.

"When'd you start carrying lube around?"

"When I got dressed this morning. Wanted to be ready for you." Zev nibbled on his ear. "So what'd you do with the alien guy?"

It took several seconds for Jonah to remember what he'd been saying.

"Well, we ran some tests. Turns out he was loaded out of his mind on meth. The hardest part was that he told us they had the equipment to do the alien removal in their basement, but it was noisy and disturbed the neighbors. So his brother told him to come to the hospital to get it done. We were wondering if the brother was drugged out too, but when we called his house, he admitted that he'd just gone along with the whole alien thing to get the guy to the hospital."

"Smart brother."

"Uh-huh."

"Hey, Jonah?" Zev's voice was husky and rough with arousal, his grip around Jonah's cock tightened, and his breath beat faster against Jonah's neck.

"Mmm-hmm?"

"Can I try something new?"

Jonah swiveled his hips to push into Zev's fist.

"You can do anything you want with me, Zev. Always. You don't need to ask."

A rough groan left Zev's mouth just as he clamped down on Jonah's neck. Jonah arched to the side to give Zev more room. He was so lost in the feeling of being with Zev again, in those teeth gnawing on him, that hand stroking him, that scent overtaking him, that he'd forgotten about Zev's question until he felt slick fingers caress his crease.

"Zev?" Jonah gasped. Zev had rubbed his cleft before, but never with lube or lotion coating his fingers.

"Just my fingers, Blondie. I gotta get in here. Figure if it's just my fingers, it'll be okay. I think I can get in deeper than with my tongue this way."

"Love your tongue."

Zev chuckled. "Yeah, I know. I think the people in the rooms next to ours know too."

Jonah laughed, enjoying the fact that they could talk and tease while they loved on each other.

"Am I too vocal, Hassick? Want me to try to keep it down?"

Thick fingers circled and massaged Jonah's entrance, causing him to push back against them, seeking more.

"Hell no. I like it. But I will admit that one time when we went for a run in the morning and saw those two little old ladies leave their room, I was a little embarrassed."

Zev pushed the tip of one finger into Jonah's hole, and both men moaned.

"When..." Jonah gasped when the finger continued its inward slide. "When was that?"

Hot suction on his neck let Jonah know he'd have to wait for an answer. And wear collared shirts for the next week.

Zev enjoyed marking him. He took the opportunity to do it whenever they saw each other. Not that Jonah objected. Hell, he encouraged it.

"It was after the night when you were working your dick and pleading with me to lick your ass. You were screaming, and I think your exact words were, 'eat my ass, fuck me with your tongue, oh yeah, I'm coming' or something like that."

The pumping of the finger in and out of his sensitive channel made it hard to respond. Jonah couldn't decide which he enjoyed more, Zev's hand stroking his cock or Zev's finger pushing into him. When a second finger joined the first, the decision was made and the conversation was forgotten.

"Oh, damn, that feels so good, Zev. Push it faster, deeper."

Zev complied. He moved his long fingers in and out of his mate, enjoying the warmth, reveling in Jonah's pleasure, thinking about how good it'd feel to do the same thing with his cock one day. Zev didn't think Jonah could look hotter than he did right then. His cheeks flushed with passion, his mouth open and gasping for breath, his shirt unbuttoned, exposing his chest, and his pants pushed down to his knees. Then Zev twisted the tips of his fingers inside and touched a certain spot, and Jonah went wild.

"Yes! Uh-huh."

Animal noises poured out of Jonah as he pushed back hard and fucked himself on Zev's fingers. When Zev added a third digit into that tight body, Jonah convulsed and came with a cry. His body went limp against Zev's, his breath ragged. Zev kept his fingers inside, moving them slowly in and out, waiting for Jonah to calm.

"Did you like that?"

Jonah snorted. "You kidding? I think you melted me."

When Zev's fingers left his body, Jonah turned around, slipped out of his shirt, toed off his shoes, and let his pants and briefs fall to the ground.

"Get naked and get in bed, Hassick. I want your dick in my mouth and this floor's hard."

"I missed you, Blondie," Zev said with a laugh.

"Missed you too."

Jonah woke in the middle of the night to feel Zev pressed against his back, sucking on his earlobe, pinching his nipples, and rutting against his ass.

"Mmm," he moaned sleepily as he thrust back against that hard cock.

"You awake, Blondie?" Zev asked gruffly.

"You didn't actually expect me to sleep through this, did you, Hassick? I think that might be a little too weird, even for me."

"Ha ha, smartass." Zev kissed Jonah's temple. "Sorry for waking you. I know you need your sleep. But I really want you."

"Don't apologize. This kind of wake-up call is always welcome."

Jonah scooted up a little closer to the headboard, reached between his legs, and took Zev's dick in his hand. He pulled it down so the crown dragged through his cleft, making both men shiver and groan, then tucked it between his thighs. A slight wiggle backward had Zev's member situated right where Jonah wanted him—enveloped snugly between Jonah's thighs.

Zev moved his hand to Jonah's hip and held tight as he began to pump back and forth between those muscular thighs. The movement had Zev moaning in no time. Jonah took himself in hand and stroked in time to Zev's thrusts.

"Fuck, yeah," Zev whispered huskily right before he grasped Jonah's shoulder between his teeth and gnawed and sucked on it, bringing blood to the surface in a deep hickey.

The pressure Zev put on his hip was sure to leave finger-shaped bruises. Jonah's arousal ramped up at the knowledge that he'd wear yet another of Zev's marks.

"Almost there, Zev. Come on, come on," Jonah encouraged through gasps before he arched his back and threw his head against Zev's shoulder.

Long streams of ejaculate shot out of his cock and painted Jonah's hand and stomach. He swiped his hand through it and reached over his shoulder, where Zev's tongue made quick work of licking his seed.

"Yes!" Zev cried as wet heat spread through Jonah's thighs.

They lay together and gulped air.

"Now I'm all sticky," Jonah whined.

"Oh, you poor thing." Zev laughed. "Let's get in the shower. I'll help you clean up."

Jonah flipped around, tucked one arm under Zev's neck, and draped the other over his friend's shoulder. He leaned in for a chaste kiss that quickly turned into two kisses and ultimately a dance of tongues. Zev squeezed Jonah's ass with both hands and pulled him close, until their reenergized cocks were pressed together.

"Change of plans. First I'm gonna get you even stickier, then we can take a shower."

"Excellent strategy, Hassick. You're getting smarter in your old age. Never thought I'd see the day."

"Yeah? Well, you aren't getting any funnier. Now stop talking and kiss me," Zev said as he nipped at Jonah's lips, catching the bottom one between his teeth and sucking it into his mouth.

Jonah didn't bother arguing. Talking really was overrated when the alternative was having Zev's tongue push into his mouth.

CHAPTER 17

BEING AWAY from his boyfriend had never been easy for Jonah, but rather than getting used to it, Jonah found it even more difficult as time went on. The constant ache and loneliness he felt due to his separation from Zev was exacerbated by the unfortunate lack-of-sleep issue. The only time Jonah was able to sleep through the night was when he was literally curled together with Zev. It seemed like it should be uncomfortable to sleep that way—legs tangled, arms wrapped around waists or chests, faces buried in each other's necks. But it was actually cozy and safe, and gave Jonah a sense of peace he wasn't otherwise able to claim.

Then when Jonah was in the final year of his residency, things took a turn for the worse. The nightmares kept interrupting the very small amount of rest he was able to get, and he was worried about his ability to care for patients without ever getting truly deep sleep. He was still plagued by that unexplained restlessness within his body, the feeling that he was being strangled somehow, like he couldn't breathe.

But the kicker was when Zev's work responsibilities changed and he wasn't able to get away as frequently.

Jonah had already been close to a breaking point from the sleepless nights and physical pain that had become his daily companion, but the reduced time with Zev pushed him over the edge.

He hadn't wanted to ask his dad about his mother, hadn't wanted to bring up painful memories. But his physical malady combined with the lack of sleep motivated Jonah to seek answers. So during one of his rare evenings off from the hospital, he went to his father's house for dinner.

"Tell me how work's going. I can see that you're tired, but I also remember how good it felt to treat patients on my own, have everyone call me doctor. How about you, Jonah? What's your favorite part of your residency?"

Kevin Marvel looked at Jonah with bright, joy-filled eyes. The man was so clearly happy to have his son over that Jonah almost changed his mind about broaching the topic that had inspired the visit. But then Jonah's muscles ached, his stomach twisted, his heart raced, and he knew he had to get to the root of the unwelcome and unexplained ailment.

"Dad, I was just, um, wondering." Jonah took a deep breath and forged ahead. "Do you know whether my mother or someone in her family had any health conditions?"

Jonah bit his bottom lip and anxiously looked across the table, hoping his dad wouldn't be too upset by the question. His father dropped his fork and swallowed the food in his mouth. It took several seconds, but eventually, the look of surprise cleared from his face.

"Why do you ask? Is something going on?"

"No," Jonah responded instinctively in an attempt to shield his father from worry. Then he reminded himself that he hadn't been able to figure things out on his own, and he just couldn't keep going the way he had been. "Yeah, Dad, something's going on. I just don't know what it is."

Kevin pushed his plate aside, propped his arms on the table, and leaned on them.

"What are your symptoms?"

"Dad, I..." Jonah dragged his fingers through his already disheveled hair in frustration. "I don't want to get into the details of it. I just need to know if there's a family history of anything."

"Jonah Marvel, stop being stubborn. I can help you. There's nothing to be ashamed of. Now, tell me your symptoms. I'm a physician."

"So am I, Dad," Jonah responded quietly. There was no way to explain his symptoms to his father. There were too many, they made no sense, and then there were the nightmares. He definitely couldn't tell his father about the nightmares.

"Listen, Dad." Jonah tried again. "I know you want to help, but I've figured out all I can based on the information I have. To be honest, I think this is probably a psychological issue more than a medical one."

The statement wasn't an attempt to avoid sharing information with his father, it was the truth. People suffering from mental illness could develop physical pain or discomfort. That was the most logical explanation for everything going on with Jonah's body and mind.

"Psychological?"

"Yes." Jonah nodded. "Do you know if there's a history of mental illness on my mother's side of the family? I don't think I've heard you say there's anything like that on your side."

Kevin shook his head. "No, not on my side. I'm not sure about Joan's, er, your mother's family. The truth is I never met any of them. They weren't really thrilled about your mother dating me, but she never explained the reason for that. I can..." Kevin stopped talking and looked at Jonah carefully. "Is this serious, Jonah?"

His father looked so worried. His lips were drawn in tight, thin lines, his forehead creased with concern. As much as Jonah hated being the cause of that worry, he was too tired to deny it.

"Yeah, it's serious."

Kevin sat up straight in his chair and seemed to shake himself together.

"Okay. Well, Joan was close to her sister. They talked on the phone regularly even when the rest of the family kept their distance. I'll track her down and ask her about the family history, Jonah. If anyone can help us figure this out, it'll be Leah."

Jonah's father was true to his word. There was no doubt that the man had been worried about his son, as demonstrated by the many telephone calls and frequent visits Jonah had received since he'd confessed his ailment. But despite his father's best efforts, months went by without Jonah getting any answers.

It seemed that Kevin was doing everything possible to find Joan's sister without going to her parents. But she no longer lived in the same town, and Kevin hadn't been able to locate her elsewhere. Jonah told his father that she'd probably married and had a different name, and the only way to get answers would be to go to his grandparents, who apparently were still alive and residing in the same place.

But Kevin admitted to Jonah during one visit that he doubted they'd be willing to see him. Apparently, Jonah's mother had been estranged from her family. At first, Jonah had accepted that excuse, wanting his father to feel comfortable, allowing him to get answers at his own pace. But eventually time ran out.

Jonah was in the last week of his residency and Zev was expecting him to move back to Etzgadol. Just that week, Jonah had opened a letter from Zev and a key had dropped onto the floor. He knew what it was before reading a single word on the page. It was a key to their home, the cabin Zev had built with Jonah's input, the space they planned to share for a lifetime. And Jonah desperately wanted to do just that, but he didn't want to saddle Zev with an increasingly messed-up partner. Sleepless nights, unexplained pains, and constant anxiety—wow, wasn't he a treat?

"What if I call my mother's parents, Dad? Maybe they'd talk to me."

"No!"

Jonah had never seen his father look so terrified.

"Why? Look, I get that you're the guy who took their daughter away, or whatever, but I'm her son, which makes me their grandchild. Surely they won't hold me responsible. Maybe they'll even be happy to see me after all these years."

Kevin shook his head and jumped up from Jonah's sofa, where the two had been sitting and talking.

"No, Jonah. They don't know about you. They can't know about you."

"She never told them she had a baby? Did they really hate you that much?"

"I don't know, Jonah!" Kevin shouted as he paced around the room. "I told you already, I never met the Smiths. She wouldn't let me. It was almost like she was afraid of something. And then she was gone and I had to protect you, keep you safe."

It didn't escape Jonah's notice that at that moment, his father sounded about as bat-shit crazy as he felt. He got up and put his hand on his father's arm. The gesture seemed to de-escalate the situation.

"I couldn't let anybody know about you. So the night your mother died, a couple of, uh, friends, helped us pack up; they had some connections in the hospital in Etzgadol and that

was that. We moved, set down roots, and you've been fine
ever since."

His father had always been overprotective, and Jonah
finally understood the reason. Despite the bad blood his
mother had apparently had with her family, though, Jonah
doubted they'd turn away their grandchild. He was certain
his father was being paranoid. But without more to go on
than the last name "Smith," Jonah didn't stand a chance of
tracking them down on his own.

"Well, I'm not fine anymore, Dad. I'm sick and I need
some help. I want you to tell me their names and where they
live, so I can talk to them. I'm not a little boy anymore, they
can't keep me away from you, don't worry."

"You think that's what I'm worried about?" Kevin spat
out, his eyes wild, his face red. "I'm trying to keep you alive,
Jonah! They killed your mother, and I'll be damned if I'm
letting them get you too."

Jonah's mouth dropped open in shock. He stumbled
backward and fell onto the couch. His father sounded
completely unbalanced, irrational and out of control. And this
was the first he'd heard about his mother being murdered.

"My mother died in a car accident, remember? Dad, are
you okay?"

"No, I'm not okay! I'm terrified." Kevin sat on the couch
and took both of Jonah's hands in his. "Listen to me, son, I
never wanted you to know this, but you're right, you're not a
child any longer, and I can see that you need to understand."

He took a deep breath and then continued speaking. "Your mother didn't die in a car accident."

"She didn't?"

Kevin shook his head. "No, she didn't. She was attacked by wolves."

"Wolves?" Jonah said, his voice sounding young and broken even to his own ears.

"Yes. Your mother was pregnant with you, due any day. I heard her shouting and ran into the living room. Someone was knocking on the door. She was frantic, said he was going to kill her, that we had to get out of there. So we went into the kitchen, hoping to get out that way, but there were three huge wolves standing in the middle of the room, growling at us. Your mother managed to make it into the bedroom. I grabbed a frying pan and tried to ward them off."

Kevin stopped speaking. His hands were shaking, his eyes glazed over. The memory of that day thirty years prior clearly still terrified him.

"I slowed them down a little, but they were huge, Jonah. They were so huge. And then someone pushed me from behind, I fell and knocked my head against the counter, and I was out."

Tears now filled Kevin's eyes.

"When I woke up, she was dead. There was so much blood. And she was dead." He raised his eyes. "I hadn't been able to protect her. But you were alive. It was a damn miracle. They put you in my arms and told me that we had to get away. That he'd kill you if he knew you'd survived."

Jonah was just trying to keep up with the surreal story.

"Who told you that, Dad? The man who'd broken into your house?"

"No, two other men. I don't know how they knew we needed help, but they did. Somehow they did. They scared off that guy and the wolves and they saved you. They couldn't save Joan, but they saved you." Kevin grasped his son's hands. "Now do you understand, Jonah? It isn't safe. If anybody finds out about you, that man could come back. He could take you away."

Taking his shivering father into his arms, Jonah tried to gather his thoughts. Either his father had completely lost touch with reality and the man was fabricating this story, which, frankly, would at least answer Jonah's question about the mental illness familial link, or his odd dreams about his bleeding mother being surrounded by wolves weren't just dreams. There was only one way to find out which was true, and Jonah was more determined than ever to understand his history.

"I'm not a weak pregnant woman. I'm strong, Dad. They can't hurt me."

For the first time since the day Jonah had asked for help learning about his maternal medical history, Kevin laughed.

"A weak pregnant woman? With an attitude like that, it's a good thing you're gay, son." Kevin shook his head. "If your mother were here right now, she'd disabuse you of that notion faster than you could say Jack Robinson. That woman was strong and brave and..."

Kevin's voice broke and tears once more gathered in his eyes. After a few seconds, he cleared his throat and slapped his hands on his thighs.

"I'll take care of this, Jonah. They can't know about you, but I'll go talk to them and find out where Joan's sister is. I'll get you some answers, I promise."

Jonah didn't have a chance to argue, because with that assertion, his father got up and left the apartment.

CHAPTER 18

ZEV ROLLED down the truck window and took in a deep breath of fresh mountain air. He missed Jonah desperately. Twelve years. That was how long it'd been since he and Jonah had shared that Etzgadol mountain air together. And Zev had missed Jonah every day that the man had been in college, and then medical school. The residency after that was almost too much to bear, especially because Zev had had to greatly reduce his out of town visits since he'd officially taken over as Alpha of the Etzgadol pack. There was too much to tend to in Etzgadol, and the pack needed to see their Alpha, know he was present and in control. Without that sense of security, shifters would panic and a pack could disintegrate.

The part of Etzgadol where most of the shifters lived had always been fairly run-down. That was common for pack towns. The belief that nonshifters were to be avoided created an insular society that didn't generate much opportunity for economic development. Plus, it'd only been a couple of generations since shifters were strictly prohibited from traveling to metropolitan areas because those were inhabited by bloodsuckers. Thankfully, the animosity between shifters and vampires had diminished over the years.

Still, having the ability to go into urban areas wasn't the same thing as having the desire. The need to see the moon and run, to smell the trees and feel the dirt under their paws, those things inherently drove shifters to remain near the woods, so they rarely sought out the metal and cement jungles. But Zev had needed to travel in order to see Jonah.

Thankfully, Zev got along well with humans. He'd gone to school with them from an early age, played sports alongside them, and learned that they weren't all that different from shifters. That open attitude allowed Zev to make contacts with distributors and retailers, and he turned the once-small family ceramics business into a highly sought after manufacturer of high-end pieces that were almost always on back order.

The influx of funds didn't just benefit Zev, though. He'd insisted on putting a lot of the earnings back into his community. Roads that used to be cracked were now paved. The shifter elementary school had all new books and even a couple of computers in every room. And with Lori's urging, Zev had funded a birthing center for the females. The space was getting a lot of use with all the new cubs being born into their pack.

The Etzgadol pack was doing remarkably well. The families that had long been in the pack had been expanding. The security and prosperity Zev created allowed them to have more young than had been possible in past years. Plus, they'd had a tremendous influx of new members moving to the area wanting to join the pack rumored to be led by the strongest Alpha in untold generations.

A lot of the growth was due to simple economics. The ceramics business was doing so well that many more pack members were being employed by the Hassick family, and their salaries were higher, giving them more to spend on businesses owned by other pack members. So everyone was prospering. The pack was successful and the members were happy. But the Alpha responsible for it was all but lost.

Ever since the day he'd realized Jonah was his mate, Zev had believed things would work out. He'd stomached the pain of separation, certain in his mind that everything happened for a reason, that Jonah's studies would benefit the greater good, and most of all, that his mate would return to him in time for them to tie and secure his human connection to the world. But Jonah had finished his residency two weeks prior, and he still hadn't come home.

Zev's mate had sounded progressively more agitated every time they'd spoken on the phone lately, and he'd refused to tell Zev what troubled him. Over the past few days, the phone calls had stopped entirely and brief texts had taken their place. It was only the fear that he'd lose control of his wolf and shift in a strange place that had kept Zev from going after Jonah himself and dragging the man back to Etzgadol.

As he neared the beautiful cabin he'd built for Jonah out of fallen timber and mountain stone, Zev wondered whether they'd ever be able to share the space. He didn't have much time left before his wolf would break free of his human's internal restraints. He needed Jonah. An all-consuming, soul-crushing, breath-stealing need. Where was his mate?

Just as Zev pulled into the carport, a wonderful scent cleared away his distraction and permeated his awareness. Lemons, grass, and mint. Jonah.

He slammed on the brakes, tore out of the truck, ran up the steps, and yanked the front door open. The living room looked exactly like he'd left it.

"Jonah?" He recognized the panic and desperation in his voice, but he had no ability to control it. "Jonah?"

Not in the kitchen either.

"Zev." The familiar voice cracked. It was weak, barely audible.

He raced to the hallway and stumbled when he saw Jonah standing naked in the bedroom doorway. His mate was clutching the doorjamb and leaning on it, as if he couldn't support his own weight. There were dark circles under those coal eyes, his breath was heavy and labored, and the pallor of Jonah's normally golden skin was disconcerting.

"Oh, Blondie," Zev mumbled when he reached Jonah. He kissed his mate's head and stroked his soft cheek. "I missed you."

"Missed you too, Zev. So much. I tried to stay away. Tried to fix it on my own, but my dad's gone, and I don't know what to do and..." Jonah swallowed hard and looked at Zev imploringly. "I can't stay away from you. Don't wanna." A cry left Jonah's lips, and he crushed his face into Zev's neck. "S-s-s-sorry. I'm sorry."

Zev held Jonah close and rocked them from side to side.

"Shh. I'm glad you're here. You don't need to apologize for needing me. I need you too. What're you trying to fix, Jonah? Where's your dad?"

The body Zev held in his arms trembled.

"I don't know. Don't know where he is. He was going to try to find my mother's family to help me. But he was scared." Jonah pulled back, clutched Zev's shirt with both hands, and looked into his eyes. "Did you know she didn't really die in an accident? Those nightmares I had were true. She was killed by wolves, so my dad hid us away. But then I made him go back and now I can't find him."

Jonah dropped his face against Zev's chest.

"I'm fucking messed up, Zev. I feel like I'm coming undone. I don't know what's wrong with me. I...I..." Jonah's entire body was trembling.

"Shhh," Zev whispered as he rubbed slow circles on Jonah's back. "There's nothing wrong with you that we can't fix together. You just...miss me, is all."

Jonah managed to push out a chuckle.

"Damn, boy, do you ever have a healthy ego. Some might even call it cocky."

Zev shrugged.

"Hey, like Kid Rock says, 'it ain't braggin', motherfucker, if you back it up.'" He half carried, half pushed Jonah over to the bed. "Seriously, though, we're together. It's all gonna be okay from now on. You'll see."

Once Jonah was lying across the bed, Zev kicked off his shoes and pulled off his clothes. Then he crawled onto Jonah and kissed the too-cold neck, the slightly stubbled jaw, and finally those pink lips. He darted his tongue out and licked his way in, grateful that his mate was finally with him, even if the man was confused.

Zev wasn't sure what to make of Jonah's statements. Wolves didn't kill humans, at least not to Zev's knowledge. The story sounded far-fetched and didn't make any sense. But then again, neither did having a human for a mate. Plus, the way Jonah looked, and his description of how he was feeling, sounded like what would happen to shifter females if they didn't tie. Not to humans.

Not that Zev had actually witnessed firsthand such a thing as a shifter who didn't tie, but he'd seen some females who tied a little later than usual, and they certainly exhibited some of the signs Jonah showed; the wolf within would become so desperate to get out that they'd lose their sanity. Of course, none of those females had been three decades old. He'd never known of a shifter who could wait that long to tie. Male or female. He laughed internally. Except himself, of course. So yeah, the rule book was completely thrown out here and anything was possible. Including murderous wolves.

But now wasn't the time to analyze the past. Now was the time to cement their future. Zev and Jonah needed to tie together and find peace. Then they could talk and figure out the rest of it.

Zev kissed Jonah soundly, tongues twining, bodies rubbing, hands caressing. Despite how tired he'd been, despite the annoying family intervention and the resulting headache, despite the concerns he'd had about his mate that had been wearing on him for weeks, despite it all, Zev hardened in reaction to Jonah's body, Jonah's scent, Jonah's taste. And he felt a similar reaction from Jonah, pressed hard and firm against his hip.

"How're you doing, Blondie?" He petted Jonah's soft, fair locks.

Jonah moaned. "I feel...I feel a little better." Jonah sounded surprised. "Like something's loosening up inside."

Yeah. Zev understood. He was feeling the same thing. The only difference was he knew what it meant. Understood that his body was anticipating the tie, relaxing with the knowledge that he would soon be whole.

He licked his way down Jonah's chest and sucked a nipple into his mouth, noticing that some heat and color were already seeping back into his mate's skin. Jonah moaned and arched his back, moving toward Zev's mouth. He answered the silent request and sucked harder, longer. When Jonah's gasps were fast, his heart pounding, Zev moved to the other nipple, giving it the same treatment.

"Zev," Jonah groaned, pushing his hard dick up against Zev, leaving a wet trail. "I want... I want..."

Zev knew exactly what his mate wanted. He leaned over to the nightstand, pulled a bottle of lube out of the drawer, and snapped the lid open. Jonah jerked, his eyes wide, hope and anticipation written all over his face.

"Turn over, Blondie."

He thought Jonah would ask for an explanation, that the man would insist on remaining as he was so they could make love face to face. Zev assumed that was how it worked with humans. But Jonah just moaned, flipped over, tucked his knees underneath his stomach, and spread them as wide as he could, leaving himself open and exposed.

Zev groaned, leaned over Jonah's back, and whispered into his mate's ear as he let the lube drizzle down that enticing cleft and then pushed it into that pink hole with his finger.

"Next time we'll have time for lots of foreplay, but right now I need you, Jonah. That okay?"

Jonah's breath was coming in gasps. He nodded and pushed his ass back in silent agreement. That was all the affirmation Zev needed.

With a trembling hand, Zev slicked his cock, then massaged Jonah's pucker. There was no fear, no tension in his friend. Just a body strumming with need and want. Zev thought he'd cry from the joy of finally being able to fulfill that want.

A slight bit of pressure was all it took for Jonah's body to open to him, welcome him inside. Then Zev was pushing in at a steady pace, not stopping, not slowing, just claiming his mate. When his balls were pressed tight against Jonah's ass, he circled his arm around that trim waist and gnawed on his smooth shoulder. He was going to leave his mark on that perfect skin. The thought made Zev growl, made him pull out and push back in again. His mate would wear his mark. Another thrust out and in.

"Zev." Jonah said his name like it was a prayer. "So good. You feel so good inside me."

With every stroke in and out of that tight channel, something inside Zev filled. The connection with his mate strengthened, their bond intensified, and with it Zev's connection, his tie to his humanity.

He pulled and pushed while Jonah met him movement for movement. They were moaning together, moving together, and Zev had never felt more complete.

"I'm gonna. Zev! I'm gonna. Gonna." Jonah mumbled the words and increased his pace, rocking back against Zev faster and faster, taking Zev's hardness into his warmth.

Zev reached around and took Jonah's long dick into his hand, stroking it in time with his penetration of that tight ass. It only took a few strokes for Jonah to push back hard, arch his neck, and shout out his pleasure.

"Yes! Oh, yes."

Wet warmth seeped over Zev's hand. He used it as lube and kept stroking, not giving Jonah a chance to rest. He was going to keep his mate aroused.

"We're not done yet. Gonna keep making love to you." Zev's voice was deeper than usual and rough with arousal.

"'Kay."

Jonah was out of breath, but his body hadn't stopped moving, rocking with Zev. When the prick in his hand firmed back up, Zev increased the pace of his strokes. He angled his hips to hit the spot that made Jonah squirm and moan the loudest, rubbed his thumb over the top of Jonah's cock, and sucked on Jonah's ear.

"Oh, my God, I'm gonna come again. How...how...oh, God, I'm gonna!"

Jonah's body rocked back and forth faster, taking Zev in, holding him tight. Zev moaned and met Jonah's passion, pushing harder, deeper, until he was slamming into that perfect ass, one hand holding onto his mate's hip, the other flying over his mate's cock. Giving no room for a break or a rest, Zev's motions became wild, animalistic.

Jonah's eyes were closed, his mouth open, and he felt like something inside him was unlocking, releasing. He was so close to bliss. He just needed...just needed... He didn't know what it was. His body shook, and he groaned in frustration.

"Help me," he pleaded with Zev, knowing the other man could give him whatever it was his body so desperately sought.

"Follow my lead, Blondie." Zev's words were almost growled.

That hard dick inside Jonah seemed to get longer, thicker, until he was completely overtaken with it. Every spot inside him was touched continuously. Every movement massaged his gland, the pressure never stopping, the pleasure never curbing. Zev flicked his tongue on the spot where Jonah's shoulder met his neck, licked his skin, and then Jonah felt a sharp pain that immediately morphed into blissful pleasure and everything his body had been seeking was right there.

Jonah felt so damn good. Incredibly good. He was free. For what felt like the first time in his life, Jonah Marvel felt freedom and peace. He howled out his pleasure when his body found release. And then he slept.

CHAPTER 19

ZEV WASN'T sure how long he sat on his bed and stared in shock at the sleeping form of his best friend. Jonah was a shifter.

It was completely unexpected, but Zev had seen it with his own eyes. They'd been making love, moving together, completely in sync, when something in Jonah had called to Zev's wolf. He didn't recognize it for what it was at the time; his brain wasn't leading the charge in that lust-filled moment. Operating on pure instinct, wanting to give Jonah what he needed, Zev's human body morphed into his wolf form and Jonah's followed suit.

They were tied together then, Zev's cock long and thick, the mating knot at the end keeping him connected with a white wolf. Zev bit past the fur into the part of Jonah's body where his neck met his shoulder, letting his sharp canines puncture the skin, completing the mating ritual. When he heard his mate howl, Zev's wolf joined the song, and they found their pleasure together.

And then, as Jonah's exhausted body softened beneath him, the muscles relaxed, Zev followed his sleeping mate downward until they were resting on the mattress, their bodies still connected. As the haze of lust and desire dissipated, Zev realized that the body in his bed was not one he'd previously seen. It was Jonah, there was no doubt about that, but instead of golden skin, there was white fur covering the sinewy frame of the most beautiful wolf Zev had ever encountered.

As the realization made its way into Zev's conscious mind, his body shifted back to human, hoping that the more logical of his two forms could make sense of the situation. But the shift in Zev's body seemed to trigger the same reaction in his mate, so he found himself lying with a very human Jonah and almost wondering whether he'd imagined the whole thing.

When the mating knot released Zev's connection to the beloved man beside him, Zev kissed the scar he'd left on that perfect skin with the mating bite. He'd had an entire speech planned for Jonah; he'd planned to tell the other man that he was a shifter, explain what that meant. But seeing Jonah shift with him, hearing that Jonah's mother passed away as a result of a wolf attack, well, the speech Zev had practiced just wouldn't do.

Jonah's analytical mind would expect an explanation, and that was something Zev couldn't deliver. People didn't just turn into shifters later in life. His kind was a different species from the humans. Shifters were born with both a wolf and a human sharing one body, inheriting that characteristic from their parents. But Zev had spent enough time with Jonah's father to know that the man was human. He knew

Kevin Marvel's scent and there was nothing about it that was anything other than a human male.

Now Jonah's mother...well, Zev didn't know anything about her. He didn't even know her last name. He thought Jonah might have mentioned it at some point, but Zev must not have considered it important at the time, because he was drawing a complete blank. Zev tried to think of everything he knew about Jonah's mother. He remembered the description of the night terrors that had been haunting his mate—Jonah's mother lying dead and bloody—and Jonah had said that in those dreams, the woman was sometimes a wolf. Could Jonah's mother have been a shifter?

Zev couldn't decide whether that explanation cleared everything up or just confused things further. On the one hand, having a shifter for a true mate was certainly more comprehensible than sharing a mating bond with a human. On the other hand, if Jonah's mother had been a shifter, that would have to mean that she'd had sex with a human, gotten pregnant, and that the baby had somehow survived.

Interspecies breeding was a feat that Zev had thought to be physiologically impossible. Such a baby was classified as incompatible with life because the wolf within the fetus wouldn't inherit genes from both parents and would therefore cease developing and cause an end to the pregnancy. There were urban legends of a few such creatures surviving in utero, but they'd never been able to actually live long enough to take a breath outside of the safety of their mothers' wombs.

But Jonah was very much alive. He was a living, breathing conundrum, and Zev needed to unravel the mystery. He needed to find answers to give Jonah. As the Etzgadol pack Alpha, Zev held all the books containing their pack's history, the information about other packs, the stories handed down from the elders. But the library was fairly thin because his kind carried on oral traditions of storytelling, rather than documenting information. And shifters were notoriously bad genealogists, so Zev would be hard-pressed to find much historical information about other packs in his books.

Still, Zev had to try. He owed it to his mate. So he slid out of bed and walked over to his home office, hoping to find a sliver of a clue that could explain the heritage of the man who was finally sharing his bed.

The first thing Jonah noticed as consciousness seeped into his mind was Zev's scent radiating from the pillow. He didn't feel the heat of his partner's body pressed against his own, so he blindly reached out his hand and grunted when he encountered nothing but empty sheets. He buried his face in the pillow and inhaled, letting the scent take him back to the previous night.

It had been so good. Shockingly good. Better than he'd ever imagined. And, damn, had he done a lot of imagining. Jonah groaned and tucked his hand under his body to adjust his growing erection. The feel of his fingers on the sensitive skin elicited another groan, and he took a few short strokes before deciding to go find his wayward partner and do things the right way. He slipped out of the bed, then turned around and fumbled in the sheets until he found the bottle of lube.

After stopping in the bathroom to splash some water on his face and clean up a bit, Jonah stepped into the hallway. He opened his mouth to call for Zev when he sensed his friend's presence in the room at the end of the hall. The feeling was at once strange and familiar. Like his body implicitly accepted the ability to home in on Zev's location even while his scientifically trained mind questioned how such a thing could be possible. Before he had time to think on it any further, Jonah was turning the door handle and walking into the dimly lit room.

Zev sat at a desk with a single table lamp illuminating a mess of papers laid out before him. He looked over his shoulder and smiled, causing Jonah's heart to thud heavily against his chest.

"Hey," Jonah whispered. "The sun's not even up. How long have you been awake?"

Zev shrugged. "Haven't gone to sleep yet."

Jonah walked over to Zev and straddled the nude specimen of perfect masculinity. He dipped his head and kissed Zev chastely. The skin-on-skin contact mixed with the taste of his man inspired a fog of lust to overtake Jonah's mind, leaving him dazed and aroused.

"You work too hard, Pup."

Zev's entire body went rigid.

"We need to talk, Jonah."

"Shhh." Jonah trembled. "We can talk later. Right now I want you." He pressed his feet flat on the floor and raised his body until the head of Zev's cock prodded his cleft. After a few grinding moves against Zev's erection, Jonah felt the other man relax.

"Mmm. We went at it pretty hard last night, Blondie. I know you must be sore," Zev mumbled into Jonah's chest, peppering it with kisses.

"Well, you know what they say helps with sore muscles?" Jonah said hoarsely as he flipped the lid on the lube and coated his fingers, then reached behind himself to rub it against his opening.

"What's that?" Zev asked breathlessly.

"Lots and lots of stretching," Jonah replied while coating Zev's hard erection with the slick liquid.

He then moved the glorious cock to his pucker and pushed down against the thick head, whimpering slightly when he felt it breach his still-sensitive body.

"You sure?" Zev gasped, his hands clinging to Jonah's hips, holding his mate in place.

"Trust me. I'm a doctor." Jonah chuckled as he pressed himself down the hard column, reveling in the sensation of his man filling his body once again.

He closed his eyes as he lowered himself, allowing his focus to narrow on the wonderful feelings in his body. Maybe it was because he was finally back home with Zev for good. Maybe it was because he'd had a long and sound sleep.

Maybe it was because he was finally getting laid. Whatever the reason, Jonah's brain was clear and his body felt light and strong. He was no longer weary, anxious, and, if he were being truly honest with himself, petrified about the unknown ailment plaguing his body and mind.

When Jonah was settled completely against Zev's groin, he opened his eyes and fell into an amber gaze full of love and devotion. Zev's hands remained on his hips, but they were no longer holding him in place. Instead, the incredible strength in those muscular arms was helping Jonah's ascent and descent along the hot cock inside his body.

Jonah dropped his forehead onto Zev's as he clung to those broad shoulders, and he cried out in pleasure at their joining. The sound of his voice seemed to trigger something in Zev. The man growled and cupped Jonah's ass, holding their groins close together; then he rose to his feet and laid Jonah down on top of the desk.

Zev caressed Jonah's thighs and then held onto the area behind his knees and pushed Jonah's legs up until they were braced on Zev's arms. Then he pulled out and pushed back into Jonah's willing body with a grunt.

Jonah lay on his back, knees bent and spread. Zev nestled between his legs, cradled Jonah's neck in a strong grip, and leaned above him, gazing into his eyes as he pumped in and out of his channel. Jonah's mouth dropped open and he stared up at the handsome man.

"'S good."

"Yeah, it is," Zev replied.

Zev gently rubbed his thumbs along Jonah's temples. The previous night had been a blur of passion and pounding bodies. This joining was different. Zev trickled soft kisses on Jonah's lips, caressed Jonah's face along his hairline with strong hands, and rolled his hips slowly, allowing Jonah to feel the hardness inside him without putting undue stress on his opening. He was infinitely tender, and Jonah fell even deeper under his spell.

"You ready to let go, Blondie?"

"Of you? Never."

Zev grinned. "Now, you know I'd never ask you to do that. No matter how cheesy you are."

Zev cupped his jaw, pressed those full lips firmly against Jonah's, then pushed his tongue into Jonah's mouth. Both men moaned at the added sensation. It was all Jonah needed to find his pleasure. He clung to Zev's broad torso and panted into Zev's hot mouth as liquid heat shot out of his dick and spread between them.

He was still trembling from his release when Zev called out his name, thrust, and then stilled deep inside his body, joining him in bliss.

Neither man moved for a couple of minutes. They just held each other, breathed together, and enjoyed their closeness. Eventually, Zev slipped out of Jonah's body, and they both chuckled at the strange sensation.

"C'mere," Zev said as he sat back in his chair and took Jonah with him, settling the man across his legs.

"I'm not exactly lap-size, Hassick. Even if you are as big as a mountain."

"You're exactly the right size for me, Blondie." Zev landed a soft kiss on Jonah's temple. "We need to talk."

Zev sounded serious and almost sad or worried. It made Jonah nervous, and he squirmed against the muscular body holding him.

"What do we need to talk about?"

Zev took a deep breath and looked straight into Jonah's eyes.

"About me. About you. About your mom."

Trying to lighten the mood, Jonah grinned and pinched Zev's nipple.

"That's a lot of stuff."

Zev shook his head without cracking a smile.

"It's just one thing, actually. A big thing, yeah, but...one thing."

His friend was clearly anxious and jokes weren't going to help, so Jonah braced himself and took a breath.

"'Kay. Lay it on me."

There was only a short pause before Zev spoke.

"I'm not exactly human," Zev said. Though his voice was low, his tone was steady and sure. Jonah didn't know how to respond. Hell, he didn't even know what that meant. Zev kept talking. "What I mean is, I'm not only human. I'm a man. And I'm a wolf."

"A wolf?"

Zev nodded, his eyes never leaving Jonah's.

"You're a wolf?"

Another nod.

"What does that mean?"

"It means that sometimes my body looks like this. But other times I change into a wolf."

"Are...are you telling me you're like a werewolf or something? When the moon is full you get all hairy with fangs and uncontrollable violence?" Jonah tried not to sound like he was making fun of Zev because, really, even though it should have been a joke, he knew Zev was dead serious.

"No." Zev shook his head. "I'm a man and I'm a wolf. I'm not some monster creature. Just a man and a wolf."

Jonah knew his jaw was hanging open, but he couldn't help himself. When had Zev lost his mind? Or was this all a fabrication of Jonah's brain? He'd been on edge for so long, and then last night, when he was finally with Zev, it all seemed better. All the pain and discomfort had magically disappeared. What if none of it was real? What if Jonah was hallucinating?

"Jonah." Zev squeezed his shoulders tight, the feeling comforting him with the knowledge that this was real, that he wasn't trapped in his own head. He focused on Zev's face. "Just...just don't shut yourself off from me, Blondie. Stop thinking for a minute and feel. There's a part of you that already knows this."

Zev was his closest confidant. His best friend. His lover. Everything in Jonah's body told him to trust this man, to believe in him. Even if everything his brain had learned through years of scientific training insisted the things he was hearing couldn't be true.

More than twenty years. That was how long Jonah had known Zev. Other than his father, Jonah had never connected with anyone on a soul-deep level like he did with Zev. Well, not anyone except... Jonah's heart slammed against his chest with the realization.

"Pup?" Jonah croaked.

CHAPTER 20

JONAH SOUNDED shocked, but the man hadn't bolted for the door, hadn't moved off Zev's lap, or looked truly horrified. Zev was endlessly relieved, maybe even a little surprised. Sure, Jonah had already called him Pup on a few occasions, including that very morning when his mate had said he worked too hard. But that name slipped out when Jonah's subconscious was filling in what his conscious mind hadn't yet processed or accepted. It was never something Jonah had truly recognized, so putting it all out there could have inspired a wave of denial and panic.

"Yeah." Zev nodded and responded to Jonah's question. "I'm your Pup."

Jonah stared at him, not saying anything, mostly just blinking and swallowing. Eventually his mate cleared his throat.

"Let me see."

Zev scooted off the chair and set Jonah down in it. It didn't look like the man had the ability to hold himself up on his own. It wasn't as if Zev hadn't shifted thousands of times before. Plus, Jonah already knew his wolf. Still, he couldn't help being a little nervous that Jonah would turn him away when he saw who Zev truly was, when he saw Zev shift.

Well, he didn't have a choice in the matter. His mate deserved to see his wolf, especially because this was only the beginning of the conversation. Telling Jonah that he himself was also a shifter was sure to be the real mind-bender portion of the day's programming schedule.

Zev laughed internally. Who could have guessed that the "your boyfriend is a shifter" topic would be the mild portion of their already "are you fucking kidding me" discussion?

"Ready?" he asked, watching Jonah's face carefully to make sure his mate wasn't about to pass out.

Jonah nodded.

"'Kay."

The word was barely out of Zev's mouth before Jonah was sitting in a chair and looking at a wolf. Or, more precisely, his wolf. He was looking at Pup.

The logical part of Jonah, the one with scientific training, the one that believed in the anatomy and physiology texts he'd read rather than in sci-fi novels—that part of Jonah wanted to leap out of his chair and back away from what he was seeing. But the rest of Jonah, his gut, his heart, the part of his brain that remembered all the times he'd spent with the wolf in front of him, and the man whose place he'd taken—those parts of Jonah wanted to drop to the floor and embrace his Pup.

The internal conflict kept Jonah paralyzed in place. That is, until Pup walked over to him and rested his head on Jonah's lap. Amber eyes looked up at him with the same loving, devoted gaze that had met him earlier that morning, except this time those eyes were in a different face. Everything that had been holding Jonah back was dismissed with that recognition.

This was his Zev, the man who meant everything to him. Okay, so what he'd just witnessed with his own eyes didn't make sense, but, hey, neither did physics at the beginning of the semester freshman year, and by the end, Jonah had earned an A. So he'd just need to learn about this in the same way, ask questions, study...whatever there was to study. Jonah was a good student; learning had never been an issue for him. Jonah took in a deep breath. Yes, this was all about learning something new. It'd be fine.

He reached out a trembling hand and stroked the soft fur on the head still resting in his lap. The wolf whimpered and turned into his hand, licking it. Then those familiar eyes looked up into Jonah's face.

"Zev, I...I..."

Okay, so it'd be fine, but at that moment he felt cold and sweaty, he was having trouble getting air into his lungs despite rapid attempts to suck it in, he was nauseous, and he thought he might faint. Yeah, okay, so maybe he was in shock. Just a little bit.

Jonah dropped to his knees and then laid flat on his back, trying to calm down. He propped his feet up on the chair.

"Blondie?" Zev's concerned face was right above him, petting his hair. "You're shaking. Oh, damn. Jonah, do you hear me?"

He hadn't even seen the wolf turn back into a man. It had happened that seamlessly.

"I... I... I'm fine. Just, um, need to lie down a little. Maybe..." Jonah tried to gather his thoughts. That effort alone was helping. "Just get me a blanket, okay? I'm cold."

Zev shot out of the room, and before he knew it, Jonah felt a blanket being tucked around him. He looked up and saw that Zev's gorgeous eyes were wide, his forehead was creased with worry, and his full lips were drawn in tight lines. Jonah tried to exude comfort.

"I'm okay, Pup. Promise. This is just a lot to take in. Give me a minute to adjust."

All right, time to man up. So his boyfriend could turn into a wolf? Hell, he'd done rounds in the ER of a huge metropolitan city at night. Some of the shit he'd seen there firsthand was way scarier than a furry woodland creature who liked to nuzzle him. That train of thought almost made him laugh out loud.

He might have even managed a smile because he heard Zev let out a relieved sigh and felt the man relax, even though they weren't touching. How could he feel what was going on in someone else's body?

Okay, yeah, that was weird. He'd need an explanation. Add it to the ever-fucking-growing list.

"All right. So you can turn into a wolf."

Jonah's voice almost sounded steady. He gave himself mental props for that achievement.

"Yeah. Are you still freaking out?" Zev asked.

"Nah. You're not the first seemingly normal guy I've seen turn into a wolf."

"I'm not?"

Jonah shook his head.

"No. Of course, it usually happens at bars late at night when the guy's had too much alcohol or controlled substances and he's making a pathetic last-ditch attempt to get laid. Still, I'll take your type of wolf over the kind that shows up right around last call anytime."

Zev's jaw dropped.

"Are you... Was that a joke, Blondie?"

Jonah nodded with exaggerated slowness.

"Yes, it was a joke. It's a good thing I'm moving back here, Pup. You're clearly starved for intelligent company if you can't even recognize humor when it's right in front of you. I blame Toby for this. The man still laughs at fart jokes. Those stopped being funny right around the time we got our drivers' permits. And don't even get me started on his taste in music. Do you think he's really a seventy-year-old hearing-impaired woman masquerading as a guy?"

Zev shook his head.

"'Fraid not. I've seen Toby in both his forms. There's no rational explanation for his unfortunate musical proclivities."

Jonah felt better. The room was no longer spinning, his body no longer shaking, and his friend looked happy. All right, time to sit up and ask some questions.

"Okay, so I gather from what you just said that Toby is a werewolf too?"

Zev cringed.

"Shifter. He's a shifter. You know, a man that can shift into a wolf."

"Shifter. Got it. Sorry. I don't have a handle on the PC terms yet. Help me up, Pup. This floor's hard and I have questions. Lots of questions."

Strong arms wrapped around Jonah's chest, and he was suddenly being carried out of the room.

"Hey, I'm perfectly capable of walking, Prince Charming."

"Can it, Blondie. You almost passed out in there. I'm not taking any chances. Besides, I like carrying you."

All right, well, truth be told, Jonah liked it too, so he stopped complaining. Zev walked into the bedroom and gently placed Jonah on the bed. Then the big man got in next to him and pulled the blankets up. They lay on their sides, facing each other, holding hands, and everything felt right. Jonah knew without a doubt that he'd never been happier. Zev leaned over and dropped a chaste kiss on his lips.

"Okay, Blondie, let's hear the questions. I'll do my best to answer them."

Three hours later, with only a short break to chow down on some cereal, the two men were still in bed, with Zev playing teacher. He explained everything he knew about shifters to Jonah—their history, their pack structure, the way their bodies worked. The last one was particularly fascinating to the young doctor, but unfortunately, Zev couldn't answer most of Jonah's questions. Hell, he had a hard time understanding the questions and most of the words in them. After Zev promised to introduce Jonah to the pack healer to get the more technical details of how a shifter's body worked, the man was finally willing to move on.

They were lying in bed, gently petting each other's bodies, everything close and warm and perfect between them. Zev was still talking, still explaining how things worked, when suddenly, a cold front came off Jonah in waves. Zev stopped talking and blinked in surprise.

"What's wrong?"

Jonah glared at him.

"You're asking me what's wrong?" His voice was loud. Then he looked around the room, not that there was anyone else there, and spoke again. "He's asking me what's wrong!"

"Um, Blondie, who're you talking to? What's going on?"

Jonah sat up in bed and pulled the blanket around him.

"What's going on? You're asking me what's going on?" The answer was yes, but Zev was afraid to say it. "I'll tell you what's going on." Jonah continued shouting.

Oh, thank goodness.

"I'm apparently the dumbest person on the fucking planet, that's what's going on."

Zev sat up and tried to pull Jonah against his chest but his mate wouldn't budge.

"Shh, Jonah, calm down. Let's talk through this, okay? I'll make it better."

"You'll make it better? Right. Is that what you tell your woman too? Or is it women? How many are there, Zev? And did you honestly think I'd be okay with this?"

"What woman, er, or women? Okay with what? Jonah, slow the fuck down or calm the fuck down, or...shit! What the fuck are you talkin' about?"

Jonah took a deep breath and squeezed his hands into tight fists.

"I'm talking about the fact that the man I'm supposed to spend the rest of my life with just told me that he plans to fuck women on the side!"

"What?" Zev was horrified. "I never said that!"

Jonah rolled his eyes.

"Okay, fine. Tie with women. Honestly, Zev, don't try to tell me there's a difference, because you know damn well there isn't. Just because your dick gets longer and thicker doesn't mean it isn't inside a vagina. Fucking is fucking!"

"Damn, Jonah, chill out. I didn't say anything about vaginas. What the hell conversation were you just involved in? Because it sure as shit wasn't with me."

Jonah looked as frustrated as Zev felt, but neither of them rose from the bed. Because being apart would have been worse than fighting. Worse than anything.

"You just said that in order for male shifters to stay human, they had to have sex with female shifters. You said that if they didn't, they'd get sick and their wolf would take over full time. You said they usually start doing it in their late teens and early twenties. That's what you said. And you're here, Zev. You're here and you're thirty and you're very clearly human. So that means..."

No longer angry, Zev gentled his voice as he said, "It doesn't mean what you think it means."

"So explain it to me, Pup." Jonah raked his fingers through his hair. "Shit, I'm trying here. I really am."

"I know you are, Blondie. C'mere, huh? I know you're pissed, but don't push me away. C'mere."

Jonah slowly made his way into Zev's lap. He put his knees on the outside of Zev's thighs, straddling his hips, and then collapsed his forehead on Zev's shoulder.

"The thought of you touching someone else makes me feel sick, Zev. Seriously, it's like a sharp pain in my chest and my stomach hurts and..."

Zev kissed the top of Jonah's head.

"I don't touch other people, Blondie, not like how you think. Do you remember what I said about female shifters?

About how they need to tie with a male shifter in order to release their wolf?"

Jonah didn't respond verbally, he just nodded, not moving his head from Zev's shoulder.

"And if they don't tie, then the wolf is trapped, it starts messing with them, makes them lose their minds, makes them sick from the inside. You heard me say that too, right?"

"Yeah, I heard you, Zev. I get it. But they can tie with someone else. It doesn't have to be with you."

"That's right. They can tie with someone else. But you can't. You can only tie with me, Jonah. Just like I can only tie with you."

"You know what? I'm tired. My head hurts. You're gonna have to talk in English, because I don't understand what you're getting at." Jonah growled out the sentences, his frustration clear in his tone.

"Yeah, you do. You're a doctor, Jonah. How long have you been feeling off, huh? How long has your body been hurting? How long have you had the nightmares? And it's all gone now, right? It's all better."

Jonah pulled his head back and met Zev's gaze. He nodded slowly.

"Right. It's better. And when did it get better?" Zev paused to let his words, the meaning of what he was saying, sink in. Then he answered his own question. "It got better last night. When we were together, when our bodies joined. That's when all the bad feelings went away. I know because the same thing happened to me. When we connected, Jonah, when we finally connected in that way, I finally felt whole. That's what happens when a shifter ties with his true mate."

"I don't..." Jonah shook his head. "I don't understand. I mean, I know what happened last night and I know it was amazing. And, yeah, I feel better now. But, Zev, it isn't the same thing as your whole tying thing. You get that, right? Because I'm not a shifter. And, by the way, I'm not a woman, either, but I'm gonna go ahead and let that implication go. Seriously, though, for a gay man you have a lot to learn. Just because a guy likes to bottom doesn't mean he's a girl and..."

Zev's hands landed on Jonah's cheeks. He sucked in a deep breath, steeling himself for the coming blow. Then he looked straight into his mate's eyes.

"You're not a girl. I know that better than anyone, considering my intimate acquaintance with your dick. But, Jonah, don't freak out now, but..." A deep breath, and then Zev finished speaking in a rush. "You are a shifter."

CHAPTER 21

BOTH MEN were quiet for a long time. Zev allowed his words to sink in, letting Jonah absorb intellectually what Zev was certain the man's body already knew innately—that he was not only a man, but also a wolf.

"I'm a shifter?"

Zev nodded.

"And you think this...why?"

"I know this because you shifted last night. When we were together, you shifted and you were beautiful. Damn, Blondie, your wolf is just as gorgeous as your man."

"I shifted?"

"Yes."

"Into a wolf?"

"Yes."

"Last night?"

"Yes."

"I shifted into a wolf last night?"

"Yes, Jonah. When you add up all three clauses they make a very pretty sentence, and the meaning stays the same."

"You know what, Zev? Can the sarcasm. My boyfriend just told me that my body turned into a wolf when we had sex. And that's coming on the tail end of said boyfriend transforming into my childhood pet, or whatever, right in front of me. So cut me some slack here if I'm a little slow in putting the damn pieces together."

Zev wrapped his arms around Jonah and squeezed him tightly. He leaned down and kissed the beloved man's forehead, the tip of his nose, and then his full lips. The kiss was sweet and loving, Zev's lips grabbing on to Jonah's bottom lip and tugging slightly every so often, his tongue darting out and licking. "'M sorry," Zev apologized quietly once their mouths separated.

"Yeah, okay." Jonah lay back down. "So tell me exactly what happened last night."

Zev's forehead creased. "You're taking this remarkably well."

"Oh, well, you know, it's just like when I'm watching a movie. Once I suspend disbelief in order to go along with a world where apes can talk, then I'm also willing to believe they took over the earth in the future. Or was it that the humans destroyed themselves and then the apes came into power? Whatever, you get my point."

"Uh-huh. I get your point. That Statue of Liberty buried in the ocean scene was epic. The remake didn't even come close to having the same impact. Now do you wanna go back to what we were talkin' about? 'Cause your analogies are a little too complicated for my simple brain to follow."

Jonah reached his hand up and smacked Zev in the shoulder.

"You're brilliant and you know it."

Zev rubbed his shoulder dramatically.

"That's not what you've been saying to me for the past couple of decades. What? All of a sudden you're changing your tune?"

Taking Zev's hand in his, Jonah yanked his man down so they were lying side by side again.

"Yeah, well, a hot night in bed with a guy will do that to you. Suddenly even a bumbling buffoon seems fascinating and intelligent."

"Last night was hot, huh?" Zev smirked.

"On fire," Jonah confirmed.

"Smokin'."

"Explosive." Jonah continued the game, his lips twitching.

Zev cocked an eyebrow in amusement. "Got another one, Blondie?"

"Nah, I'm all good. Go on and tell me about my miraculous transformation."

Zev caressed Jonah's hip and relaxed.

"There's not much more to say. We were having sex and I felt your wolf calling me. It was like I could sense it, desperately trying to get out. And my wolf responded instinctively to his mate. So I told you to follow me, or maybe I thought it, I dunno. Anyway, I started shifting and you did too."

"Your mate? Is that, like, wolf-speak for boyfriend?"

"Ah, Jonah," Zev said huskily. "Don't you get how much more you are to me than a boyfriend? How much more we are to each other?"

Jonah nodded, then whispered his response. "Sometimes it's like I can hear you talking in my head. Or like I can feel you or something, you know?"

"Yeah, I know. That's the mating bond. It's always been strong with us. Stronger than I've ever heard of. And my guess is that because we've tied now, it'll get even stronger. That's why I was never willing to do this until you were here to stay. Being separated from you all these years was barely tolerable as it was. I didn't think either of us would be able to survive it once we tied and connected on a deeper level. And that was before I knew you were a shifter."

"You didn't know?"

Zev shook his head.

"So you can't tell when another person is like you?" Jonah asked.

"Actually, I can usually tell when someone's a shifter. I can smell it. Everyone has a different scent, and I can usually spot a shifter's scent before I lay eyes on him. But your scent has always been human." Zev nuzzled into Jonah's neck. "Delicious and addictive, but human."

"Maybe you turned me into a shifter. Maybe when we were having sex and you bit me..." Jonah rubbed at the mark on his shoulder and remembered the feeling of Zev's teeth sinking into him. The memory inspired a shiver through his body and a hardening in his groin.

"No." Zev was absolutely firm in his response. "You can't just turn someone into a shifter. That's, like, a movie thing. We're a different species, Jonah. Different chromosomes. A bite isn't gonna change that. Besides, you shifted before I bit you."

Jonah sighed.

"And you're sure I smell completely human."

"Uh-huh. Well, you did, anyway. Now our scents are woven together."

"What do you mean?"

"When true mates tie together and complete the mating bond, their scents combine." Zev shook his head. "No, I'm not explaining it the right way, because neither scent disappears. It's more like the two scents are braided together so you can still tell they're distinct, but you can only smell them in unison. Like they're inextricably joined."

"Okaaay." Jonah drew out the word. "We'll have to go back to that one, because I don't fully get it. But first I need to understand how I can be what you say I am. It doesn't make sense. Well, it makes less sense than the rest of this, anyway."

Zev chuckled.

"Well, there's one explanation that comes to mind. It probably raises more questions than it gives answers, considering the impossibility of interspecies breeding, but..." Zev's voice trailed off. He looked at Jonah meaningfully.

"You think my mother was like you, don't you? You think she was a shifter?"

"I think it's a good possibility. You told me that, in your dreams, your mom was sometimes a wolf, right? Dreams aren't always just dreams. Sometimes they're a way for the truth we know innately to come up to the surface of our consciousness."

"Wow, that's deep, Pup. I didn't know you had it in you."

"Keep makin' jokes, Blondie. Go ahead. I dare ya."

Jonah rolled over and straddled Zev's body. He twined their fingers together and pinned both of the bigger man's hands against the bed.

"Not so tough now, are ya, big guy? Whatcha gonna do to me, huh?"

"I'll do anything you want, Blondie." Zev sounded like he was speaking through gravel. "But if you keep grinding your sweet ass against my dick that way, there are some ideas that will definitely need to be addressed before others."

The arousal wasn't one-sided, and Jonah found himself panting. His cock was hard, and he felt that moving, clenching feeling inside his body, like he needed to be filled again. Zev pulled his arm free of Jonah's grip and wrapped a big hand around Jonah's cock, stroking it gently.

"I love how you feel. So soft, but hard at the same time. Your body turns me on so much. I want you."

"Ungh. Zev." Jonah whispered the name reverently. "I want you too, but I..." He swallowed so he could keep talking. "I wanna shift. I wanna see myself as a wolf."

"Go ahead."

"But I don't know how. Tell me how to do it."

"Explain shifting?" Zev stopped stroking Jonah's cock and dragged his fingers through his hair. "That's like telling someone how to swallow or breathe. Your body does it instinctively."

"Clearly, that's not true." Jonah arched his eyebrows meaningfully.

"Fair enough." Zev grinned. "Umm. Let me think." He pressed his lips together and his forehead creased in concentration. "Okay, you just sorta relax and think of your wolf form, and then your body changes to match the picture in your mind."

"But I've never seen my wolf form."

"It shouldn't matter. It's like an internal picture, yeah? You feel your wolf inside and you focus on him."

Jonah closed his eyes and concentrated. He willed his body to relax, willed himself to find that internal wolf. But it wasn't working. He opened his eyes and looked at Zev imploringly.

"It isn't working. Are you sure I did this last night? Because I don't know how. I can't feel a wolf inside."

"Yeah, I'm sure. Your wolf is there. You just need to recognize him." Zev chewed on his bottom lip, a thoughtful expression on his face. "I'm not sure why this isn't working; let's try a different approach." He placed a big, warm hand on Jonah's chest, over his heart. "Can you feel me inside you, Blondie? Can you feel our bond?"

Jonah nodded. Now that he knew it was real, now that his analytical brain wasn't blocking him from admitting it, that ability to feel Zev was right there. It was just like being aware of his own feelings. That was how connected he was to the other man. It should have been scary, but it wasn't. It felt right.

"Okay. Close your eyes and concentrate on me. Concentrate on what you can feel inside me and follow that trail, 'kay? Just stay with me."

Jonah closed his eyes and focused on his boyfriend, his mate. He felt the warmth of that hard body, felt the strength of the man he knew would be by his side forever, felt how deeply he was treasured, how vital he was to Zev. And then he felt something cold and wet on his nose.

He opened his eyes and saw Pup in front of him. The wolf was crouched down and he was nudging his nose against Jonah's. Jonah reached his hand out to pet the beautiful animal, but instead of fingers, he saw a paw. His own paw. He had a paw.

Startled, Jonah pushed back and looked down his body. There was white fur covering a canine form. Dear God, he'd done it. He was a wolf. He'd transformed into a wolf. Shifted. Whatever.

Jonah jumped off the bed and walked into the closet. He remembered seeing a full-length mirror there earlier. It should have been shocking to see his own coal-colored eyes looking at him from the body of a white wolf, but it wasn't. It felt right somehow, almost like it was a relief.

Pup walked in, bumped his body against Jonah's, and mouthed the white wolf's muzzle. Jonah tossed his head and whimpered before pressing close to his Pup, his Zev. He nibbled on the other wolf's coat and enjoyed the low rumble he could hear in that large chest.

A big tongue swiped across Jonah's face, and then Pup walked out of the room, turning amber eyes back to look at Jonah expectantly. Jonah was following his mate before his mind had even processed what was happening. Zev led them through the house and into the mud room, where he pushed open an unlatched ground-level window with his nose and then stepped outside. Jonah was right behind his mate when they left the house, walked off the porch, and ran into the woods.

They'd lost track of time, having spent the day in bed, talking. The sky was now black, the only light coming from the bright moon above. It felt like an adventure, running through the forest with his mate, exploring new smells, seeing nature in a way he'd never imagined—like he was part of it.

Sometimes they'd walk slowly, smelling every tree, seeing every nocturnal creature hiding in the trees or among the shrubs on the ground. But when the mood struck, they'd stop exploring and start running, chasing each other through the forest, pushing their muscles, enjoying the burn. And every so often, Pup would jump on Jonah, tackle him to the ground and roll around with him, nipping at his neck, pushing his snout against him.

The only word to describe their night together in wolf form was fun. Jonah was having the time of his life. He was finally himself, finally free, finally whole.

After spending hours in the woods enjoying their wolf forms, Zev and Jonah made it back to the cabin. They walked in through the window on four legs, but as soon as they were inside, Zev shifted into his human body. Jonah's reaction was instantaneous as his body instinctively followed his mate's internal directions, and he found himself back in his familiar skin.

He looked over at Zev's nude body and groaned. All those rippling muscles, the dark hair on that broad chest, those amber eyes that always looked at him like he was a prize or something. Damn, but Jonah wanted Zev. He wanted the man in a hungry, primal, desperate way that couldn't be denied. He thought he might actually die if Zev didn't touch him.

Thankfully he didn't have to find out, because his mate seemed to be just as aroused. Zev had him backed up against the counter before he could say a word. Those long fingers tangled in his blond hair, that hot mouth chewed on his shoulder, his neck, his ear, and finally covered his mouth, swallowing his whimpers. And all the while, Zev's big, hard dick was pressed against Jonah's erection, rubbing and thrusting.

"Can ya go again, Blondie? 'Cause I want inside real bad."

The hand that wasn't clutching Jonah's hair caressed his ass, dipping into the cleft, pressing against the puckered skin. Jonah managed to spin around. He leaned over the counter and reached his hands back to clutch at his own ass, pulling his cheeks apart and exposing his entrance.

"Yeah, we can go again. I need you."

Zev kissed and nibbled on Jonah's neck as he ran his large hand over the small of Jonah's back, across his ass, down his thigh, and to the back of his knee. He bent that knee and pushed it up to the counter, leaving Jonah spread.

"Oh, God, Zev," Jonah moaned when Zev's kisses went lower, moving into his cleft.

"Think you're stretched enough from earlier that you can take me on spit or should we go into the bedroom where we have the slick?"

"It's good. We don't need to move. Damn, Zev, please lick me. Wanna feel your tongue pushing into me. Wanna..."

Jonah lost the power of speech when Zev gave him exactly what he wanted. That talented tongue lapped against his cleft, laved his entrance, and penetrated his body with darting swipes. It felt so incredible that Jonah's entire frame shook, his legs trembled, and he moaned almost continuously.

He didn't know how long Zev had been working his ass when he felt the man rise. Then a strong arm gripped his shoulder and that thick cock pushed into him with one smooth, steady stroke.

"Oh, you feel so good inside me, Zev. Damn."

Jonah braced himself with his left elbow on the counter and used his right hand to clutch the edge and meet Zev's thrusts. The sound of skin slapping against skin harmonized with their almost constant grunts and groans. Jonah could smell their passion, their arousal for each other, and it turned him on even further. He could feel his release in his gut, making every moment even more intense, bringing the pleasure up to fever pitch.

"Yes. Yes. Yes," Jonah chanted as their bodies moved in concert, Zev's thick cock dragging in and out of his body.

When Zev wrapped his hand around Jonah's dick, the reaction was almost instantaneous. Jonah called out Zev's name and shot so hard that he almost blacked out. And Zev clutched Jonah's hips tightly and gave two more thrusts before he held his position deep inside, arched his neck, and cried out in pleasure.

The upper portion of Jonah's body collapsed onto the counter, his cheek resting on the cool granite as his heart rate slowed, and he dragged air into his lungs. Zev's big frame blanketed him, and he heard his mate sucking in air like it was about to be discontinued.

"Holy shit, it just keeps getting better," Jonah finally wheezed out.

"Yeah, it does. That's how it's supposed to be, Blondie, how it'll always be with us. I'm gonna make you so happy. I'll be the best mate you can imagine."

"You already are, Zev. You've made me happier than I could've dreamed."

CHAPTER 22

BY THE time they'd eaten enough to replenish their energy and taken a long and not-just-to-get-clean shower, both men were exhausted. They dropped into bed, immediately rolled toward each other, tangled their bodies together, and fell asleep.

Zev's empty stomach eventually woke him from a deep sleep. He could feel Jonah's hand on his hip, Jonah's left knee pressed between his thighs, and Jonah's right leg draped over his calf. He dipped his head and kissed the top of that blond head, and Jonah's hand immediately moved over his body and started caressing his chest.

"Mmm. I love sleeping with you. I've been so damn tired all these years. I couldn't ever get a decent night's sleep, except when you were with me. But now...now it's even better. It's like my whole body can finally rest," Jonah mumbled, his words thick with sleep.

"Me too, Blondie. I swear, I've felt like shit for so long that I'd forgotten what it was like not to hurt," Zev said as he rolled onto his back and pulled Jonah on top of him.

Jonah raised his head, cupped Zev's cheek gently with his hand, and searched those amber eyes.

"But you're okay now, right? Your body doesn't hurt anymore?"

Zev nodded and smirked. "Yup, I'm all better. You're a great healer, Dr. Marvel."

The hand against Zev's cheek was gone for a second before it landed again, not so gently this time.

"Why didn't you tell me, Zev? All these years you were hurting and I was hurting. Why didn't you tell me what was going on?"

Zev threaded his fingers through Jonah's hair.

"What would you have done if I'd told you?"

"What do you mean? I would've believed you just like I did when you told me yesterday."

"And then what?" Zev pushed.

"Then I would've moved back here with you and everything would've been fine."

"And that right there, Blondie, is exactly why I didn't tell you."

Those blond eyebrows scrunched down in confusion.

"You had a goal. You wanted to be a doctor. I couldn't stand in your way, Jonah. Doesn't mean I was happy about it, especially at first. I wanted you by my side. But I had to trust that we'd be strong enough to handle the separation, and then you'd have the career you wanted, the pack would have a great healer, and I'd have my mate with me."

"You risked being trapped as a wolf for the rest of your life so I could finish med school? I don't know whether that's the sweetest, most honorable thing I've ever heard, or the stupidest, most reckless decision of all time," Jonah said. "Seriously, it's a toss-up."

Zev chuckled.

"Well, it doesn't matter now. You're here, I'm here, your medical degree is here, metaphorically speaking. All's well that ends well, right?"

Jonah buried his face in Zev's neck, inhaled deeply, as if taking in his scent, and then trembled. "Yeah. You're right. I'd still like to figure things out about my mom, though. And I need to understand how it's possible for me to be half shifter if shifters can't reproduce with humans. And did you just say that I'm going to be the pack's healer? What does that mean?"

Zev rolled so he was on top of Jonah, pinning him down. He kissed Jonah's brow, then his nose, and smiled.

"You're adorable with all those questions," Zev said.

"Fuck you."

That reply cracked Zev up. He had missed his friend so desperately over the years that having Jonah home was causing a giddy sensation all through Zev's body. He felt like he was floating.

"All right, I'm gonna answer your questions in backwards order. I know you can get a job at the hospital and probably lots of other places too, but the pack's healer is getting up there in years and we'll need someone to replace him. Our kind can't go to human medical centers; we need one of our own to care for us. Usually healers apprentice for years before they work independently, but you've gone to medical school, so you'll have a lot of knowledge they don't. I think you can work with Doc Carson for a little while, learn about how we're different from humans, and then you can take over. If you want to, I mean."

"I'd have to learn a lot about shifters. Medically speaking, it's incredible that a body can change forms. I'm itching to understand how that works and what it means from the standpoint of illnesses, injuries, life expectancies..." He drew in a deep breath and continued more slowly. "I guess what I'm saying is, I like the intellectual part of it, and my competitive side likes the idea of learning things my colleagues won't ever conceive of, but that's not the biggest reason the job appeals to me."

"What's the biggest reason?"

"I don't really know how to explain it. Even though I didn't keep in touch with people here and there are plenty of them I've never met, it's like there's this driving force inside me that says I should be a contributing member of the pack."

"That's natural. All wolves want to better the pack. And you're a great doctor. I'm sure you'll be able to learn everything you need to treat shifters with the same skills you mastered in your treatment of humans."

"Thanks for the vote of confidence." Jonah grinned. "I think I'd like being the pack doctor. I have a lot to learn, obviously, but I'm up for it. Hell, as good as I feel right now, it's as if I can do anything. You're like a damn drug, Pup."

Zev dropped his head and rubbed his cheek against Jonah's.

"I'm your true mate. That's better than any drug."

"Don't let the pharma companies hear that. They'd make sure we're drowning in complimentary pens and free lunches until their product gets top billing." Jonah laughed at his own joke, then shook his head. "Don't mind me. Doctor humor. Keep going. You were addressing all points in backwards order, right?"

"The rest of it is all pretty much the same. We need to go through the paperwork I have in the office and talk to the elders if we have more questions. Maybe you can ask Doc Carson about the more technical stuff. We'll just dig until we find answers about your mother and until we understand how you survived conception, pregnancy, and birth."

Jonah nodded.

"Okay. Let's get some grub, and then we can start going through the documents you have. I just need to try my dad again. It's not like him to be out of touch for so long, and I'm starting to get really worried."

Zev was in the kitchen frying up bacon when Jonah walked in holding his cell phone. Warmth flowed through his chest at the sight of his...mate.

"Need help?" he asked as he set the phone down on the table and walked up to Zev, molding his chest to that strong back and resting his cheek on Zev's shoulder.

"Did you get ahold of your dad?"

Jonah kissed Zev's nape. "No. But there was a message from him. He must've called when we were out running last night. Said he's getting closer to some answers. I tried to call him back to tell him not to bother because I'm fine now, but he didn't answer."

Zev put the bacon on paper towels to drain, and then turned around, wrapped his arms around Jonah's waist, and tugged him forward until they were pressed together. "I don't like the idea of your dad out there asking questions. If we're right about your mother being a shifter, it would mean her family is too. Shifters don't interact well with humans anyway, but if your dad starts digging for information about them, they're liable to get really agitated."

Jonah sighed. "Yeah, I get that. He's pretty scared of them because of what happened to my mom, so I'm sure he'll be really careful about what he says. I don't think he's asking a bunch of questions. He's just trying to track down my mother's sister because he thinks she's safer than the rest. But I'll call again in a little while and try to get him on the line. Then I'll tell him to call off the search."

A telephone ringing interrupted their conversation. Both men looked at the table, but Jonah's phone was dark and silent.

"Must be mine. I'll be right back," Zev said.

Zev walked out of the kitchen in pursuit of his phone. He was back a few minutes later, his forehead creased with worry.

Concerned, Jonah asked, "What's up?"

"That was Toby. Something's going on with Lori. I need to get over there."

"What's wrong? Is she sick?"

Zev shook his head. "No. She's not home or something. Toby was really freaked out so it was hard to understand him. I better go check it out. I'm sorry. I know we planned to spend the day going through those papers."

Jonah took Zev's hand in his and kissed it. "No worries. Unless you need my help, I'll just stay here and get started while you figure things out with your sister. That okay?"

"Of course. I'll try not to take long."

Zev yanked on Jonah's hand, bringing him crashing against Zev's chest, and then cupped the back of Jonah's head, brought it forward to meet his own, and sucked Jonah's tongue into his mouth.

Eventually, the need for air separated them. "Love how you taste." Zev lapped at Jonah's lips. "Smell." He buried his nose against Jonah's skin and inhaled. "Feel." He ground their hips together.

"Go on, horn-dog," Jonah panted. "Go deal with your sister. Then get your ass back here and take care of mine."

"Toby?" Zev called out as he knocked on the door to his sister's house and pushed it open.

"In here."

Zev followed Toby's voice to the living room and found him pacing a trail on the floor.

"What's going on? Where're Lori and the kids?"

Toby raked his fingers through his already disheveled hair.

"Your mom just left with the kids. I'm not holding it together so well here and I didn't want to worry them, so I called her and asked her to pick them up. And I don't know where Lori is."

Well, that was about the most useless answer ever. Zev sat down on the couch, rested his forearms on his knees, and clasped his hands together.

"Come sit down and talk to me, Toby. You're not making any sense."

"I was only gone for a few hours. She'd never leave the kids alone. Doesn't make any sense." He continued pacing, pulling on his hair, and mumbling almost incoherently.

"Toby!" Zev's deep voice boomed, causing Toby to jerk his gaze over to Zev. "It was an order, not a suggestion. Sit your ass down on this couch, take a breath, and tell me what's going on."

Zev knew using that tone would register to the wolf inside Toby, bringing him comfort and assuring him of safety.

Sure enough, Toby immediately responded to his Alpha. He walked over to the couch, took a deep breath, let it out, and started talking. "I went fishing with my dad, his brothers, and their boys this morning. Most of those guys are camping out, but Lori's been having so much trouble keeping anything down that I didn't want to leave her alone with all four kids for that long."

"Why's she been throwing up? Is she sick...?" Zev changed tracks midsentence when he saw Toby blush. "I see. I'm gonna be an uncle again, huh? I thought you said you were done after four."

"Yeah, well, this one wasn't planned. Aaaanyway, I got home about an hour ago and the kids were all alone. They were in the family room watching cartoons and they seemed fine, so I figured maybe she just ran out for like a minute or something." He paused and looked up at Zev. "Not that she'd ever do that, you know? It seemed weird, but..." Toby shrugged. "I don't know. Anyway, when she wasn't back after thirty minutes, I asked the kids if they knew where Mommy was. They said she went for a drive with the men."

"What men?" Zev's eyebrows bunched together.

"That's just it!" Toby cried, "I don't know. They didn't know who the men were, and I didn't want to push too much and worry them. What the hell's going on, Zev? I'm scared."

"I don't know." Zev stood. "Did you look around, see if maybe you could recognize a scent that shouldn't be here?"

"Yeah, 'course. I did that right away. I smelled four males, but none of them were familiar. They're not from our pack. I know I don't have your nose, but if they were from around here, I'm sure I'd have recognized at least one of them."

Zev nodded. "I know you would. I'm gonna shift and give it another go, just in case." He squeezed Toby's shoulder. "It's gonna be okay, Tobes. We'll find her."

Though he meant the words, Zev was more worried than he let Toby see. It really wasn't like Lori to leave her children or to take off without telling anyone where she was going. And there was absolutely no reason for unknown males to be at the house.

Zev walked to the front door, opened it, and then shifted into his wolf form, letting his clothes fall to the ground. He immediately smelled four male shifters, and just as Toby had said, they weren't from the Etzgadol pack. With his nose close to the ground, Zev first moved inside the house, wanting to follow the trail, but it ran cold at the end of the entryway. Zev then turned and walked outside, again following the scent of the intruders to the long driveway, where the scent ended. He walked back to the house, shifted into his human form, and then yanked on his clothes hurriedly.

"That was fast," Toby said, unable to hide the disappointment in his voice. "I guess you couldn't follow the trail either?"

Zev shook his head and pulled his shirt on.

"The reason we can't follow the trail is that they drove. That's why their scent ends at the driveway. And I don't think they got any further into the house than the entryway, so they couldn't have been looking for something inside."

"What the hell does that mean?" Toby asked in a panic.

"It means they got what they came for. They got Lori. But we're getting her back." Zev finished tying his shoes and started walking out the front door. "Let's go."

"Where're we going?" Toby followed him, his entire body trembling.

"Brian Delgato's." Zev slammed the truck door, waited for Toby to scramble inside, and then peeled out of the driveway.

"What's Brian got to do with this, Zev? We're not friends with the guy, you know? He's had a thing for Lori for years and he's kind of an asshole to boot. There's no way she'd tell him shit about where she was going."

"No, she wouldn't. But one of those men who was at your house is his kin. There was a similarity in their scents that only happens with family."

"You're amazing, you know that?" Toby shook his head in awe. "I've never heard of a shifter with stronger senses. Recognizing the scent of littermates is, well, not common, but some shifters can do it. But recognizing distant kin..." Toby's voice softened. "You're incredible, man. I hope my boys inherit some of your strength."

There was nothing he could say in response to the admiration, so Zev stayed quiet. The Etzgadol pack knew it had a strong Alpha. Zev couldn't hide his power; it rolled off him and was obvious to other shifters. Not that Zev would want to hide it. Having a strong Alpha was important to a pack's security. It let them feel safe and cared for.

But Zev had never told anyone about how deep that strength ran. They didn't know how quickly and painlessly he could shift, or just how well he could see in pitch dark, or hear across long distances, and until that moment, nobody knew that the Alpha could differentiate the individual components of each shifter's scent, that he could literally trace a shifter's line to his parents and grandparents.

Yet with all that power, Zev hadn't smelled a trace of wolf in his own mate. The scent that he knew better than all others, the one that had intrigued him for as long as he could remember, that arousing perfume of freshly mowed grass, lemons, and mint; that scent he couldn't dissect, couldn't recognize as anything other than home and comfort and wholeness. He would've chalked the block in his abilities as something mate-related, like maybe his mating bond prevented him from focusing on anything other than the man himself. But that wouldn't explain why the other shifters had never recognized Jonah as one of their own.

No, the reason Jonah smelled completely human wasn't the mating bond; the reason was something inherent within Jonah. It probably stemmed from the man's human father, though that same factor should have made shifting impossible.

How had Jonah been able to shift without the necessary shifter chromosomes from both parents? Zev didn't have more time to ponder the question, because they'd reached Brian Delgato's house.

CHAPTER 23

THE TRUCK windows were open, and as soon as they turned onto the long driveway, there was no mistaking Lori's scent. His sister had been there recently. Zev glanced over to Toby to see whether the other man picked up the scent. His nose was in the air, and then he turned his head to Zev, the question in his eyes. Zev nodded, confirming what Toby already knew.

The truck hadn't even stopped moving before Toby flung the door open and shot out like a rocket. He ran for the front door and growled in frustration when he found it locked. With his fists pounding on the wood, Toby started shouting.

"Open the door, Delgato." He kicked the bottom of the door with all his strength and continued pounding. "You hear me, Brian? Open the fucking door!"

Zev got out of the truck and smelled the air, recognizing the scents of the four males who'd been to Lori's house. But those scents were weak and they didn't emanate from the house. Only Brian's and Lori's scents came from inside, letting Zev know they were the only ones still present.

He approached Toby quietly, took hold of the man by the shoulders, and firmly moved that furious body to the side.

"Stay," Zev said, leaving no room for argument.

He glared at Toby, making it clear to the other shifter that there was no other choice. Toby stopped shouting, but his hands remained clenched into fists and his body vibrated with anger. Zev tilted his head to the side and listened carefully. He could hear whimpering, but it wasn't coming from Lori.

Suddenly, the door swung open and Lori stood before them. Her wrists were raw, showing signs of being bound, there was blood on the side of her head, and her left eye was sporting the beginnings of what would probably become a pretty decent shiner. With all that damage, his sister still managed a little smirk.

"Oh, thank God, the cavalry's here," she said, deadpan. "Come on in, boys."

Lori stepped aside and Zev walked into the house. He heard Toby's body make contact with Lori's and knew the man was checking his wife over, making sure she was okay.

"Where is he, Lori?"

When she didn't answer right away, Zev turned around and got caught in a misty gaze. Lori walked right up to him and pressed her face to his chest, inhaling deeply. She smiled and gave Zev an approving squeeze, but didn't verbalize what they both knew she'd smelled: her brother's scent braided with Jonah's.

"Brian's in the kitchen. I just finished getting him... situated."

Zev nodded, gave Lori a quick hug, and walked toward the kitchen. He almost laughed when he found Brian hunched on the floor. His legs and arms were tied behind his back with a rope that was also wrapped around his neck. Other shifters couldn't change forms as quickly as Zev. If they tried making the change while clothed, the fabric would tear and the wolf would often find himself tangled in cloth, which wasn't so much dangerous as it was uncomfortable and embarrassing. But being bound like he was, if Brian shifted, there was a good chance he'd break a limb or choke.

"This your work, Lori?" Zev shouted over his shoulder. "Nice."

Lori and Toby walked into the kitchen, and Toby gasped at the sight that greeted him.

"Yeah, it's not bad for a weak, defenseless girl, is it, Brian?" she said sarcastically.

"I swear, Zev, I didn't have anything to do with this. I refused to help them when they asked. But then they said they had Lori and I didn't want them to hurt her. That's the only reason I got involved." Brian was shaking and pleading. "You have to believe me. Lori, I was just trying to help you."

"Help me? They came into my house and threatened to hurt my kids if I didn't go with them! My kids, Brian!" Lori's voice rolled with anger.

All three men were stunned by that revelation. Shifters didn't hurt their young. Cubs were treasured and protected by their packs. Brian tried to shake his head in denial, but the rope prevented him from moving. Suddenly Toby sprang forward, going after Brian.

"You bastard! I'm gonna take your head off."

Zev got his hand on Toby's shirt and pulled him back, keeping his arm around his brother-in-law's chest.

"All right. We're all gonna take a deep breath and calm down." He gave Toby a small tug. "You hear me, Tobes? Calm your shit down. Your kids are fine. Your wife kicked his ass. It's all good. Now we just need to figure out what the hell's going on and get these men away from the rest of our pack before they hurt someone."

Toby nodded reluctantly and returned to his spot by Lori's side.

"No. He wouldn't hurt any shifters. He wouldn't. He'd never do that, Zev." Brian was shaking and whimpering, his words running together.

Zev combed his fingers through his hair. Brian was an ass. Zev had never liked the man. But he was part of the Etzgadol pack and that made him Zev's responsibility.

"All right, Brian. I'm going to untie you now. Then we'll all sit down and have a nice little talk. But one thing you need to understand is that your kin and his friends have already hurt a shifter. They hurt Lori. And they put four cubs in danger. I can't let that go, and if you're loyal to this pack, neither will you."

By the time Zev was done talking, the ropes were loose and Brian was able to stand. Zev helped him up, knowing the man's legs would be shaky. Once Brian was sitting down at the kitchen table, Zev sat across from him and appraised the situation.

Brian was looking down, clearly ashamed and scared. He had his head tilted to the side, leaving his neck exposed, showing his submission. Well, at least some things had improved over the years.

"Look at me, Brian," Zev ordered.

The shifter raised his eyes and looked at his Alpha.

"Did you hear what I said? I need to know where your loyalty lies."

Brian didn't hesitate.

"With you, Alpha. My loyalty is to this pack. I didn't mean for any of this to happen. I swear."

Toby snorted, and Zev turned to glare at him. Toby raised his hands in surrender and sat down quietly. Lori settled on her husband's lap and watched Zev work.

"That's good, Brian. That's real good. You know our pack is only as strong as its weakest member. I need you to tell me what you've gotten yourself into here. That's the only way for me to help you and take care of our pack."

Brian nodded, twisted his hands together, and bit his lip. He looked at Lori with longing and then moved his gaze down to the table. This sad, meek version of Brian was a far cry from the arrogant loudmouth Zev had grown up with. When he looked at Brian now, Zev felt only pity.

"I got a call from my father's cousin last night. He said there was a human coming to see Leah Harrison, and he wanted me to keep an eye out for him."

Toby's head snapped up as soon as he heard his mother's name. A growl rumbled in his chest, but he managed to keep his mouth shut.

"Keep an eye out for him? That's it?" Zev asked carefully.

Brian's neck heated up.

"Well, he asked me to watch for him, and when I saw him, I was supposed to, uh, get a hold of him and keep him until Jimmy got here." Brian swallowed hard.

Hearing about a shifter trying to trap a human engaged all of Zev's protective instincts and made him want to lash out, but he kept his feelings in check for the moment. He needed more information and scaring Brian wouldn't get him anywhere on that front.

"Jimmy's your dad's cousin?"

"Uh-huh." Brian nodded.

"And what does he want with the human?"

"I don't know, Alpha. The guy's a little off. He's always been kind of an extremist, and he has a real issue with humans. More than usual, I mean."

For Brian to say those words meant this Jimmy was flat-out dangerous. It wasn't unusual for shifters to look down on humans or avoid them, but the Etzgadol pack was more tolerant than others, even more so in recent years as a result of Zev's leadership. Yet, despite being part of their pack, Brian was one of those shifters who clung to the old ways, refusing to engage in any interaction with humans unless it was absolutely necessary. The bottom line was that, in their pack, Brian was an extremist. So if Jimmy was worse, that could mean real trouble.

"Okay, so what happened? He asked you to grab the human and then what?"

"I refused." Brian looked up at Zev, clearly hoping his leader believed him. "I promise, Alpha, I said I wouldn't do it. I'm happy here. And even though I've never understood it, I know you always want to protect the humans. I remember how pissed you'd get in school whenever we gave them a hard time, and I didn't want any trouble with you. So when my cousin asked for help going after a human, I said no."

Zev nodded, letting his pride show in his eyes. Brian needed to know he'd made the right choice, even if things deteriorated at some point. And Zev needed Brian to keep talking so he'd understand exactly what had happened. The shifter seemed to gather courage from his Alpha's approval, so he kept telling the story.

"When I said no, he got all pissed off at me. Told me I was supposed to help my family. Then when guilt didn't work, he offered me money, but..." Brian laughed ruefully. "It's not like I need anything. I mean, look at my house." He waved his arms around the clean, modern space. "I never imagined living in a place this nice. I know it's because of you, because of what you've done for our pack. And I didn't want to let you down."

Brian took a deep breath and then continued. "Then, today, Jimmy called again, and this time he said he had Lori. He...he knows how I feel about her, and he said he'd give her to me unharmed if I did him one favor; all I had to do was get the Harrisons out of their house."

Brian looked at Zev and then at Lori and Toby, willing them to understand his plight.

"I didn't think he'd really hurt her, but like I said, he's not all there, and I couldn't take the chance, not with Lori. So I said I'd do it. It's not like it was all that hard anyway, 'cause Jeremiah was already out, so I just called Leah and told her that I ran into Lori in Summerberg and her car was broken down, but I couldn't fit the kids on my bike so she asked me to let Leah know 'cause she has that big van for carting the kids around. I figured with an hour's drive each way, Leah would be gone long enough for Jimmy to do whatever he had planned."

"Damn it, Brian!" Toby finally lost his temper, the combination of his injured wife, the risk to his children, and the manipulation of his mother clearly more than he could take. "You should have called Zev. You can't just run off half-cocked. If people are making threats, forcing you to lie to your pack, you call your Alpha."

"I know. I know." Brian buried his face in his hands. "I get that now, I do. But at the time I just wanted to get Lori away from Jimmy, and I thought that was the fastest way to do it."

Zev sighed. Brian was an idiot, but he was a well-meaning idiot. Zev would never truly like the guy, but he believed Brian's story, believed he was a committed member of the pack, and believed that his long-standing crush on Lori combined with his subpar decision-making skills were the only reasons he'd participated in...whatever the hell had gone down that morning.

"I believe you, Brian. It was the wrong decision, and I expect you to come to me first thing if anything like this ever happens again, but I believe you."

Brian's posture visibly softened, tension flowing out of his body.

"All right, here's what we're going to do," Zev said as he looked at the three people gathered around him. "Toby and Lori will take my truck and go see Doc Carlson." Zev held up a hand before he'd even finished the sentence. "I know you're fine, Lori, but you're going to humor me here and go see Doc. If nothing else, it'll help Toby relearn the ability to breathe. The man has been functioning without oxygen since he found you missing, and pretty soon that'll impact his already frighteningly weak brain. I have real concerns that if he loses any more brain cells, he'll turn into one of those yahoos who takes pictures of himself pretending to copulate with inanimate objects and then shows them to his friends." Zev faked a shudder. "Nobody wants that."

Lori grumbled and frowned, but she didn't argue. Toby just flipped Zev off, his expression remaining completely unchanged.

"I'll borrow Brian's bike and head on over to the Harrisons' place. I need to see what this Jimmy fool and his goons are up to over there and make sure they don't hurt anyone else, including that human." Zev rubbed his palms over his eyes, wondering how a blissful day with his mate had suddenly turned into some sort of made-for-television drama.

"What should I do, Alpha?" Brian asked quietly.

"Well, for right now, I just need you to tell me whatever you know about this human," Zev answered. "What's his name? Why was he going to see the Harrisons? And what'd the human do that got your dad's cousin hot and bothered enough to violate pack law by assaulting a female and endangering her young?"

"I...I don't know. Jimmy didn't tell me any of those things."

"All right," Zev said, trying not to let his frustration come through in his voice. "What did he say? Come on, Brian, think back to the conversation. Anything you know could help."

Brian bit his lip and twisted his hands nervously.

"Umm, Jimmy's from the Miancarem pack, and I got the feeling he knows Leah from there."

"Yeah, my mom grew up in that pack," Toby confirmed.

Brian brightened suddenly and sat up straight.

"Oh, I remember now. He said something about not wanting the human to give Leah information about her sister."

"That can't be right, Brian," Lori said, her annoyance clear. "Leah doesn't have any sisters, only brothers."

Zev would have let it go, would have just given up the conversation and headed over to the Harrisons' place, but the terrified look on Toby's suddenly pale face stopped him.

"Toby? Something you want to share with the rest of the class, man? You look like you've seen a ghost."

Toby blinked a few times, swallowed hard, and then said in a cracked voice, "My mom had a sister. A twin. But she died thirty years ago. Joan was murdered."

CHAPTER 24

JONAH GOT up from the office floor and stepped over the stacks of papers he'd spent hours organizing. He needed to stretch his legs and clear his mind. All that reading and the only thing he'd learned was that shifters were shitty historians.

There were lists of names with dates of birth and death along with ancestors' and children's names, but most of the information was incomplete. Sometimes part of the name was missing, sometimes a date. Still other times, everything seemed to be in order until Jonah would come across another paper and see that a person who was listed as having two siblings shared the same parents with three other people. Plus, everything was handwritten and not always in legible penmanship. And coming from a doctor, a complaint about indecipherable handwriting was really saying something.

But the most frustrating part of the search was that Jonah hadn't found a single reference to anyone named Joan Smith. Zev had warned him that the records were thin and that there was almost no documentation about other packs. And since his mother wasn't from Etzgadol, the chance of finding anything about her in Zev's documents was very low. Still, Jonah had hoped for a better outcome.

Pacing around the room loosened Jonah's muscles. He was breathing easier, feeling a bit less frustrated, and that was when it hit him. There hadn't been a Joan Smith mentioned in the documents, but that wasn't the only name he knew. Jonah's father said his aunt was named Leah. Jonah was sure he'd seen a Leah mentioned somewhere among the papers.

He sat back down and flipped through them until he found a clue in a document at the bottom of the third stack. It was Lori's family tree. It showed her and Toby, their kids, and both sets of parents. Toby's mother was named Leah. The family tree used her married name—Leah Harrison—so there was no reference to Smith. But at least it gave Jonah an idea of where to start. He'd come across a few marriage papers, and those had listed the bride and groom's parents. Maybe he could find Leah Harrison's marriage papers, and then he'd be able to learn her maiden name.

Ten minutes later, Jonah was clutching a piece of paper that held the closest thing he'd ever had to an answer about his mother's family. Leah Harrison's maiden name was Smith. Before marrying Toby's father, she'd been Leah Smith. Sure, it was a common name, and there were probably tons of Leah Smiths out there. But it was a start, and it was the only lead he had at the moment. Besides, there was no harm in going over to the Harrisons' place and saying hello, maybe asking a few questions, dropping a name.

With that decision made, Jonah found the Harrisons' address in the phone book and left a note telling Zev where he was going in case his lover beat him home. Then he headed over to the Harrisons' house, hoping to find some information about his mother.

Jonah had left Etzgadol a dozen years prior and he'd spent those years in a highly populated metropolitan city, surrounded by bumper-to-bumper traffic, foul-smelling smog, and buildings so tall and condensed that it was sometimes hard to see the sky. Being back in the forest, inhaling the bouquet of fresh air and trees, seeing the bright blue sky, and hearing the sounds of birds chattering all around him—all those things made Jonah wonder how he'd ever survived all that time away from the place that was unquestionably his home. All the reasons his eighteen-year-old self had had for wanting to escape the small town—the slow pace, the simple lifestyle, the quiet surroundings—now sounded like a slice of heaven.

The rocky road curved and led a smiling, happy Jonah to a barn-red farmhouse. He found himself whistling as he pulled his car up next to a nondescript white sedan. The sun was setting in the sky, covering everything in a hazy, orange glow. It was beautiful.

Had he ever felt so fulfilled and whole? He didn't think so. He knew it wasn't really the location that had settled his once restless body and cloudy mind; it was Zev. Being with his boyfriend, no, his mate had put Jonah at peace.

He got out of the car and started walking toward the front door, wondering if it really mattered what he would learn from the people inside. Yes, Jonah was curious about his heritage, curious about how he could suddenly turn into a canine, and curious about why this new ability was, according to Zev, a complete contradiction to how things usually worked for shifters. But at the end of the day, the curiosity just seemed idle now. With the fear over losing his mind gone and the deep connection he'd always felt with Zev cemented, Jonah realized that even if he never understood the why and the how of his birth, he'd still be happy with his life.

"Maybe I should just turn around and go home." He smiled at how quickly he thought of Zev's cabin as home.

Of course his mate had built the space for them both to share, even showing Jonah the plans during his visits and insisting that they confirm the layout and choose fixtures and furniture together. So, yeah, the cabin was home, their home. Before Jonah could make a final decision about whether or not he should stay at Leah Harrison's house, a noise caught his attention and sent a shiver of unease down his spine.

He looked around and didn't see anyone, but he could still hear sounds. He stood still and cocked his head until he heard the sounds again and determined that they were coming from the side of the house. Zev had mentioned the whole heightened-senses thing during the previous day's impromptu Shifter 101 tutorial, but actually experiencing it was a bit of a shock. Shocking or not, Jonah thought it was pretty cool. He felt a bit like a superhero with special powers.

He smiled at the thought of himself wearing tights and a cape as he walked toward the strange sounds. Jonah's light, happy feeling vanished in response to the sight that greeted him as soon as he rounded the corner of the Harrisons' house and stepped into the shadowy side yard.

His father was slumped on the ground, surrounded by four large men. Jonah could see his father's chest moving up and down, and the knowledge that the man was still breathing went a long way in easing his panic.

The situation got infinitely worse when one of the men towering over Kevin Marvel's body bent down, hooked beefy arms around his chest, and began dragging the unconscious man toward a large SUV that was parked nearby. Everything Jonah had ever heard on television said getting into a car with a kidnapper was a sure recipe for defeat. He couldn't let these dangerous men put his father in their vehicle, but his chances of overpowering four men by himself were pretty slim. But whatever the odds, Jonah didn't have a choice; he had to step in.

"Hey!" Jonah shouted, hoping the knowledge that someone else was there would be enough to scare the men away. "What're you doing to him? Let him go!"

He walked toward the men as he spoke, getting closer to his unconscious father with every word. Unfortunately, he didn't get close enough to do much good. As soon as they heard his voice, the four men stopped their walk toward the car and jerked their heads over to look at Jonah.

"Well, look at that. Guess the human wasn't traveling alone," the biggest, meanest-looking of the men said. "Chuck, get that one too. We'll take them both with us."

One of the men in the group broke away and walked up to Jonah, clearly intending to follow his leader's order. But this wasn't Jonah's first rodeo, and he knew that if he could face off against the men one at a time, he stood a good chance of defeating them. As soon as Chuck, the man sent to retrieve Jonah, was within reach, Jonah clenched his fist and took a swing. His powerful right hook connected with Chuck's jaw and the man fell to the ground, looking dazed.

The other three men growled, obviously surprised and angry at that unexpected defeat of their comrade. They left Kevin Marvel on the ground and marched toward Jonah. Unfortunately, it seemed that his plan of dealing with the men individually wasn't going to come to fruition. On the plus side, however, his father was no longer being carted toward the vehicle. Of course, Kevin's freedom would be just a brief respite if Jonah couldn't scare off the men or at least slow them down enough to get his father out of there.

He tried to think through the situation. Was there any strategy that would allow him to get his father into the car and away from that yard? Was there anything lying around that he could use as a weapon? Neither question inspired a useful answer, and Jonah's stomach clenched with worry.

Just as the three oafish bodies were getting uncomfortably close, a dark figure seemingly flew through the air and knocked one of them to the ground. Jonah saw the tall, strong body and long, flowing black hair, and felt a hint of recognition. He didn't have a chance to think too much on it, though, because seconds later, a brown wolf darted out of the forest and jumped on one of the other men, wrestling him down.

Everyone seemed startled by the unexpected visitors, and for a few seconds, everything froze. Then mass chaos exploded. The hulking man Jonah had hit was still on the ground, but the action around him seemed to have snapped him to attention, because he suddenly began removing his clothes with a speed that reeked of desperation. The two men who'd been taken down tried to do the same while defending themselves against the brown wolf and the incredibly strong black-haired warrior. And the leader of the ruffians took in the scene with wide eyes, momentarily distracted by the unexpected attack on his gang.

Jonah had no doubt the distraction wouldn't last long and he wanted to take advantage of the situation by going after the mean-looking thug. That was when he saw the man on the ground begin awkwardly changing into a wolf. Jonah wondered why the shifting process he was witnessing looked so much less fluid than what he'd experienced, or, for that matter, why he was witnessing it at all. He'd shifted into a wolf and then back into a human twice, and the changes had been so seamless that the first time he hadn't even been aware it had happened and the second was done in the blink of an eye. Of course, both times his body had been following Zev's, acting on instinct rather than changing forms on his own. Still, the writhing man on the ground seemed to be going through a completely different process, one that was uncomfortable at best and painful at worst.

Now was not the time to ask questions. He was dealing with shifters rather than humans, as he'd originally thought. Beating a man in a fistfight was one thing, and even if he had to go up against the two men who weren't currently being occupied by the brown wolf and the dark-haired man, he might have stood a chance. But these were shifters, not humans, and once they changed into their wolf forms, they'd have claws and fangs, thereby becoming significantly more dangerous.

Jonah's best odds against them would be to fight as a wolf, rather than as a man. He thought about what Zev had taught him about shifting. He visualized his wolf, tried to reach the animal and talk him into taking over their body. But no matter how hard he concentrated, Jonah couldn't shift.

Zev. He needed Zev. Just like the night before, Jonah wasn't able to uncage his wolf on his own, and though he didn't understand why, he knew his mate was his only hope of drawing out his animal form.

When the man on the ground finally completed the oddly lengthy and wince-inducing change, he looked straight at Jonah. Seeing that vicious glare coming from the massive wolf made Jonah realize his time was almost up. He clenched his fists and held his head high. Whatever else happened, he wouldn't go down without a fight.

CHAPTER 25

WITH DUSK already settled around him, Zev sped through the familiar streets and prayed that he'd get to the Harrisons' place in time to stop the rogue shifters from hurting Jonah's father. He had no doubt that was who the endangered human was. After all, Jonah had said his father was trying to track down his aunt. Well, it looked like Kevin Marvel had succeeded in locating Leah's address. Now Zev had to save the man from having his persistence rewarded with violence from a group of unstable shifters.

As he navigated the motorcycle toward the Harrisons' house, Zev wondered why Lori hadn't known that Leah Harrison had had a sister. There was no way Toby and his family had inadvertently forgotten to mention a murdered aunt. That kind of crime in a shifter community was extremely rare, and for the victim to be a female, and a pregnant one at that, was unheard of. But why would Leah withhold that information? Did she know that Jonah was her nephew? And if so, why was she hiding that knowledge?

Zev's mental ponderings were interrupted by a cry for help. He could hear Jonah calling from within his own head, their mental link providing a source of communication almost as strong as verbal conversation. He sensed frustration and fear from his mate, which immediately brought his own hackles up. Jonah was in danger.

Suddenly, Zev felt his wolf coming to the surface, responding to his mate's call. Jonah's wolf wanted to be released, but for some reason he couldn't shift on his own. It was the same unexplained issue that had plagued Jonah when he'd tried to shift the prior night.

Zev came to a skidding stop and leaped off the bike. He ran through the woods, knowing that the rest of the trip would have to be on foot. There was no way for a wolf to operate a motorcycle, so Zev shifted as soon as his human body left the bike.

His mate seemed unable to shift independently. So far, Jonah's wolf had managed to surface only by using the connection between them. So Zev had shifted, hoping that, despite being in a different physical space from Jonah, the open communication link between them would be enough to inspire Jonah's wolf.

Though it likely took only minutes, Zev's run through the forest seemed interminably long. When he reached the Harrisons' place, he followed Jonah's scent and dashed around the side of the house, ready to destroy anyone threatening his mate. But in typical Jonah fashion, the man already had the situation handled. Though from the look of things, he had had some help.

A striking man with hair as black as night held a half-naked shifter by the neck. At first scent, Zev identified the handsome man as a bloodsucker. He gave himself an internal reprimand for thinking that derogatory term. Vampire. The man was a vampire.

Zev looked at the sky. The sun had set, but there was still residual light around them. Because of their inherent allergy to the sun, it was highly unusual to see a vampire out before all traces of light were gone from the sky. Just as unusual was seeing one of their kind on pack lands.

There was something different about this vampire's scent, Zev realized. It seemed to be twined with the scent of a shifter. And finding that very shifter was easy because the same combined shifter-vampire scent resided in the body of a small brown wolf who, at that moment, had his sharp teeth clamped over another partially dressed shifter's throat. It seemed that the two thugs who were being held by the vampire and the brown wolf had tried to shift, but then given up when they realized they were overpowered.

Zev became distracted from his confusion over the vampire and brown wolf by another wolf with fur as white as snow. Jonah's beautiful wolf stood over a third shifter, who was in the process of changing back into his human form, his body limp with submission. And the fourth goon, who Zev identified by scent as Brian's cousin, was trapped in the middle of the group, his eyes darting around, trying to chart an escape. Well, it looked like things were well under control.

Zev shifted back into his human form and noted that Jonah's change mirrored his own, just as it had the previous two times his mate had shifted. He gave himself permission to steal an admiring glance at Jonah's gorgeous, gloriously nude body, then forced his eyes away from the arousing sight and glared at the good-for-nothing shifters who'd attacked his sister.

"You're not so tough when the odds are closer to even, are you? Turns out taking on three males isn't as easy as overpowering a pregnant female. Not that I can understand why any shifter would do such a thing," Zev said, causing all eyes to turn toward him.

Jimmy stiffened and his eyes widened with fear when he saw Zev and heard his words. The other three members of Jimmy's gang also tensed briefly, but then their postures slumped and whatever fight they still had left their bodies. One of the men turned his head toward Zev but didn't make eye contact, attempting to show his submission and respect to Zev's more powerful wolf.

"We had no idea he was going to kill her. He said we were just going to get her away from the human and take her back to the pack," the shifter closest to Jonah said. "She'd stopped attending pack functions and nobody had seen her in months. When word got out that she was shacking up with a human, we knew we had to save her. We couldn't let her soil herself that way."

Zev realized that his comment about overpowering a pregnant female had been misconstrued to be a reference to Joan Smith. Well, it looked like he'd confirmed that these were the shifters responsible for murdering Jonah's mother.

"Let me get this straight: you didn't like who she chose to sleep with, so you killed her? And now you're saying that you were, what, doing her some kind of favor?" Jonah said incredulously.

"Shut up, Harry! Just shut the fuck up!" Jimmy shouted. His voice shook, betraying his continued anxiety.

"No, you shut up!" one of the other shifters yelled at Jimmy. "You're the one who got us into this mess, and I'm done listening to you! It's over now!" The man's voice actually seemed to soften, and he almost sounded relieved as he finished speaking. "It's over. I'm telling them what happened, and I'll face the consequences. I'm tired of always looking over my shoulder, tired of hearing her screams in my head."

But before the clearly weary shifter could say anything further, Harry started talking again.

"We thought it'd be easy. We'd go in, grab Joan, and leave. It's not like a human and a female could put up any real fight. We didn't think anyone would be hurt. But when we saw Joan, we realized how much worse things were than we'd realized. She was pregnant. She ran out of the room and Jimmy chased her. Chuck, Walter, and I were standing there, trying to figure out what to do. Then we heard a door slam. After that, there was banging and screaming." He swallowed hard, clearly struggling to continue. "By the time we got to the bedroom, it was too late. Jimmy had broken the door down and torn her apart. It was like he was rabid or something; we couldn't get him under control. Then we heard a car pulling up, and that seemed to snap him out of it. We all ran out of there."

"And we've been running ever since, at least in our minds," the third shifter said, finishing up the story. "We were constantly afraid someone would find out what we'd done. And when the human came back around, asking questions about Joan, we thought he'd figured out who we were. Jimmy said there was only one way to stop him, so we came here, but then it all blew up in our faces." He rubbed his eyes, looking exhausted to his core. "Enough's enough. Like Chuck said, it's over."

Everyone was reeling from the revelations, and Jimmy took their momentary distraction as an opportunity to make a run for it. He had almost managed to reach the car before Zev realized what was going on. But before Zev could do anything to stop the escape, Jonah had pounced on Jimmy and knocked the bastard out with one punch.

Zev felt absurdly proud of his mate. He knew that he was supposed to protect Jonah and shield his mate from danger. But, damn, Jonah's strength made Zev's blood run hot.

Zev had been raised to believe an Alpha would naturally be attracted to a submissive person, one who relied on him to stay safe and who innately recognized and acknowledged his position as the leader in all things, their relationship included. But Zev found that he greatly preferred what he actually had: an independent mate who could hold his own in any situation and would go toe to toe with Zev if warranted.

Jonah was no weakling, not in body, mind, or spirit, and Zev wouldn't change that for the world.

After calling a handful of men over to the Harrisons' and ordering them to detain the hateful thugs who had murdered Jonah's mother, Zev helped Jonah load his still unconscious father into the backseat of the car. Zev got behind the wheel, and Jonah climbed in with his father.

"Is he going to be okay?" Zev darted his eyes to the rearview mirror and back as he asked the question.

"I think so." Jonah glanced down at his lap, where his father's head was resting. "His vitals are strong, his breathing's even. Now he just needs to wake up."

"Why hasn't he done that? Do you think they drugged him?"

"It's possible, but I don't think so. The swelling on the back of his head makes me think that they managed to knock him out with a blow to the head. Again." Jonah sighed.

Zev hated how broken Jonah sounded. It had been a day full of upheaval, and Zev wanted nothing more than to scoop his mate up and lock them away in their cabin, where they could find comfort in each other. But there was still more to do before they could rest. He pulled over to the side of the road where he'd left Brian's motorcycle and his own clothes, dashing out of the car and getting dressed as quickly as possible.

"Sorry about that. I don't think they'd appreciate having a naked guy walk into the hospital," Zev said when he got back into the car and started driving.

Jonah cracked up.

"I didn't even think about that. Fuckin' A, Zev. If I'm too distracted to notice your fine self in the raw, then the situation must be truly dire."

"This day has been for shit, but I think we've got the situation under control. And no worries, as soon as we get your dad checked out, I'll make it my personal mission to make sure you know where to put your priorities."

"Oh, yeah? And where would that be, Hassick?"

Zev swore he could hear the leer in Jonah's voice.

"On my dick," he answered, deadpan.

"Works for me, Pup. Definitely works for me." Jonah's voice dropped off. He sounded completely exhausted.

"Go ahead and rest, Blondie. I need to make some calls anyway. I'll wake you up when we get to the hospital."

He looked into the rearview mirror and saw his mate nodding, then tipping his head back and resting it against the seat. All right, it was time to deal with the ne'er-do-well shifters they'd apprehended. Zev fished his cell phone out of his pocket and dialed the Alpha of the Miancarem pack. He didn't know the man well, but they'd met several times over the years at interpack meetings.

Dirk Keller had always struck Zev as being a fairly strong and decent leader, but the man was definitely a traditionalist. He'd never supported Zev's pushes for the packs to move toward a more egalitarian organizational structure, though he hadn't actively opposed the idea, either. In any event, Zev knew Dirk would be appalled and horrified by the news that four members of the Miancarem pack had butchered one of their own females and then hidden the crime for decades. Deciding this was definitely not the type of news that should be communicated over the phone, Zev told Dirk that he was holding the four men and he needed Dirk to come collect them in person, along with reinforcements. The other Alpha was taken aback by the demand and briefly tried to get more information, but he didn't push too hard.

Despite the years of working with, and sometimes even befriending, other pack Alphas, the men had always kept a slight distance from Zev. He was well liked and highly respected, but every other Alpha knew that Zev stood a good chance of winning in a challenge, and nobody wanted to upset the powerful young Alpha enough to instigate such a situation. Well, the hint of fear seemed to work in Zev's favor this time, because after a phone call that lasted less than five minutes, he had assurances that Dirk would be in Etzgadol by morning along with five of his best men.

The crimes Jimmy and his crew had committed would need to be addressed by the interpack council leader. Normally, Alphas had jurisdiction over pack discipline, but this situation fell way beyond a bar brawl or property dispute. Although the Alpha of the members responsible for the crimes would likely be consulted about their punishment, the ultimate decision would have to be made by the council itself. Rather than calling the interpack council leader directly, though, Zev decided to wait until the following day so he could give Dirk the opportunity to participate in the call.

Just as they pulled into the hospital's parking lot, Zev heard a moan from the backseat, followed immediately by Jonah's concerned voice.

"Dad? Can you hear me?"

"Jonah?" Kevin Marvel's voice sounded hoarse and weak. "Where am I? What're you doing here?"

"Shh. You're fine. We're at the Etzgadol City Hospital. You, um..." Jonah paused briefly before continuing. "You hit your head and passed out. Do you remember what happened?"

Kevin shook his head, then moaned again and kept still.

"No. I think I found your aunt, and, you won't believe this, but it turns out she lives right here in Etzgadol. I remember walking up to her house, and then I woke up here. Maybe I fell. I haven't been getting much sleep."

"Well, you can rest now. I think you might have a concussion, maybe slight dehydration. We'll get you admitted and make sure everything's okay." Jonah kissed his father's head. "Thank you for finding her, Dad. I have a feeling everything's going to be okay from now on."

CHAPTER 26

TWO HOURS later, Jonah fought to keep his eyes open as they drove over bumpy roads into the part of the forest where Zev had built their home. "I'm so damn tired. Working a triple shift in the hospital has nothing on this day." He leaned his head against the window and wondered when he'd managed to gain ten pounds in each eyelid. They were too heavy to keep open, so he gave up and closed his eyes. A large, strong hand squeezed his knee, then rubbed up and down his thigh.

"Emotional upheaval can take its toll. You've had a lot dumped on you in a short time, Blondie. Especially today. Are you okay?"

"Yeah, I am. I really am." Jonah nodded. "It's a lot, but then it isn't, you know? My dad will be fine in a few days. They'll monitor him, pump him full of fluids, and make him rest, and then he'll be back to normal. It sounds like there's finally going to be justice for my mother. And I'm here with you. Not just for a couple of stolen days, but for good." He scooted closer to the driver's seat and rested his head on Zev's shoulder. "So, yeah, I'm okay."

They completed the drive in comfortable silence, and Jonah even managed to drift off. He woke up when he heard Zev growl.

"Shit. Will this fuckin' day never end?"

Jonah sat up quickly and looked around. "What?" They'd pulled into their driveway, right next to an unfamiliar truck. "Whose truck is that?"

"My father's." Zev sighed. "I was hoping to do this after we rested and figured out everything with your mother and all that, but I guess there's no time like the present. Ready to meet the family, Blondie?"

"Oh, come on. It's not that bad. I've met your dad lots of times. We don't need to tell him anything's going on between us right now." After a dozen years feeling resentful that Zev hadn't told his family about the nature of their relationship, Jonah surprised himself with his own suggestion. "He knows we're friends, so it shouldn't be a total shock to see me here."

"Doesn't work that way," Zev said as he shook his head. "We're true mates. I told you about the scents. Ours have joined together. My dad'll know who you are to me as soon as he smells us." He took Jonah's hand in his. "Besides, I won't hide you, Blondie. I've hated doing it all these years, but I had to. Now that we have proof of what we are to each other, I'm done pretending. I'll never deny you again, Jonah. Not ever."

Okay, yeah, that was romantic as hell, and it made Jonah's heart flutter. Not that he'd ever admit to having a fluttering anything. Even if it did feel good.

"Yeah, I forgot about that scent thing. But none of those guys today seemed to notice, so maybe he won't either."

"Those guys today were distracted by everything that was going on. They were too overwhelmed by their own fear to notice our scent. Besides, my dad's a hell of a lot stronger wolf than those pathetic haters."

Gregory Hassick stepped out of his truck and looked at Zev through the windshield. He tilted his head, twitched his nose, and a look of confusion washed over his face.

"Time's up, Blondie." Zev sighed. "Let's do this thing."

They got out of the car and walked over to Gregory.

"Jonah, you remember my father, Gregory Hassick. Dad, this is..."

"Your true mate." Gregory's voice shook.

"That's right. This is Jonah Marvel." Zev put his arm around Jonah's waist and pulled him close. "We've had a long day, Dad. I don't think either of us has the strength to have this conversation outside. Come on in and we can sit and talk for a few minutes." Zev walked to the front door, never releasing his grip on Jonah.

Once they got inside, both men flopped on the sofa, remaining close together. Jonah briefly considered sitting in a chair so Zev's father wouldn't be made uncomfortable by their show of affection, but he dismissed the idea right away. Why should they hide their feelings for each other? If Zev wasn't worried, Jonah sure as hell wasn't going to push the issue. He needed Zev's touch and comfort more than ever.

It took Gregory a couple of minutes to walk into the house, and when he did, he headed straight for the kitchen. "I'm getting a drink. You boys need anything?" His booming voice drifted over.

Jonah shook his head, and Zev responded for both of them.

"No, thanks. We're good, Dad."

Zev's comments that shifters believed their kind couldn't be gay had made Jonah realize they certainly weren't the most tolerant bunch around. He scoffed internally at the understatement. Shifters had killed his mother because she was sleeping with a human. Knowing their Alpha was gay had to rank even higher on their "oh, no fuckin' way" list. Thinking about whether Zev would be uncomfortable with essentially being outed to his entire community, Jonah nuzzled into Zev's neck, enjoying the feeling of the strong arms that immediately wrapped around him.

"It's amazing how your dad knew about us before we'd even said a word. This whole joined-scent thing is going to complicate things, isn't it?"

Zev combed his fingers through Jonah's hair and massaged his scalp.

"I think it'll make things easier, actually. It's irrefutable proof that you're my mate. There's no way for them to hide from it or deny it."

"No, there's no denying it." Gregory's voice interrupted their conversation. The large man walked over and sat in the armchair, looking down at the glass he held in his hand and swirling liquid that looked like Scotch. "He's a male and he's a human and he's the Alpha's mate. Mind telling me how in the hell that's possible?"

"We're still trying to figure some of this out. But, frankly, it doesn't matter. Jonah's mine and I'm his. Folks are just gonna have to deal." Zev's voice was tight. "I'm too tired to have my soul questioned, Dad. And that's who he is to me. He's my true mate, which means he's the other half of my soul."

Gregory threw his head back and emptied the glass into his mouth, swallowing the gold-colored liquid in one gulp. He set the glass down on a side table and got up.

"Well, I'd say that's just about right." He walked over to Jonah and held his hand out. Jonah took it and they shook. "Welcome to the family, Jonah." Gregory turned toward his son. "I need a night to rest on this, and then we'll celebrate. Finding your true mate is a blessing, and your family will share your joy." His voice lowered as he finished speaking. "We'll adjust, Zev. It might take a little time, but we'll adjust."

He had begun walking out of the room when he seemed to remember something. "Oh, with all of this true-mate excitement, I almost forgot the reason I dropped by. Your mother tells me that Toby asked her to get the grandkids, and that when she got to the house, Lori was gone and Toby was a mess. Care to fill me in?"

Zev sighed and rubbed his hands over his eyes. "Yeah, I will, but not right now, okay? Lori's fine. Toby's fine. The kids are fine. But it's a long, complicated story and we're beat."

Gregory nodded, raised his hand in a silent wave, and then left. Jonah and Zev stayed on the couch, their hands clasped together.

"That went better than I thought it would, given all your warnings over the years," Jonah said.

"Well, now that we've tied together and completed the mating bond, there's no way for him to keep burying his head in the sand." Zev shrugged. "Gay is unheard of in our community, Blondie, and so is mating with humans. But the bond between true mates is revered. He smelled that bond and knew he'd have to set everything else aside."

Jonah nodded in understanding. Sure, there were still a lot of questions left unanswered, but so many things he'd wondered about over the years made sense now. Zev's unwillingness to have intercourse had seemed like an old-fashioned notion, but now Jonah realized that sex would have included the tying that a wolf shared with his mate, an act that changed them both forever. Waiting had been in turn frustrating and physically debilitating, but they were both better for it.

Zev was the respected leader of his pack and the head of what was an increasingly successful family business. And Jonah had gotten his medical degree and seen a world outside their small town. With his urge to experience new places and meet new people sated, Jonah felt right coming home to Etzgadol and settling down. Especially now that he realized there was a wolf living inside him.

"Your dad seemed as confused about me being human as he was about me being a guy. Why didn't you tell him that I'm a shifter too? Maybe it would've helped make him feel better."

Zev dropped his head onto Jonah's shoulder. "Yeah, it'll make him feel more comfortable about our mating, but it'll also raise a lot of questions that we can't answer. And right now, I'm not in the mood to get into it. Besides, whether he feels comfortable or not isn't going to change a thing. I meant what I said, Blondie—you're mine. Being with you comes above everything and everyone else."

Jonah rubbed his cheek over Zev's head and squeezed his hand.

"I feel the same way. But being together and putting each other first doesn't mean we have to forget other people, especially family. Your dad seems like a good guy, Pup. He was really great tonight."

"Yeah, he was," Zev agreed. He squeezed Jonah's hand, stood, and pulled Jonah off the couch too. "You hungry?"

Jonah nodded. They walked into the kitchen and quickly made sandwiches, then stood at the counter as they ate.

When they finished, Zev took their dishes to the sink and then tugged Jonah into an embrace. "'S bed time. Tomorrow's another busy day, and we need to get some rest."

After a quick stop in the bathroom, they stripped off their clothes and crawled into bed, immediately finding their way into each other's arms.

"Mmm. You smell so good, Pup." Jonah sniffed and nuzzled Zev's neck. It wasn't long before the nuzzling turned to licking and sucking. "Taste good too."

"I would have sworn I was too tired to get it up, but you're a potent aphrodisiac." He rolled on top of Jonah, pinned his wrists to the bed, and moved his neck out of reach of Jonah's mouth.

"Why'd you move away?" Jonah whimpered at the loss and looked at Zev in confusion.

"'Cause you were poking a bear there, Blondie."

"I thought you were a wolf." Jonah smirked.

"Very funny. I know you're too tired to get into anything tonight, but if you keep kissing me and moaning like that, I won't be able to hold myself back from ravishing you."

"You never have to hold back those kinds of instincts, Pup." Jonah arched his back and pushed his hard cock against Zev's hip. "I promise that I'm right there with you. But if you're worried about me overexerting myself, I'm happy to just lie back and let you do all the work." He wiggled a little, settling himself on the bed. "All right. I'll stay right here and you come on up. I want to taste you."

Zev cocked one eyebrow. "You sure you're up for this? I know it's been a really long day."

"I think I already proved that I was up. Quit being an old lady and come shove that thick dick down my throat. And no holding back, Pup. If I'm still able to talk when you're done, then you didn't do it right. Got it?"

A smile spread over Zev's face. "I adore you."

"Because of my charming wit?" Jonah joked.

"Among other things." He dropped a soft kiss onto Jonah's lips. "You're strong, smart, handsome, and funny as hell."

"Uh-huh. That's nice. Now fuck my mouth."

"Yes, sir," Zev said with a laugh. He released his grip on Jonah's wrists, straddled his body, and knee-walked up the bed until he knelt over Jonah's chest.

Jonah raised his head, tried to catch a swipe of Zev's dick with his tongue, and then grumbled when he couldn't reach. He flung one hand up and smacked Zev's ass.

"Hey! What was that for?"

"Seems like you forgot who's in charge of this operation. Stop teasing me and get that dick over here."

"Oh, I know who's in charge, Blondie."

Before Jonah could argue or come up with another smart remark, Zev followed his instructions. One more step forward put Zev's knees on either side of Jonah's head. He threaded his fingers through Jonah's hair, cupped the back of his head, and then slowly slipped his dick into Jonah's waiting mouth.

"Oh, damn. Feels good."

Jonah worked Zev with his tongue, swiping back and forth over his glans and then sucking hard, all the while moaning and whimpering, his arousal too high to keep inside.

"Those noises make me crazy." Zev pumped his hips until his balls rested on Jonah's chin. "Your mouth is amazing, Blondie. I swear you were made to suck my cock." He pulled out so Jonah could get some air into his lungs, then plunged back in. "Can't be gentle." He increased his pace, plowing into Jonah's mouth. "It's too good." His motions became progressively more brutal as he pushed himself deep into Jonah's throat, pulled out, and then drove back in again. "Is this what you wanted?" he asked in a rough voice as his hips snapped, his cock moving in and out even faster. "You like this, Blondie? Like feeling me take you?"

A muffled shout was Jonah's only response.

"I can feel that noise. Damn, Blondie." Zev pushed deep inside Jonah's mouth, held his head still, and shot down his throat. He shook for several long moments before moving off Jonah and sitting down on the bed.

Jonah lay on his back, gasping for air.

"I didn't hurt you, did I, Blondie?" He pulled Jonah's head onto his lap and swiped his thumbs over Jonah's cheeks. "You're crying."

Jonah opened his mouth but only a rough sound came out. He shook his head and cleared his throat. "That's exactly what I asked for, Pup." His voice sounded like it was being dragged over gravel, but he managed to smile. "And I think this confirms how much I liked it." He pointed at his cum-coated belly.

"I aim to please." Zev grinned and rubbed his thumb over Jonah's mouth. "No more talking, 'kay? I think your throat's a little sensitive right now."

Jonah closed his eyes and sighed contentedly. "That was fuckin' awesome. Glad I've got a man who can deliver the goods."

CHAPTER 27

"Your dad looked pretty good, don't you think?" Zev asked as he drove down the familiar roads leading to their cabin.

"Yeah, he definitely did. The attending doctor told me they were keeping him for another couple of days because of the exhaustion and dehydration, not the concussion." Jonah raked his fingers through his hair. "As soon as he feels better, I'm going to let him have it. I don't know what he was thinking, driving himself that hard. I think he hadn't slept in days."

Zev reached across the front seat of the truck and squeezed his mate's arm.

"I'm pretty sure he was thinking you were a mess and he needed to find a way to help you. Sounds like a pretty good dad thing to do, if you ask me."

Jonah didn't respond, he just grumbled quietly.

"I'll take that as a sign of agreement. In fact, I believe those little grumbles actually translate into, 'Oh, you're absolutely right, Zev. You're the most brilliant, perceptive man I've ever met. Thank you so much for gracing me with your infinite wisdom.'"

One side of Jonah's mouth turned up. "Was that supposed to be an impression of me? Because I'm pretty sure I don't sound like a cross between a woman and a hyena."

Zev laughed, but he didn't have a chance to launch a defense, because just then they turned into their driveway and saw Leah Harrison's car parked under their carport. Leah was standing next to the car along with the black-haired vampire Zev had seen the previous day, and a small, brown-haired shifter who Zev quickly realized was the human form of the brown wolf who had helped Jonah in the fight with Jimmy and his gang.

"You ready to meet your aunt, Blondie?" Zev asked, pulling in next to Leah's car and turning off the truck's ignition.

"Yeah, I am. Not for the same reasons I had before, 'cause I don't feel like I'm crawling out of my skin anymore, but... yeah, I wanna meet her." Jonah turned to Zev. "Do you think she knows who I am, Pup? Do you think she's always known?"

Zev took a moment to think about Leah. They weren't contemporaries, but he knew the woman fairly well. He'd spent a lot of time with Toby as a youth, and even more since he and Lori had gotten married. So, yeah, he felt like he knew Leah Harrison. And what he knew, he admired.

"Yes, I think she knows." He nodded. "I think she's probably always known."

"Then why didn't she ever say anything? All those years she saw me at soccer games, baseball games, school carnivals. Why didn't she tell me?" Jonah's frustration came through in his voice.

"That's not a question I can answer, Blondie. But it looks like you have your chance to find out. Come on, let's get out of this truck and get some answers."

Zev stepped out of the truck and walked over to Leah, noticing that Jonah was heading straight for the front door. He didn't know whether his mate was anxious about finally meeting a maternal relative, or whether Jonah was upset with Leah for keeping her connection to Joan Smith under wraps for all these years. Well, either way, he knew that his mate just needed a few moments to pull himself together, and then the man's natural curiosity would come to the forefront, motivating Jonah to talk with Leah. In the meantime, Zev would just have to get everyone inside and settled. That should buy Jonah enough time to get his emotions under control.

"Sorry to keep you all waiting. We didn't realize you'd be coming by this morning, and we needed to go into town to check on Jonah's father."

"That's all right, Alpha. I know you weren't expecting us and that you've probably got a lot going on today, but I hoped you could spare a few minutes." Leah's voice shook slightly as she spoke. Zev had never heard the strong female sound frightened. Leah Harrison was usually a force to be reckoned with. It was one of the things Zev had always admired about her and a big reason why he had always supported his sister's relationship with Toby Harrison. He'd figured a man with Leah for a mother would treat his wife like an equal, something that couldn't be said for a lot of shifters. Though he certainly hoped strides were being made in that direction, at least in his pack.

"It's always nice to see you, Leah," Zev said as he pulled the female in for a brief hug. "You know you're always welcome here." When he looked up, he noticed that the two males hadn't moved from the car. They'd also been completely quiet, just as they had during their brief encounter the previous day. Plus, the vampire was once again out during the day. Yes, he was standing in the shade. But shade wasn't night. "What's the deal with them?" Zev asked Leah, tipping his head toward the males.

Leah immediately stiffened and raised her chin, a determined glint in her eye.

"They're with me. That's their deal. Is that going to be a problem, Alpha?"

Zev was taken aback by the angry, defensive tone. He shook his head and spoke slowly, carefully measuring each word. "It's not a problem, Leah. But I'd like to go inside, maybe get a drink and something to eat. Don't your guests want to join us?"

Leah looked truly surprised by that response. "They can come into your house?"

Zev smiled and nodded. "Of course they can come in." He walked over to the two males and held his hand out. "Zev Hassick. Welcome to the Etzgadol pack. I'm grateful for your assistance yesterday. My mate was in danger, and from what he tells me, it could have been very serious if you two hadn't jumped in."

From the looks on their faces, the two males were just as surprised by Zev's polite behavior as Leah had been. The shifter stepped forward. He cleared his throat, blinked away tears from his coal-black eyes, and held out his hand, putting it into Zev's and shaking it.

"It was our honor, Alpha. We only wish we could have been there sooner. I'm Ethan, and this is my mate, Miguel."

It seemed as if the small shifter held his breath after that introduction. And the vampire, Miguel, had his arms hanging by his sides and his hands clenched in fists, as if he were primed for a fight. Hearing that the two men were mates was a surprise. Of course, Zev had smelled their interwoven scents the previous day, and there was only one possible explanation for that phenomenon. All right, then, another gay shifter, and this one was mated to a vampire who could somehow tolerate at least some vestiges of sunlight. Would wonders never cease?

"Nice to meet you guys. Let's head inside. I imagine being out here during the day is uncomfortable for Miguel, even if he is standing in the shade."

Ethan swallowed hard and nodded. "Yes, thank you, Alpha." His eyes still looked a little wet, which his mate must have realized, because the vampire immediately wrapped a long, muscular arm around Ethan and stroked his waist.

"Thanks for your hospitality..." Miguel hesitated, and Zev almost laughed. Vampires were so very different from shifters, and the whole pack structure was something completely foreign to their kind.

With all the traveling into big cities he'd done over the years, Zev had met more than his share of vampires. In the beginning, he'd made an effort to find the local coven whenever he'd arrived in a city, seeking permission to remain in their territory for a few days. But he soon realized vampires weren't like shifters—they didn't take ownership over certain areas of land, didn't have designated leaders, and most certainly didn't call anybody Alpha. He guessed it was the latter issue that was making Miguel's words stick in his throat.

"You can call me Zev, Miguel. No need for formalities. Let's head inside where you'll be more comfortable." Zev walked toward the front door. "How is it you're out before night, by the way?"

He didn't mean to be nosy, but he couldn't help but ask, since he'd previously thought vampires and daylight were a nonnegotiable don't-mix.

Miguel looked at him carefully before he answered. "I think the explanation that'll make the most sense to you would be to say that it's because of my mating bond with Ethan."

Zev hesitated. No, that didn't make sense. Then again, a shifter mating with a vampire didn't make sense either. Speaking of mates, it was time to focus on Jonah, not deviations in vampire behavior.

He reached for the front door and held it open for the visitors, pointing toward the living room.

"Go on and have a seat. What can I get you to drink?"

Leah immediately got up from the chair she'd just occupied.

"Oh, I'll take care of drinks, Alpha."

Zev shook his head and waved her back to her chair.

"Please sit down, Leah. I've got this."

Once everybody had placed their drink requests, Zev turned to leave the room and found himself looking into the coal-black eyes that were the center of his every fantasy. Just the sight of his mate made Zev's heart rate increase, his breath come faster, and his dick harden.

"You ready to join us, Blondie?" he asked quietly, putting one hand around Jonah's neck and the other on his waist. He stroked his mate's skin softly as he spoke. Jonah took a deep breath and nodded.

Zev turned back to face their guests, keeping his hand on Jonah's waist.

"Jonah, you remember Toby's mother, Leah Harrison." Zev tilted his head toward Leah. "And these two gentlemen are Ethan and Miguel."

Both men got up and walked to Jonah, but when they got within arm's reach, Ethan put his hand on Miguel's arm and stopped him. He looked up at Zev, but kept his head lowered respectfully.

"Alpha, may we approach your mate and shake his hand?"

Zev almost laughed at the formality of Ethan's request. Sure, shifters could be ass-backwards, and he knew the Etzgadol pack was more forward-thinking than most, but it had been many years since a shifter had dominion over his mate's body to such a degree. Jonah must have been just as surprised by the request, but he handled it with his usual sense of grace and decorum.

"He's my mate, not my fuckin' keeper. Now get over here and give me a hug. You boys saved my life yesterday. Don't think I don't know that." Jonah bridged the distance between himself and the two males and pulled each of them into a hug. "Hey, Zev, bring some chips or something too, would ya? I'm hungry."

Zev grinned and nodded as he walked out of the room.

"I don't know about that." It sounded to Zev like Ethan was responding to Jonah's comment. "I've never seen a shifter change forms as quickly as you did yesterday. Something tells me you would have been fine even without our help."

A deep sense of pride flowed over Zev. He'd known that his mate was a strong man, but hearing that he was also a strong wolf felt good. Jonah truly was amazing.

Zev was still in the kitchen when he got the call from the pack member he'd tasked with meeting Dirk Keller and the other males from the Miancarem pack. He put some snacks together and loaded them onto a tray along with several bottles of water and cans of soda. He'd just set the tray down on the ottoman in the living room when the doorbell rang.

"Leah, I know you wanted to talk with us, so I apologize for the interruption, but that's Dirk Keller and his men. I need to fill them in on what happened yesterday." He couldn't help but notice the disappointed look on Leah's face, and he didn't understand the cause until he noticed that Ethan and Miguel had gotten up from their places on the loveseat. "Oh, I didn't mean you have to leave. In fact, I hope you'll stay. Miguel and Ethan were there yesterday, so they might be able to share some details I missed. This shouldn't take terribly long; then Dirk will be on his way, and we can talk about whatever it was you came here to tell us."

"Thank you, Alpha," Leah said. "We'd be happy to stay."

Zev walked over to the front door and opened it, seeing Connor, his pack member, along with Dirk Keller and five other males.

"Thank you, Connor," he said. "I appreciate you taking the time to meet Alpha Keller and his men and guide them here."

"Of course, Alpha." Connor nodded. "If it's okay with you, I need to go pick up a few things at the store and bring them home for Mary, but then I'll be back to help with whatever you need."

Connor's wife was pregnant with their second set of twins and she'd been on bed rest for over a month. From what Zev had heard, she was taking it well, but things weren't easy with two other little ones at home.

"Of course, Connor. We'll be talking for a while anyway, I'm sure." Zev then turned to greet his visitors. Dirk Keller was a good fifteen years older than Zev, but the other Alpha didn't match up to Zev in height or strength. "Dirk, thank you for coming." He shook Dirk's hand and then greeted all of the other Miancarem males.

"You're welcome, Zev." Dirk nodded and got right to the point. "Now, what's all this about some members of my pack causing trouble?"

"Come on in. Have a seat and I'll explain," Zev said.

Dirk and his men followed Zev into the living room, but they stopped abruptly when they saw the other people already gathered there. Zev turned around and glared at Dirk.

"Have a seat, Dirk," Zev repeated. The words no longer sounded like a polite request; they were an order, and Dirk responded accordingly, with his men following. "Let me introduce everyone..."

Unable to keep his temper or anxiety in check, Dirk interrupted. "No need. I know everyone here. Now I'd like to know why you called me here."

Zev realized Dirk didn't know everyone in the room, because the man had never met Jonah. But it seemed that the time for social niceties was over. Zev sat on the end of one couch, right next to Jonah.

"I called you here because last night four of your pack members assaulted my pregnant sister and kidnapped her. Then they attacked a human, injuring him significantly enough to require hospitalization. I have no doubt they would have done much more, but these men"—Zev pointed toward Jonah, Miguel, and Ethan—"stopped them, at which point they confessed to having murdered a pregnant female from your pack about thirty years ago."

CHAPTER 28

DIRK AND his men were staring at Zev, slack-jawed. He grinned inwardly. *That's what you get for pushing me to talk at your pace, asshole.*

"I don't, uh, I don't understand. Killing a pregnant female, kidnapping and hurting another one... Why would they do that?"

Zev noticed that Dirk had made no mention of the attack on a human. Apparently, that piece of information hadn't registered as significant.

"From what we've been able to piece together, they kidnapped Lori, that's my sister, in order to force one of my pack members to help them isolate Kevin Marvel, that's the human. And the reason they wanted the human is because they thought he was going to tell Leah Harrison that they were the ones responsible for butchering her pregnant sister all those years ago. To be fair, it looks like one of them, Jimmy Delgato, acted alone when he killed Joan Smith; the others had been on board for kidnapping, not murder. At least that's what the three of them said."

The room was so quiet that the grasshoppers outside the door sounded like a stampeding herd of cows.

"You're telling me that Jimmy Delgato murdered Joan Smith and her unborn cub?" Dirk asked incredulously.

"I'm not dead," Jonah mumbled under his breath.

Zev saw Leah lean close to Jonah and whisper something into his ear.

"That's the story Chuck Hanson, Harry Ballings, and Walter Ford told us. They admitted to being there, but said they had no part in the actual murder."

"But why would Jimmy kill one of our own? And a pregnant female... That just doesn't make sense." Dirk still sounded shocked.

Zev took a deep breath. He supposed saying Jimmy—and the other three shifters, too, for that matter—were closed-minded, hateful pieces of shit wouldn't be a productive answer.

"According to them, they did it because Joan Smith was living with the human they attacked yesterday. They didn't want a female shifter having a relationship with a human, so they broke into Joan Smith's home and incapacitated the human, intending to return the female to pack lands by force. When Jimmy Delgato saw that she was pregnant with the human's child, he shifted into his wolf, chased her through the house, and tore her apart." Zev used a calm, even tone when he spoke. The facts were horrific enough on their own; there was no need to add extra drama to the situation.

Dirk shook his head. "I still don't understand why they would do that and how they could have kept it hidden all these years."

"I think the answer to both of those questions is exactly the same," Leah Harrison said, her voice full of rage. She had jumped to her feet and her hands were firmly rooted on her hips in a pose Zev remembered from his childhood. It had scared the shit out of him when he'd been playing ball in her house or dipping into her cookie jar back then, and the extra couple of feet he'd gained on Leah in the intervening years hadn't changed his reaction one bit.

Dirk glared at Leah, clearly not happy that a female had dared to speak to him in that tone. Or perhaps he wasn't happy that a female had spoken to him at all.

"Leah, please tell us what you mean," Zev asked gently.

"The reason they killed my sister is because they're so damn afraid of anything or anyone that's different. And that's the same reason they've been able to keep it hidden for thirty years." Every man from the Miancarem pack growled when they heard Leah's words, but she continued, completely undeterred. "Yes, afraid. You heard me right. Jimmy Delgato and those idiots weren't the only ones who were all up in arms about Joan taking up with a human. They were just the first ones to try and stop her with something other than words. And when witnesses came forward about the murder and we tried to tell the Miancarem Alpha what happened, he called them liars and turned them away."

This was the first Zev had heard about witnesses. He furrowed his brow in concern and looked at Leah, hoping she would elaborate. She glanced at Miguel and Ethan. The men looked at each other, their hands clutched tightly together, and Zev was sure they were communicating through their mating bond. After a few seconds, they turned back to Leah and nodded. She looked at Zev and continued talking, her voice sounded calmer, or maybe it was just sad.

"Joan called me right before she died. She was screaming hysterically, saying she'd locked herself in her bedroom because shifters had broken into her house and hurt Kevin. She wasn't living on pack lands, obviously, so there was no way for me to get to her in time to help. But our kin were visiting and they always stayed in town, because they weren't allowed on pack lands either." Her voice became deeper, her lips tighter with those words. "So I called Ethan and Miguel and asked them to go help Joan. They got there just as the shifters were leaving. They saw their truck, and Ethan could have identified them by scent, had he been given the chance. But the Alpha at the time refused to see them, refused to hear their testimony, even after I begged. He said he wouldn't degrade himself by giving counsel to a bloodsucker and an abomination."

Leah was shaking by the time she finished talking. Jonah pulled her down to the couch and put his arm around her slender shoulders. Given everything else they were addressing, Zev decided it wasn't the right time to ask how it was possible for Ethan to have witnessed a murder thirty years earlier. Miguel was a vampire, which made ascertaining his age impossible. But Ethan was a shifter and he looked to be about the same age as Zev and Jonah. So unless he had witnessed the murder from the safety of his mother's womb or a stroller, something didn't add up.

Dirk barely spared Ethan and Miguel a glance before he looked at Zev and responded to Leah's accusations. "I think we can all understand my predecessor's reaction. An Alpha can hardly allow himself to be influenced by...um, by those types of people."

Zev vaguely registered Ethan sinking into the couch and Miguel wrapping his arms around his trembling mate. He wondered how often the small shifter had heard this type of animosity from his own community. With the desire to belong to a pack being such a deeply ingrained part of a shifter, that rejection had to be tremendously painful.

"You know what, Dirk? You've been going on and on about how you don't understand why your pack members behaved as they did. I think Leah's absolutely right in her assessment. Those types of people are just people, no better and no worse than you and me. And if you continue to treat everyone who is different from you as if they're lesser, then your pack will follow and do the same." Zev took a moment to let his words sink in. "I think we've all been given a horrifying example of what can happen if this type of hate is allowed to persist. It drove four of your men to murder a pregnant female. Is a life full of anger, hatred, and violence really what you want for your pack? Don't you think they deserve better?"

It was impossible to know whether Dirk took Zev's words to heart. Not much more was said after that. Dirk joined Zev in his office, where they called the interpack council president and filled him in on what had happened. They all agreed that Dirk should take custody of the men responsible for the unusual violence and hold them until the interpack council could meet and determine their fate.

Connor, the shifter who had led Dirk and his men to Zev's cabin, returned while Dirk and Zev were on the phone, apparently having confirmed that his bedridden wife had everything she needed. He escorted Dirk and his men to where their pack members were being held. With the Miancarem contingency gone, the air in the cabin felt somehow lighter.

Zev walked back into the living room and collapsed on the couch next to his mate. He rested his head on Jonah's shoulder and his hand on Jonah's thigh.

"Well, that was a party and a half. What else do you have lined up for tonight, Pup? A disembowelment? Maybe a root canal?" Jonah said with a laugh.

Zev couldn't hold back his smile. He'd never stop being amazed at Jonah's ability to make him feel happy under any circumstance. And he'd never stop being grateful that he had this man in his life. He truly felt like the luckiest shifter around to have been blessed with Jonah for a mate.

"You know, as strange as it sounds, I think that went well." Leah's voice sounded tired, but more upbeat than it had earlier. "Other Alphas aren't like you, Zev. They're not even like your father. So other packs aren't as open and accepting as ours. You'd be surprised at how much animosity still exists toward humans and vampires, and well, anybody that isn't a typical shifter. I think Dirk Keller left here today realizing that he's got a lot to think about. And I hope the same message makes its way to the other packs once they hear about what happened to my sister." Leah sniffled and wiped away tears that were falling freely from her eyes. "It'd be her ultimate legacy—forcing those old dinosaurs to open their damn minds and stop their hateful behavior. Joan would've loved that."

Everyone sat quietly for some time after that, each lost in their own thoughts. Eventually, Jonah broke the silence.

"Leah, earlier you said you'd tell me what happened after Jimmy Delgato killed my mother. I'd like to know, if you're up for talking."

So that was what Leah had whispered to Jonah while they were talking with Dirk. Zev was curious about what had happened that day too. He wanted to know how Jonah could have survived in utero when, by all accounts, his mother's entire body was savagely attacked and torn apart. And that didn't even get into the question of how Jonah had lived at all without having shifter chromosomes from both his mother and his father.

"I think now's when we turn things over to Ethan and Miguel," Leah replied. "They were there and they've been waiting a long time to meet you and tell you what happened."

Jonah turned to Miguel and looked at the handsome man carefully. "You look familiar to me, you know? Like I've seen you somewhere." He bit his bottom lip and then looked over at Ethan. "Actually, so do you. Have we met?"

Ethan shook his head.

"No, we haven't met. But Miguel and I have been keeping tabs on you ever since you moved away from Etzgadol. I'm sure you've seen us once or twice over the years."

Jonah cocked an eyebrow.

"Keeping tabs on me? Why? Were you worried that Jimmy and those guys would find me or something? I know my dad was terrified of that happening. I still need to figure out how to tell him the guys who killed my mother have been caught without there being a trial or anything." Jonah shook his head to clear his own thoughts. "Sorry, one thing at a time. So what happened when you got to my parents' house that day?"

Ethan took a deep breath, seemingly gathering his courage, and then he started speaking.

"Your mother was already dead. There was nothing we could do. Actually, we didn't think we'd be able to save you, either. When Jimmy bit her and clawed her and...uh, anyway, her stomach had been sliced, so you were lying there, but you were all cut up too. You had huge gashes across your stomach and you'd lost so much blood."

Ethan shook his head, apparently too upset to continue, so Miguel picked up the thread.

"But we had to try. You were breathing a little. Not much, but enough so we had hope. We'd brought our emergency bag with us, not knowing what we'd find. So we got a line in you and started pumping blood in while we healed your gashes."

"You're saying you gave me a blood transfusion on the spot? Where'd you get the blood? And how'd you learn to do that? Is one of you a doctor? Oh, and how'd you manage to stitch up what sound like some pretty serious wounds without leaving any scars? 'Cause I can tell you that my stomach doesn't look like I had any kind of trauma." Jonah fired the questions off one right after the other, not even stopping for air in between.

"It was my blood," Ethan said. "I'm not a doctor, but I've had a lot of experience with transfusions. When vampires get really sick, they sometimes have a hard time feeding, and when that happens to Miguel, I need to get blood in him as fast as possible to help him heal. Going straight into the vein is the best way for me to feed him my blood in those circumstances."

Zev's list of questions kept growing. From everything he had ever heard, shifter blood was poisonous to vampires. But if he got into vampire physiology at that point, the conversation would be completely derailed, so Zev kept quiet and let Jonah continue to lead the conversation.

"And the scars? Or rather lack of scars?" Jonah asked.

"That was Miguel," Ethan answered. "Vamps have a special property in their saliva to close wounds without leaving marks. They use it when they feed. We didn't know whether it'd work on such extensive damage, but it did. He closed the wounds and I pumped in the blood. It worked. We couldn't believe it, but it worked."

Even though they were sitting right next to each other, pressed together, Zev still felt like Jonah was too far away. Hearing how close he'd come to losing the person who meant everything to him, who made him whole, was terrifying. He put his arm around Jonah's muscular frame and pulled Jonah onto his lap. Jonah didn't resist or complain. He just cuddled up and nuzzled into Zev's neck.

CHAPTER 29

"THAT EXPLAINS so much." Zev said, after they'd sat in silence for several minutes and he'd had a chance to ponder Ethan's explanation of what had happened the day Jonah was born.

Jonah pulled his head back and examined Zev's face.

"How? I mean, yeah, we know why I didn't die from the attack on my mother, but the rest of it..." Jonah buried his face in Zev's neck. "We don't really have an explanation of how I was able to survive," he mumbled.

"You know you have Ethan's coal-black eyes," Zev responded. "I'm guessing the similarities aren't just external. From the sound of it, they replaced almost all your blood with Ethan's just as you were born. Maybe that gave you enough of what you needed to get from a male shifter, which could explain how a product of an interspecies mating survived." Zev stroked his mate's face. "You're not half shifter. The percentage is higher. You have your mother's half and whatever you got from Ethan pumping you full of shifter blood."

Ethan and Miguel nodded.

"We thought the same thing. At first we were just so happy that you were alive, Jonah. We gave you to your father and helped him get away. But then we started worrying about whether you were a shifter or a human. We'd sent you off with a human father. What would Kevin have done if his son suddenly turned into a wolf? So Leah kept an eye on you, and we all thought everything was fine. You smell completely human, you never shifted. We figured that your human side was so strong that it had overridden the wolf somehow."

Jonah shook his head.

"No, the wolf was there. I didn't realize what it was. I just felt like I was going crazy, like I was coming undone. From what Zev's explained to me over the past few days, I think I was experiencing the same thing female shifters go through if they don't tie and their wolf can't get out."

"That's because tying isn't about connecting males with females," Miguel said.

Zev scoffed. What could a vampire possibly know about how shifters were made? The tie between shifter males and shifter females was the very basis of their society. Vampire culture was completely different. They didn't have commitment to a pack or even to each other. With vampires, it was every man for himself. They fed and had sex, without any care for who shared their beds, male or female, human or not.

"Hear the man out, Zev." Jonah frowned at him, making him realize he had been projecting his disbelief to the entire room. "In case you've forgotten, Miguel's mate is a shifter.

His male mate. Seems to me that Miguel and Ethan may have figured some things out, and we need to keep an open mind."

Well, he might be different from other Alphas, but Zev was ashamed to realize he still carried some old prejudices. After all, Miguel had saved Jonah's life and he'd been keeping track of Jonah for years. Plus the vampire was mated to a shifter. Okay, so maybe Miguel did have a commitment to something other than himself. And maybe he did have insight into shifter tying.

"I apologize, Miguel. I was being an ass. Please tell us what you mean about tying not being about males connecting with females."

Ethan beamed, and Miguel gave Zev a little nod in silent thanks.

"I don't think it's a male or female thing at all. I think tying is a wolf and human thing. Shifters think that a male shifter has to tie with a female to bind his humanity, right? Well, even with Ethan's blood flowing through Jonah's veins, Jonah is more human than most male shifters. So his wolf was a part of him, but it was trapped inside. It's the same thing that happens with female shifters, but it's not because they're females, it's because their human is stronger than their wolf."

Jonah nodded furiously, his eyes gleaming. Zev could see the joy his mate gained from solving a puzzle. It was what'd made Jonah such a good student.

"I think he's right, Zev. Your wolf is stronger than your human, so you needed to access humanity to bind your human half. And I'm more human than other shifters, so my wolf couldn't surface on his own. He was trapped inside me and he needed your strong wolf to wake him up. I think that's why we were both so sick when we were apart and why we felt better right after we..."

Jonah darted his eyes toward Leah and squirmed.

"I think the word you're looking for is 'fucked,' dear," Leah said calmly.

Jonah almost choked on his tongue. "I was going to say 'had sex,' but thanks for that." He chuckled and turned back to Zev. "You know I can't shift on my own, but your wolf is strong enough to draw mine out. I think the reason I can't do it myself is because I have so much human in me. But that works because it's exactly what you need: someone who has a human side strong enough to bind your human and keep you from becoming a wolf full time. So you see, Miguel's right, it isn't about being male or female, it's about connecting with someone who can give you what you need and inspire all parts of you—human and wolf. It makes perfect sense."

Zev stared at Jonah, amazed at the man's ability to deduce logical conclusions from completely confounding information.

"My brain hurts," Zev groaned.

Jonah patted his head.

"Of course it does. It's a sad little organ that isn't used to getting this kind of workout. But don't worry, Pup, I'm well aware of your mental shortcomings, and I'm not in this relationship because of your brain." Jonah gave an exaggerated leer and dragged his eyes down Zev's body. "I'm here because your important organ is deeply satisfying."

Leah Harrison coughed and got up from the couch. Her face was distinctly rosy.

"I suppose I have only myself to blame for that last comment. I did egg you on. Let's just go back to you feeling like you need to watch what you say around me, dear. I think that'll be more comfortable for everyone." She turned toward the loveseat. "Miguel, Ethan, are you ready to go? I think Jonah needs some private time with his mate."

The house cleared out in a matter of seconds, leaving Zev and Jonah alone for the first time all day. Jonah hadn't finished flipping the lock on the front door before Zev crowded behind him, draping that broad muscular frame over Jonah's back while his remarkably limber fingers made quick work of Jonah's shirt buttons. When the shirt was open, Zev ripped it off and spun Jonah around, covering his mouth with his own in a bruising kiss.

Jonah clutched Zev's arms and hung on, leaving himself completely pliant and letting Zev lead their coupling. Zev growled deep in his chest and nipped Jonah's lips while his hands roamed over Jonah's smooth, firm skin. He pushed his tongue past Jonah's lips and plundered that delicious mouth.

"So damn hot," he mumbled against Jonah's jaw as he licked and sucked his way down his mate's neck.

It didn't take Zev long to unfasten Jonah's pants and push them down his mate's thighs until they dropped to the ground, where they pooled around Jonah's ankles, caught on his shoes. With another growl, Zev kissed Jonah deeply and pulled him down to the floor. He pressed Jonah's chest, guiding that strong body until Jonah was lying flat on his back in the entryway, with Zev holding him down by his shoulders.

All that golden skin was irresistible to Zev, and he couldn't stop himself from exploring with his lips, tongue, and teeth, leaving marks in his wake. He licked around one pink nipple until it puckered and turned into a hard little nub. Then he moved to the other and repeated his actions, reveling in the happy moans streaming from his mate.

"Stay," he whispered into Jonah's mouth.

When Jonah nodded and whimpered, Zev grinned inwardly, proud that he could put Jonah into a lust-filled haze with such ease. He moved down Jonah's body, sniffing, licking, tasting, until Jonah's hard, dripping cock bumped against his chin. A slight tilt of Zev's head was all it took for Jonah's erection to push into his mouth.

"Zev! Ungh. Feels so good."

It felt good to Zev too. He loved sucking Jonah's dick, loved how it stretched his mouth, loved how it felt sliding against his tongue, loved how it tasted. He grunted and bobbed his head as he increased the suction. He kept one hand on Jonah's chest, making sure those nipples continued to get stimulated, rubbing and pinching them. His other hand was busy with Jonah's full balls. He rolled them in his palm and tugged gently on the sac.

"I can't..." Jonah clenched his eyes shut and swallowed hard. "It's too good, Zev. I wanna come with you inside me, and I can't hold back if you keep doing that."

Zev took a final plunge down onto the hard cock in his mouth and kept his lips tight as he pulled up. When he reached the glans, he increased the suction and finally pulled off with a pop. Jonah's hips flew up.

"Pup! So good." The man's entire body trembled.

"It's gonna get even better." Zev's voice was deep with arousal.

He stood and lifted Jonah's legs so they were resting on his thighs. Then he unlaced and removed the sneakers and yanked off the jeans so he was left towering over his naked mate. Jonah's legs were spread wide and resting against Zev's, leaving his puckered opening exposed.

With one arm holding Jonah's ankles in place, Zev unzipped his pants and snaked his hard dick out of the fly. He spit into his hand and rubbed the saliva over his cock, hoping it would be enough.

"You want me to get some lube, Blondie, or can you take me like this?"

Jonah shook his head and raised his ass so his ankles rested on Zev's shoulders. He plunged two fingers into his mouth, got them wet, then pulled them out and reached between his legs to push them into his body. His eyes were wild with passion.

"Don't stop. I need you now."

Zev understood the sentiment. He needed his mate just as badly. With his hands grasping Jonah's knees, Zev squatted down until he was bent over his mate. Jonah's legs were spread wide, resting against the sides of Zev's shoulders. The man looked completely wanton, and it turned Zev on even more.

"Put it in, Blondie." Zev's voice was low and husky, and he spoke through gritted teeth, the need to pump his seed into the willing body beneath him arousing him to the point of madness.

Jonah pulled his fingers out of his body, wrapped his trembling hand around Zev's erection, and guided it against his pucker. Both men grunted when Zev pushed past the resistant muscle and into Jonah's tight heat. He pulled out slowly, then snapped his hips and shoved his cock back home, grazing Jonah's prostate as he passed.

"Feel good, Blondie?" Zev panted.

"Fuck, yeah." Jonah wiggled and clenched, and the resulting tightness enveloping Zev's dick almost made him come right then.

"Oh, shit. You're so tight. I love doing this." Zev turned his head and kissed Jonah's calf.

Jonah just nodded and moaned, seemingly beyond words.

Zev's quadriceps and hamstrings trembled from the intense workout, but he couldn't have stopped if his life depended on it. He plowed in and out of that hot channel, dragging his dick over Jonah's spot over and over again, rejoicing in his mate's pleasure and the blissful expression on that beautiful face.

"There, there, there," Jonah chanted, taking his dick in hand and pumping in time with Zev's thrusts. "Oh, damn! I'm there!"

White seed shot out of Jonah's dick, painting his chest and neck. Zev stood above his mate, groaning as he filled that tight passage with wet heat. Both men shook and gasped for air.

"Yours." Jonah's voice trembled. "I'm so yours."

Zev lowered Jonah's legs and wrapped them around his waist. He fell to his knees and blanketed Jonah's body with his own.

"Yes, you are. And I'm yours."

THE END

REVIEWS

He Completes Me: When I'm in the mood for a romantic, highly entertaining story, time and time again I'll reach for a book written by Cardeno C.

— *Top2Bottom Reviews*

The One Who Saves Me: This author has a way of making every story unique, sexy, loving, emotional, and just plain wonderful.

— *Rainbow Book Reviews for*

Walk With Me: Whew. Cardeno C. knows how to write those sex scenes.

— *The Romance Reviews*

McFarland's Farm: The romance was fabulous, sexy and so hot.

— *The TBR Pile*

The Half of Us: Gah! If you want good MM Contemporary than Cardeno. C is your go to.

— *Live, Read, Breathe*

Jumping In: Loved, Loved, Loved this book! It was the perfect Valentine's week read and hit all my squishy feelings.

— *Guilty Indulgence*

ABOUT THE AUTHOR

Cardeno C.—CC to friends—is a hopeless romantic who wants to add a lot of happiness and a few *awwws* into a reader's day. Writing is a nice break from real life as a corporate type and volunteer work with gay rights organizations. Cardeno's stories range from sweet to intense, contemporary to paranormal, long to short, but they always include strong relationships and walks into the happily-ever-after sunset.

Email: cardenoc@gmail.com

Website: www.cardenoc.com

Twitter: https://twitter.com/cardenoc

Facebook: http://www.facebook.com/CardenoC

Pinterest: http://www.pinterest.com/cardenoC

Blog: http://caferisque.blogspot.com

OTHER BOOKS BY CARDENO C.

SIPHON
Johnnie

HOPE
McFarland's Farm
Jesse's Diner

PACK
Blue Mountain
Red River *(coming soon)*

HOME
He Completes Me
Home Again
Just What the Truth Is
Love at First Sight
The One Who Saves Me
Where He Ends and I Begin
Walk With Me

FAMILY
The Half of Us
Something in the Way He Needs
Strong Enough
More Than Everything

MATES
In Your Eyes
Until Forever Comes
Wake Me Up Inside

NOVELS
Strange Bedfellows
Perfect Imperfections
Control (with Mary Calmes)

NOVELLAS
A Shot at Forgiveness
All of Me
Places in Time
In Another Life & Eight Days
Jumping In

AVAILABLE NOW

Until Forever Comes

(A Mates Story)

A sensitive wolf shifter and a vicious vampire challenge history, greed, and the very fabric of their beings in order to stay together until forever comes.

Plagued by pain and weakness all his life, Ethan Abbatt is a wolf shifter who can't shift. Hoping to find an honorable death by joining his pack mates in a vampire attack, Ethan instead learns two things: draining his blood releases his pain and his wolf, and he has a true mate - a vampire named Miguel.

Over four centuries old, strong, powerful, and vicious, Miguel Rodriguez walks through life as a shadow, without happiness or affection. When a young shifter tells Miguel they're true mates, destined to be together, Miguel sends him away. But Ethan is persistent and being together comes so naturally that Miguel can't resist for long. The challenge is keeping themselves alive so they can stay by each other's side until forever comes.

In Your Eyes

(A Mates Story)

Two very different men with a tumultuous history must overcome challenges from all sides and see past their society's rules to realize they are destined for one another.

Raised to become Alpha of the Yafenack pack, Samuel Goodwin dedicates his life to studying shifter laws, strengthening his body, and learning from his father. But despite his best efforts, Samuel can't relate to people, including those he's supposed to lead.

When Samuel meets Korban Keller, the son of a neighboring pack's Alpha, he reacts with emotion instead of intellect for the first time in his life. Resenting the other shifter for throwing him off-balance, Samuel first tries to intimidate Korban and then desperately avoids him. What he can't do is forget Korban's warm eyes, easy smile, and happy personality.

When a battle between their fathers ends tragically, Samuel struggles to lead his pack while Korban works to break through Samuel's emotional barriers. Two very different men with a tumultuous history must overcome challenges from all sides and see past their society's rules to realize they are destined for one another.

Johnnie

(A Siphon Story)

A Premier lion shifter, Hugh Landry dedicates his life to leading the Berk pride with strength and confidence. Hundreds of people depend on Hugh for safety, success, and happiness. And at over a century old, with more power than can be contained in one body, Hugh relies on a Siphon lion shifter to carry his excess force.

When the Siphon endangers himself and therefore the pride, Hugh must pay attention to the man who has been his silent shadow for a decade. What he learns surprises him, but what he feels astounds him even more.

Two lions, each born to serve, rely on one another to survive. After years by each other's side, they'll finally realize the depth of their potential, the joy in their passion, and a connection their kind has never known.

Strange Bedfellows

Can the billionaire son of a Democratic president build a family with the congressman son of a Republican senator? Forget politics, love makes strange bedfellows.

As the sole offspring of the Democratic United States president and his political operative wife, Trevor Moga was raised in an environment driven by the election cycle. During childhood, he fantasized about living in a made-for-television family, and as an adult, he rejected all things politics and built a highly successful career as far from his parents as possible.

Newly elected congressman Ford Hollingsworth is Republican royalty. The grandson of a revered governor and son of a respected senator, he was bred to value faith, family, and the goal of seeing a Hollingsworth in the White House.

When Trevor and Ford meet, sparks fly and a strong friendship is formed. But can the billionaire son of a Democratic president build a family with the congressman son of a Republican senator? Forget politics, love makes strange bedfellows.

Blue Mountain

(A Pack Story)

Exiled by his pack as a teen, Omega wolf Simon Moorehead learns to bury his gentle nature in the interest of survival. When a hulking, rough-faced Alpha catches Simon on pack territory, he tries to escape what he's sure will be imminent death. But instead of killing him, the Alpha takes Simon home.

A man of action, Mitch Grant uproots his life to support his brother in leading the Blue Mountain pack. Mitch lives on the periphery, quietly protecting everyone, but always alone. A mate is a dream come true for Mitch, and he won't let little things like Simon's rejections, attacks, and insults get in their way. With patience, seduction, and genuine care, Mitch will ride out the storm while Simon slays his own ghosts and Mitch's loneliness.

Made in the USA
Lexington, KY
13 September 2019